blond boy

A 90s Romance

britt zane

Blond Boy

one

. . .

SMACK!

Instead of turning the corner of the science building and continuing my frantic jog to class, I ran right into another student, knocking both of our books to the ground.

"Hey," a stocky, twenty-something guy with round-rimmed glasses wheezed, as he bent over to pick up his scattered books and papers.

Not even giving the poor person an apology or a second glance, my face heated. I snatched my things from the ground and zipped into the women's restroom. As the door whooshed shut behind me, I heard the wheezing student mutter, "Fuck you, too."

Lovely. I was too late for my Spanish class to care what that guy thought of me. Shimmying out of my work uniform, scratchy polyester pants and a loose smock top, I donned my worn jeans and oversized sweatshirt. A small sigh escaped my lips at the pleasure of soft denim on my skin. After eight hours on the job as a maid at the Seaside Motel, it was a relief to get back into my own clothes.

As I stuffed my uniform into my backpack with one hand,

the other hand quickly yanked out the rubber band holding my hair in its ponytail. My hair cascaded onto my back and shoulders. Hurriedly, I ran my fingers through it and burst out of the bathroom door, hoping to make it to class only five minutes late this time.

No signs of the student I knocked down.

Thank goodness. I hated confrontations, especially when I was the one at fault. I always ended up stumbling over my words, making things worse, never able to say exactly what I meant. Surprise situations inevitably made me look foolish.

Sailing into the foreign languages building, I elbowed my was past other students who filled the hallways after an earlier class.

As quietly as I could, I pushed open the door to my Spanish 200 class. Half the class turned to see who had interrupted their academic pursuits. Professor Aguilera glanced up from her notes on the podium, spied me sneaking in, and cocked an eyebrow in annoyance.

Not good.

I slid into the first empty desk I could find, pulled out my notebook, and waited to take notes. The other students in class, there were about twenty-five, turned back to their note-taking.

The professor continued her lecture, in Spanish, of course, about conditional tense, as if nothing had occurred.

Scribbling down the main points of the lecture, I couldn't help but notice the guy sitting next to me. He was slumped curiously in his seat, blonde hair mussed, sunglasses on.

He was attractive in that 'bad boy' kind of way—black leather jacket, a small gold hoop in one earlobe, and a lanky physique. Perched on his small desk was a red plastic party cup, filled with what looked like orange juice. But, as he brought the cup to his lips, I smelled the strong odor of alcohol.

He took a sip, noticed I was watching, held the cup out to me and softly slurred, "Would you like some?"

A cloud of boozy breath drifted my way.

"No, I don't think so," I whispered. How embarrassing that he had caught me staring at him! I returned to my notes, trying to write as fast as Professor Aguilera spoke.

To stay focused, I ignored the intoxicated, but cute, guy next to me.

Not an easy task.

The professor droned on, pencils and pens scratched along paper to keep up. Blond Boy—that's what I named my new drunk acquaintance—slumped further into his seat, and then I could have sworn he fell asleep. It was hard to tell behind those dark lenses of his sunglasses whether his eyes were open or closed.

After forty-five minutes of lecturing and note-taking, Spanish 200 ended. Blond Boy stirred from his drunken sleep as the rest of the students gathered their notes and backpacks to leave. He, too, grabbed his belongings, leaving the red plastic cup on the desk, and made his way into the aisle to leave the classroom. His walk was stumbling, uneven. I followed right behind him, anxious to get some homework done before my next class at seven- thirty that evening.

Blond Boy looked a bit pale to me—paler than he had seemed in class. But he managed to weave his way down the hall to the end of the building, where a pair of double doors separated the hallway from the main entrance of the building. When Blond Boy was within two feet of the swinging doors, he stopped, gulped, held his hand to his mouth, and wildly looked around.

But it was too late. Orange-yellow vomit burst through his hand, leaving a large, spreading puddle on the tile floor.

A series of groans echoed through the hallway as students entering from the building lobby came upon the nasty mess. Other students, who had been following behind Blond Boy, immediately turned around and headed for the other exit at the far end of the building. I just stood there. Disgusted, but strangely sympathetic.

I had seen my own mother in that state more times than I could count. It wasn't pretty, but I felt compelled to help. More than likely because it was my typical behavior at home after my mother went on a bender.

She got stinking drunk, and I picked up the pieces. I had the routine down pat.

I ducked into the bathroom, which Blond Boy had failed to find in time, and came out with a stack of brown paper towels. Blond Boy made it to the garbage can for his second bout of heaving, and I handed him a few.

"Here," I said. "Take these."

Then, I spread the rest on the mess on the floor.

Blond Boy said nothing, but he gazed at me through his dark sunglasses as he wiped his mouth.

Aware he was looking me in the eye, I felt a twinge of discomfort. I wasn't used to such direct male attention. My mother had always been the man-magnet—and a bad man-magnet at that. Not knowing how to handle his piercing gaze, I turned abruptly away from him, picked up my books and backpack from the floor, and escaped to the far end of the hall. My face burned hot, and I stumbled, my tennis-shoe-clad feet squeaking on the tile. I could sense Blond Boy's eyes following me. The double doors at the opposite end of the hallway appeared further and further out of reach; the walk stretched on and on.

God, please let me get to the doors. Please.

That moment, with his eyes burning into mine, stuck in my head. How could anyone, without saying a word, affect me like that?

When my fingers pushed the swinging doors open, my breath rushed out. As I passed through the doors, I searched blindly in my backpack's side pocket for my keys. When my hand found the cold metal, I jingled them reassuringly.

A warm hand touched my arm. I jumped and dropped my keys. As I bent down to pick them up, I imagined those sunglass-shielded eyes staring down at me. Trying to think of something clever to say, I took a deep breath, snatched up my keys, and turned around as I stood up.

"Señorita Fuller..." A more feminine voice than I was expecting. A pair of high-heeled shoes and a brown tweed skirt hiding chubby knees...

"Professor Aguilera?" I peeped.

"I will not have you continually disrupt my class. Do you have a problem with scheduling?" Professor Aguilera's brown eyes snapped, and her fat fist clenched a ball point pen. "Maybe you should drop my class and find one at a more convenient time."

"I, uh..."

"I don't want an excuse; if you are one minute late for class on Wednesday..."

"I-I'll be on time. I promise Professor."

The overweight woman hesitated as if she had more to say, instead she looked me directly in the eye and pushed past me out the front door. "I hope so," she tossed over her shoulder.

As soon as Professor Aguilera was out of earshot, I cursed under my breath, "Dammit!" The two-thirty Spanish class was the only one that fit into my hectic work schedule. I needed the language credit to finish off my Associate's Degree and had already paid for the class. Switch to another class halfway through the short summer semester? No way. I would be on time for the next class if it killed me.

———

Vacuuming the worn carpeting earlier that afternoon, I started to think moving to Monterey was not such a good idea. The maid's job at the grungy Seaside Motel had not been part of my plan.

The work was hard, dirty, and sometimes downright disgusting.

I flicked off the vacuum and pulled at my uncomfortable polyester uniform: navy blue polyester pants and a striped smock-style shirt with two large pockets on the front. I had stuffed garbage liners, my rubber gloves, and a dusting rag in those big pockets to save me some time while cleaning each of the motel rooms I had been assigned.

I brushed the wisps of hair away from my face that had escaped my ponytail. My least favorite task was next: cleaning bathrooms. Donning my yellow gloves, I grabbed a bucket near the doorway and sighed.

The thought of cleaning a toilet in my own place never appealed to me, but cleaning a toilet that *someone else* had used—the urine spills, the stray hairs of unknown origin—repulsed me to no end. And for what? Seven dollars an hour? It seemed almost criminal.

I carried the bucket full of cleaning supplies into the dingy bathroom. How easy it would be to give up and go back home. Well, not my home exactly, but my mother's house in Santa Clara. Going to community college at night and working in my mother's sandwich shop during the day—was that so terrible?

"Yes, it was Sabrina," I reminded myself as I scrubbed at the stained toilet bowl.

Scrub, scrub, scrub.

My mother, Mickey, started drinking early in the morning and kept on drinking until she passed out at night, sometimes in her bedroom, sometimes on the kitchen floor. Every two months a new 'dad' would move in with us, usually unemployed, always rude and fond of expletives. After the two-month trial period, either my mother would find out the guy had been stealing from her or that he was already married/engaged/dating some other, much younger woman.

Yeah, she had a real knack for picking losers.

No, going back was definitely not an option. I would make this work. Somehow.

After a few silent minutes of cleaning someone else's toilet I could stand it no longer. "These hideous pants are so damned itchy!" I pulled at the polyester fabric and caught sight of my disheveled self in the mirror.

Polyester pants have got to be the most unflattering clothing a pear-shaped woman could wear. The clingy fabric emphasized all the wrong parts. I glanced quickly at myself, but then had to look away. It was a pretty unflattering figure. A shower and a pair of jeans would do wonders once work was over.

When I first arrived in Monterey, I had a hard time finding work. This town is a tourist destination, which means the cost-of living is high and most jobs were in the tourist industry—hotels, restaurants, trinket shops. And without much experience and no references, the job at the motel was the best I could do on short notice.

And it was pretty short notice.

It takes a lot for me to lose my temper, for me to get fed up. But one day I couldn't stand it anymore—the beer, the men, the anger. The night before I left home, I finished my Psychology exam at school, knowing I barely passed the test. Working sixty hours a week at my mother's sandwich shop, I hardly had any time to study, much less make it to class three nights a week. In fact, my mother wanted me to stop going to class altogether.

"What good is all that doing you? Huh?" Mickey yelled one Sunday morning when I was trying to squeeze in a few minutes of studying before having to open the shop. "How much do you pay to sit in that damn class and laze around for a few hours while I work my ass off to keep a roof over our heads?"

That was the moment. Right there.

I decided to move out and get away from my mother. I kept the shop open and running for years while Mickey drank and smoked away most of the money the business brought in. She spent her days in the back of the store, smoking cigarettes and flirting with the delivery men. In fact, recently, her habits had gotten worse. More hangovers that lasted all day. More whining and complaining about her life.

So, I made a decision. Some might call it a reckless one. I packed up my '88 Ford Festiva with the few clothes I owned and decided to leave.

Yep, just drive off and find somewhere new to be—where no one knew my mother was a drunk. Where no one knew my father had run off when I was a baby.

Even then, Mickey couldn't resist one last barb.

"You hear me Sabrina?" She yelled from the small covered stoop in front of our tiny house. It was early morning, and Mickey stood there in her faded housecoat. "Anyone calls here asking for you, I'll tell 'em I don't know anything about you. You're nothing to me. Nothing. You listenin'?" Arms crossed over her flat chest, the standard cigarette hanging loosely from her mouth, the rage barely suppressed.

All on my own, with only a few hundred dollars to my name, I managed to find a job, an apartment, and enroll in Monterey Community College. The first few months had been rough, lots of macaroni and cheese and washing dirty clothes in the bath-room sink, but I had made it.

And now, here I was, working harder than a dog.

But at least my money was my own. I could spend it however I pleased.

I finished up my first room and returned to my cart in the hall. To push it to the next room on my list, I had to pass by Conchita.

As usual, her cart was parked smack in the middle of the

hallway, so I had to abandon my cart and move hers out of the way.

That's when I saw Conchita in Room 214. She was rummaging through an open suitcase on the unmade bed inside. It was difficult to see exactly what she was doing as her portly body partially blocked my view.

Busy staring, I lost control of Conchita's cart and rammed it into the wall.

BANG!

She looked up, caught me watching, and slammed the suitcase shut. Her dark eyes narrowed at me, and then she screamed in her heavily accented English, "*Loca*! What the hell do you think you are doing? Spying on me? Eh? Get out of here, *puta*!"

She secreted something in the pocket of her smock, rushed to the door, and whipped it shut in my face.

For a moment, I contemplated knocking on the door of the manager's office downstairs to report Conchita's stealing. But what would be the use?

Bob, the manager, was rarely in the office And when he was, Bob enjoyed belittling and ogling the girls who worked for him rather than resolve problems or confront petty thieves.

I needed my paycheck, and it wasn't worth risking my job. Keeping my mouth shut was the smarter thing to do.

But I would soon find out, it wasn't all that smart.

two

. . .

TODAY WAS DEFINITELY A COFFEE-AND-SCONE
DAY.

I had just left Professor Aguilera in the foreign languages building, so I was in need of a place to relax and to study.

Shifting my car into gear, I pulled out of the tight parallel spot.

The fog was thicker than when I drove to the college earlier that afternoon; my headlights probed the gloom, barely lighting up the edges of the road. As I came down the hill, heading toward Monterey Bay, the fog lightened some. I took in the view of the city sheathed in swirling fog. The bay was invisible, but the buildings appeared and reappeared in the gray mist, taillights glowed eerily from the traffic in front of me.

I loved the fog. Mysterious and cool; damp and alive. It softened the ugliness and slowed the world down.

After a few minutes of dodging the evening traffic, I turned my car into a municipal parking lot behind Alvarado Street. Parking was terrible on weekends in Monterey.

It was usually better to park several miles away from downtown and hike it in, rather than fight the tourists for parking spots. Mondays, though, were slow days. I almost immediately found an empty space.

I grabbed my books and purse out of the back of my car and headed out to find a secluded spot to reflect on my stressful day, complete my homework for tomorrow, and catch up on my reading for my Meteorology course. That class was at seven, so I only had a couple of hours free.

Some days I would sit in one of the cheaper restaurants and order breakfast food (my favorite thing to eat). Some days it was eggs, toast, and bacon; others it was pancakes and several cups of coffee to wash it down. I kept very little food in my studio apartment. For one, I hated to spend time there. It was lonely and dark in that small space. And for another, I despised cooking for one person. It never seemed worth the effort of dirtying pans and dishes for a few bites of food.

I could eat more cheaply at home to be sure, but eating out was the one luxury I afforded myself—besides the occasional movie on a Friday, my day off. I found it was possible to spend very little on food throughout the day. Breakfast was typically something I grabbed at the 7-Eleven across the street from the motel, like a Pop-Tart or muffin. Work started at 6 am, so coffee was the most essential part of breakfast. Lunch I skipped—I finished my rooms much more quickly when I didn't take a lunch break. So, dinner became a sort of 'lunner' for me. Part lunch, part dinner.

Right now I hankered for a scone and a rich, dark cup of java.

The coffeehouse I preferred wasn't on Alvarado Street, it was a few blocks north on Washington: Morgan's Coffee and Tea.

Morgan's sat on a busy corner of downtown. It had large plate glass windows with small tables and chairs outside to enjoy the weather when it was fair, so it was the perfect place for people-watching.

When I pulled my car up to the curb, only a few surfboards propped up against the exterior stone wall were outside. Too cold and foggy for anyone to enjoy sitting outside today. Inside, my favorite spot was in the smaller of the two seating areas, next to the gargantuan coffee roaster. It was warm in there on cool days, and most people enjoyed sitting in the larger, more social part of the coffeehouse. I liked the intimacy of the few tables and chairs in the smaller room. Some customers never even knew the room existed, so, at times, it would be completely empty.

I dropped my stack of books on one of the small, round tables to stake out my studying territory and then grabbed a place in line by the counter to order. A typical, young California couple were in line in front of me—both blondes with dark tans. Most likely the owners of the surfboards outside. Bad day for surfing; good day for staying in and sipping on a latte. The couple gave their order and then sat by the window to keep an eye on their expensive boards.

I stood at the counter with my hands behind my back, waiting for the tall, dark-haired barista to turn around and ask for my order.

When he returned to the register, I raised my voice, making sure I could be heard over the alternative rock music that filled the room, "A tall house coffee and a—"

"Blueberry scone?" The barista finished for me.

"Yeah," I said. How did he know...?

"That'll be $3.50."

Absentmindedly, I gave him the bills I had in my hand. I didn't remember him...or did I? There were so many coffee places I used for studying it was hard to keep them straight.

He only grinned at me as he handed me my change. Another customer was waiting for his help.

I returned to my chair in the other room wondering how many blueberry scones I could have possibly consumed in the three months I'd been in Monterey. But my rumination was interrupted the minute I entered that back room.

It was no longer empty—someone with messy blonde hair was seated at another table with his back to me.

Blond Boy!

I gasped audibly. Then, I cleared my throat to try to cover it up. Thank God he didn't seem to hear the bizarre sounds I was making, or he would think I was an absolute lunatic. To meet him again face to face after the incident in the hallway...well, what were the chances?

And I had run off like a frightened deer. What an idiot!

What to do? For a second, I contemplated waiting out in the main room for my order, but my books were still on the table next to him. I would at least have to go in there to retrieve my books.

Crap!

I could pick up my books and pretend I didn't recognize him. Or could sit in the other room, leaving my books abandoned in hopes he would leave in a few minutes.

Now *that* was just plain crazy.

"Large coffee! Blueberry Scone!" the barista yelled out. I twirled around, rushed to the counter, and grabbed the heavy white mug filled to the brim with hot liquid. Then, I snatched the glass plate, which held my scone with my free hand.

Decisions, decisions...

I stood there at the counter, not moving.

"Did you need anything else?" the barista asked with a smile. I looked up anxiously, only able to concentrate on his Morgan's name tag.

"Uh, no, Tim—I'm fine. I don't need anything else." I nervously blew a wisp of hair out of my eye, and, when that didn't work, tried brushing it out of my face with the back of my hand holding the steaming mug.

Before I could spill any hot coffee on myself, Tim reached out and took the mug from me, "There you go."

Smiling at his unexpected assistance, I tucked the stray hair behind my ear. "Thanks."

"No problem," Tim smiled back. "We offer full service to our regulars."

So nervous was I about heading over to the tables in the back where Blond Boy waited, that I laughed without really hearing what he was saying to me. After an awkward silence, I noticed Tim waited patiently for me to take my mug from his hand.

Feeling stupid, I thanked him quickly, snatched my drink, and made my decision about my perplexing situation. Making sure not to spill my coffee, I walked directly to my table, immediately opened my weighty compilation Shakespeare book, and began reading.

No looking, no glancing, eyes on book only. Eyes on book only…

Blond Boy's sunglass eyes were looking at me; I could sense it even with my head buried in my book.

Just say something, dummy! Pull your eyes out of your book and say something!

Tension was as thick as the fog outside. How could I casually acknowledge our recent encounter?

'Hey, I'm Sabrina, the girl that gave you a paper towel in the hall after you threw up."

Not the most elegant way to begin an introduction to an attractive guy.

Turning my head slightly, I tried to catch a glimpse of Blond Boy through the falling strands of my hair as I read the same lines of Shakespeare over and over again. I picked up my mug to take a sip of my steaming coffee, but I wasn't looking. The mug was fuller than I anticipated, and the hot coffee spilled onto the leg of my jeans.

"Ouch! Dammit!" I stood up and managed to bump the small table, spilling even more coffee. A classic Sabrina move. Grabbing several napkins, I blotted at the hot stain on my pants with one hand and cleaned up the spill on the table with the other hand.

Idiot! Idiot! Idiot!

"Here, do you need some more?" Blond Boy handed me a stack of white napkins from across the aisle. He seemed much more sober than during our encounter in the hallway only thirty minutes earlier.

Once again, the heat invaded my cheeks, "Thanks."

Guys like this one never had shown interest in me before. I tended to attract the nerdy, plain-looking type. Blond Boy was the kind who was dark, rebellious, and a little dangerous.

I grabbed the offered napkins and avoided eye contact. I didn't want him to see how he affected me. I finished blotting and sat down to continue my assigned reading for tomorrow's English Lit class.

Now would be a good time to get up and leave, Sabrina. Now, before you make a bigger fool of yourself. It's not like the guy asked you out on a date. He's just being polite.

"Wanted to return the favor," Blond Boy's voice interrupted my thoughts. "I'm Patrick."

I could only manage a faint, "Hi."

Without being able to help myself, I glanced at Patrick. His mussed blonde hair fell into his eyes, which were finally free of the dark sunglasses. He was a bit pale and thin, but his features were striking—aquiline nose, high cheekbones—and there was a bit of a smile to his bright blue eyes.

"And you are—?"

"Oh! I'm—my name's Sabrina." I reached out my sweaty palm to shake his hand in a sort of manly fashion. I hated wimpy, feminine handshakes.

"Hello, Sabrina," he said with mock formality.

Patrick seemed a bit amused by the vigorous handshake, so I dropped his hand rather abruptly. He sort of half-smiled and turned back to his newspaper and small espresso cup. Like me, he also had a stack of books on his little table. I couldn't read all the titles, but a few were interesting:

The Artwork of H.R. Geiger

Vampire: The Masquerade

Siddhartha.

Patrick was all in black. He wore a black leather jacket, black steel-toed boots, and a black t-shirt and jeans. With his pale complexion, the color didn't really suit him. In fact, he appeared to be working a little too hard to make some sort of statement with his mode of dress. Considering I never made any sort of statement with my clothes or anything else, it intrigued me.

He continued with his newspaper reading, so I turned back to my large Shakespeare text. This was my favorite study spot, and I wasn't about to leave just because a good-looking guy was sitting next to me. I was determined to get some of my homework done.

However, I couldn't concentrate. I was too aware of his presence—the sweaty handshake and the feel of his palm in mine stuck in my memory.

Instead, I dashed into the main room to find one of the free local papers that filled a basket near the entrance of the coffeehouse. I grabbed one and returned to my seat. Maybe I could do the crossword puzzle or read the restaurant reviews. Something that took a lot less concentration. Looked as if studying wasn't going to happen until either I or Patrick left.

I took a bite of my scone and flipped through the paper to search for the crossword puzzle. A good crossword puzzle always calmed me down and took my mind off of my problems.

When I found the puzzle, I folded the paper back, rummaged through my purse for a ball point pen, and began reading the clues.

After a few minutes working on the crossword, my mind felt less cluttered, my emotions less jangled. Sighing, I sat back in my chair and took a few sips of the rapidly-cooling coffee in my mug. The scone was long gone, consumed between crossword clues. Now I felt ready to tackle my Shakespeare homework. I had succeeded in ignoring the hot guy next to me.

If I could just keep it up until my homework was done…

Opening to the sonnet that was our assignment, I hunched over the book scanning the lines in an attempt to analyze them for tomorrow's class discussion.

"Shakespeare?" Patrick's voice broke the comfortable silence. "The man who invented every cliché of the 20th century? How's the class?"

Darn.

My success was short-lived. Didn't he know I was trying my hardest to forget he was even there? I cleared my throat, wondering how to respond to his friendly gesture of conversation. Maybe this was my chance to prove I was normal and not some Nervous Nelly like the person he met in the hallway after class.

"Uh, well, it's all right." Oh, that was brilliant, Sabrina, you sound like a genuine scholar of literature. "I like some of his plays, but it's poetry that kills me. I never get it, you know?"

"What is there to 'get'? Isn't poetry just whatever you interpret it to be?"

Could it be he doesn't think I am a complete dolt? "Not according to half the students in my class—or my professor. Everything has hidden double meanings. Sometimes even triple meanings."

Oh, no! What happened to my plan to ignore him? To get my homework done? We were starting to have an interesting conversation. I was doomed.

three

$\cdot\ \cdot\ \cdot$

DISCUSSING a neutral topic like Shakespeare made me momentarily forget my nervousness. As long as he didn't ask anything about my family, my personal life, I was good to go. I liked to keep private stuff private. If he asked if I had any siblings, where I grew up, or what kind of childhood I had, I would be out the door. Those questions were taboo in my book. Why would I tell a stranger anything about my messed up life and crazy mother?

But Patrick hadn't done that—yet. He asked about Shakespeare. That kind of question I could handle. I warmed to the conversation and turned my chair in Patrick's direction. "It makes my head spin. What's wrong with taking the words at face value?"

My hands have a tendency to fiddle with whatever happens to be around when I am talking. This conversation was no exception. I repeatedly took the pen cap off my ball point pen. For some reason, this helped me think straight.

"Yeah. I think poetry is a bunch of shit. Have you read any of that modern crap? Anyone could write that," Patrick kept a cool demeanor, one that matched his goth garb. He didn't seem personally involved in the discussion. Unlike what was typical in my English Lit class when the 'smart' students latched onto a topic, he made his statements free of any overwrought emotion. In class there was an intellectual fervor among the students to outdo each other; Patrick had none of that.

I wished I could so freely discuss my feelings on the topic in class. I always felt so inferior to most of the students.

Patrick appeared to have no cares about what I or anyone else thought of him. I wasn't about to let this opportunity slip through my fingers. He was good looking, talking to me, and finding me interesting, and not digging relentlessly into my background. He was worth keeping.

Plan One, the Ignore Plan had failed. Now it was time for Plan Two: befriend and keep my emotions neutral. Most likely I was the only one in the room feeling some attraction. How could I not? He was gorgeous to look at.

"No, I don't read much poetry," I admitted. Secretly, I was pleased we shared the same view on the subject. "I really don't like poetry much, to tell the truth. I'm more of a novel reader." Right after it came out of my mouth, I wondered if he thought that was too mainstream and dull. He had a very unique idea of what was worthy reading material, judging by the stack of books on his table.

I read some, although I didn't have a lot of free time with my class load and full-time job. Mostly, I stuck to the bestseller list, occasionally branching out into the public library's Book of the Week table. I definitely didn't have the money to purchase novels that interested me, so the library was my only source.

"You're not one of those Grisham fans, are you?" He squinted one blue eye at me. I thought I detected a small glimmer of hope in his voice.

He seemed to want to include me as a part of his world. As if it was us against all the mainstream, plain vanilla people. So, although I had just finished a Grisham novel only a month ago, I quickly answered, "No."

I tried to think of a book I had read in the past six months that might impress him. To be part of something different, something unique would be a good change in my life. Even if we could only be friends. But my mind was a blank, and I continued to pluck the pen cap off of my pen. Old habits die hard.

"Good, I can't stand him," he sounded pleased with my answer "You seem a little too smart for his brand of shit." He stood up quickly, winked at me, and snagged his espresso cup off the table. He carried it into the next room and left it in the self-busing bin under a side counter. He paused beside the small, black stand that held the CD they were playing over the sound system. He read the label, then gave a derisive snort and returned to his table.

"I thought that's what they were playing," he announced as he gathered his books and newspaper. "And everyone who comes here thinks they are being so 'alternative.' They play the same Top 40 shit that everyone else plays."

"Guess they're just trying to appeal to the widest audience," I countered. "Don't want to scare any possible customers away."

He rolled his eyes, "What's the point of luring people in with the medieval stone walls outside and the industrial art on the walls, when that's not really what this place is all about?" He looked at me for some confirmation of his annoyance. "I'll bet they have jazz trios in here on Sunday afternoons and slam poetry for the kiddies on Friday nights."

The idea he even considered me as not part of the 'regular' people was flattering. I was wearing jeans and a sweatshirt with Mickey Mouse embroidered on it, for heaven's sake I was the opposite of the cool, anti-establishment man next to me. And, yet, he continued to talk to me.

"I don't come here when there are crowds," was all I could think to say. I hurriedly threw my things together, worried he would disappear before I found out more about him This was the first chance I had since leaving home to make a friend who didn't delve into my personal life as if it were a trashy novel he couldn't put down. And I wasn't about to screw it up.

―――

"Yeah, I can see why," he said contemptuously.

After gathering my books I stood and found myself awkwardly close to him. The room was tiny, and the tables were much closer together than I'd realized.

He was about my height, and I was quite tall for a woman, and thin. Sort of the wiry type. He must weigh at least twenty pounds less than I did. And, boy, did he smell good, like soap and incense. Smoky. Mysterious.

"Um," I stepped back from that intoxicating smell and looked for a way to continue our discussion. "So, did you like Professor Aguilera's class?"

"What? Who? Oh, you mean that lard-ass from Spanish?" He laughed, stepped back, and gave me a sort of half bow, encouraging me to exit the room first. More of a gentleman than I expected from his penchant for vulgarities. "I think I'm dropping that class tomorrow. I don't have time to deal with her shit."

We walked out of Morgan's together.

"Oh," I thought for a moment. "So you don't need the class for credit?"

We stopped at the corner. My heavy Shakespeare text made my shoulder zing with muscle fatigue, but I was determined to dig more information out of him before I got in my car.

"No way. Just thought the class would be interesting. I'm already busy enough."

"With what?"

"Korean. I'm up at DLI. You know, up the hill?"

I had only recently moved to Monterey, but I was already

familiar with DLI, the Defense Language Institute, a government-run language school for all the branches of the military. It sat on the top of a hill overlooking Monterey and the bay. I wasn't very clear on what exactly they taught them up there, but I knew DLI was considered the expert when it came to teaching foreign languages. Supposedly, a student could reach fluency in Spanish in six months; some of the harder languages, like Chinese or Arabic, fluency could be reached in little over a year.

"You're in the military?" I was very surprised. His mode of dress gave me the impression someone with his interests would never consider signing up for the military.

I sensed a bit of embarrassment in him. "Yeah, I'm in the Army, if you can believe it. Not many jobs where I come from for a college dropout. I'm putting in my time, and then I'm outta there. I just wanted to learn Korean."

"I think that's pretty admirable. Serving your country." I could tell the moment I said this that serving his country was definitely not Patrick's motivation behind joining the Army.

"Yeah. Right." He said nothing more on the subject. "Well, I have to get going. I'm meeting a friend." With that, he turned with a salute/wave and headed down Washington.

I wanted to follow him, find out more about who he was where he came from, and maybe how to get a hold of him. But he was a block away before I could work up the courage to move from my spot on the corner. The first friendly face in months—and one that seemed marginally interested in me—and he slipped away.

But my Shakespeare homework was waiting. Although I considered going somewhere else to study, I didn't have the time to wander back to Alvarado Street and find another place to sit. My Meteorology class started at seven o'clock. Only ninety minutes from now. Back into Morgan's I went, returning to my recently vacated seat in the back room. No one had taken my spot, or Patrick's. The room was empty and silent.

I plunked my Shakespeare book on the small table and turned to the sonnet I needed to review. Scribbling some of my thoughts in a notebook, I thought about my conversation with Patrick. He was right. Poetry was whatever I wanted it to be. Writing whatever came to mind, I hoped in class I had the courage to speak up. Maybe I wouldn't look like the Shakespeare Dummy this time.

Finishing my assignment, I shut my notebook. Since the tables at Morgan's were so small in diameter, I placed the large Shakespeare text and my notebook on the floor next to my backpack. When I pulled out the syllabus for my Native American Religions class, I saw it. A scrap of paper on the floor, folded in half. I picked it up, curious, and opened it.

PATRICK 408-661-0991

My heart fluttered.

Had he put it in my backpack on purpose? Was it a mistake? Maybe he was thinking of giving me his number, but after our conversation thought the better of it?

Hesitating, my first thought was to keep it.

Nah.

I began to crumple up the bit of paper, but, then I had a change of heart. How am I ever going to meet people if I don't take a chance?

I pocketed the paper in my jeans.

four

· · ·

"HEY, BOB," I greeted my boss with feigned pleasantness. "What do you have for me today?"

Bob, a fifty-something potbellied man wearing stained khaki pants and a short-sleeved button-up shirt, glanced up at me from his cheap fiberboard desk, which was covered in papers and dust. Before answering, he smoothed a strand of greasy hair across his forehead and scanned me slowly from head to toe.

Yuck.

"Oh, I'll tell ya what I got for ya, honey." He laughed at his own raunchy joke and reached for a printout from the stack under the printer near his desk. Still laughing, he handed a paper to me and a large ring of keys, "Anytime you want it, baby, anytime."

I was disgusted, but, sadly, used to Bob's less than professional behavior. He behaved that way with all the girls: fat, thin, pretty, ugly. It didn't matter. Bob liked making us as uncomfortable as possible. As if it was the only pleasure he got from his work day. And I could see why that would be true. Being manager of the grungy Seaside Motel was not exactly anyone's dream job.

I snatched the piece of paper out of Bob's hand and left his office without saying a word. His laughter followed me down the hall.

Since my schedule lasted from six to two every day, I was the designated "lobby girl." It was my duty to straighten the lobby, empty the trash containers, set out newspapers for the day, and clean the restrooms. Then, I could start cleaning my rooms.

During the week, most guests left pretty early, around seven or eight in the morning, so I could start in on my list right after my lobby duties. Check-out time was officially eleven o'clock, so the rest of the guests filtered out between eight and eleven. The beginning of the day started slowly, speeding up to a hectic pace around noon.

How nice it would be if I could sleep in like some of the guests at the motel. This morning I had woken up late, again. Five-thirty was just too darn early to roll out of bed. But that was about the latest I could sleep and still be on time for work.

―――――

I had yawned through my Meteorology class the night before, trying to concentrate on low pressure and high pressure fronts. Then, I stayed up until midnight completing homework due on Tuesday. A whole five hours of sleep. Some would consider that plenty, but I needed at least seven or eight hours to function well.

Oh, well, just have to drink more coffee than usual.

My futon bed had been so comfortable and warm, but I forced myself to emerge from my blanket cocoon. Opening my backpack, I pulled out my wrinkled work uniform. Well, not all of it was wrinkled, thanks to the fabric technology that allowed polyester to remain wrinkle-free.

My smock top, however, was pretty badly in need of an iron. I laid the horridly wrinkled shirt on top of my cardboard box table, as if it would magically straighten itself by the time I brushed my teeth. Then, I gathered my books for the two classes I had later today and stacked them by the door.

This was my new system. There had been more than one occasion that I, in a sleepy haze, had driven off to work without my books. So, the new system was to set them in front of the door. Pretty hard to miss them now.

I quickly brushed my teeth. Then, with my toothbrush clenched in my teeth and my mouth leaking toothpaste foam, I expertly whipped my hair into the usual ponytail. Done.

I threw my uniform on, slipped on my tennis shoes, scooped up my purse and books, and dashed down the stairs to my car. Some would call it chaos, but I called it my routine.

I threw my books on the seat next to me and put the key in the ignition.

"Dammit!"

I had forgotten to toss some clothes in my backpack for the quick change at school later that day. No way was I wearing this uniform in class. I raced upstairs, leaving the driver's side door wide open. Fumbling with my keys, I jammed the apartment key into the lock, opened the door, and tossed the same jeans and sweatshirt I wore the day before into my backpack.

That was when I noticed the scrap of paper sticking out of the right front pocket of my jeans. Patrick's phone number. For a split second, I hesitated.

Then—

"Yeah, right, Sabrina. What are you thinking?" I quickly crumpled the paper into a wad and tossed it in the direction of the paper bag that served as a wastebasket in my kitchenette.

What a freak he would think I was...or a stalker. How could I explain to him how I got his phone number?

That small delay threw my whole morning out of whack. I had that routine down to a science, there was no margin for error.

Returning to my apartment for those clothes cost me my breakfast at 7-Eleven. No coffee, no Pop-Tart.

Maybe I would get lucky and find some unopened food in one of the empty rooms. It happened on occasion. Guests left unopened cans of soda, still-factory-sealed bags of chips, and other odds and ends. I had no shame in taking advantage of free food, even if some people considered it trash. Food was food, and I didn't have to pay for it, so why be picky?

I had made it to the designated employee spots in the parking lot right on time. One minute more and Bob would have declared me "late for work."

God, this job stunk.

———

When I finished cleaning the lobby, I headed for the large storage closet where all the girls' carts were kept overnight. I found 'my' cart, the one with the "I brake for sea otters" bumper sticker plastered on the front, and filled it with supplies for the day.

I glanced at my list. Mostly turnovers—people leaving instead of staying over for another night. I made sure to stack plenty of clean towels and sheets on my already laden-down cart.

Slowly, I wheeled it to the first room on my list, 122, dragging a vacuum cleaner behind me. I knocked crisply on the door, "Housekeeping!" I hoped no one would answer.

"Go 'way," a sleepy voice grunted from behind the door of 122. A shoe or some other hard object thrown by the annoyed guest banged on the opposite side of the door, and I jumped back.

All righty. Guess this one was still occupied.

I pushed my cart to room 124 and tried the same polite knock. No answer. Thank goodness.

Unlocking the door with my set of room keys, I stuffed my smock pockets with the usual cleaning supplies and grabbed two sets of sheets and some towels off the stack on top of my cart.

Methodically, I began to tear the bed sheets off of the bed, collect the dirty, damp towels from the floor and chair, and remove the half-full garbage bag from the can. Dust. Vacuum. Clean the bathroom. Move on to the next room. Hour after hour went by that way.

Physically tiring the job was, but mentally stimulating, it was not. As I removed a garbage bag that reeked of stale cigarettes and beer, I found my mind wandering to my life back in Santa Clara. The small two-bedroom house with the rotting garage door. My tiny bedroom constantly smelled of my mother's cigarette smoke. Beer cans piled up on the kitchen table and around the sink. Open bags of potato chips littered the counter. Empty containers with remnants of yesterday's or even last week's Chinese food dotted the living room. It was disgusting, but I knew better than to complain about the state of my mother's cramped, filthy home.

I also knew better than to complain about the constant stream of men in the house. It had been that way ever since I could remember. My mother, Mickey, would go out most nights, and I would walk into the kitchen the next morning to see a stranger drinking coffee and smoking a cigarette. The stranger might stay for just one night or a few weeks. I never could tell how long.

Every single one of her short-lived relationships ended in bitter arguments—yelling, cursing, tossing of dishes. And I'd hide out in my room, hoping the cheap lock on my door would hold until Prince Charming #12 (or was it #13?) decided to give up and leave before the neighbors called the cops or Mickey's aim improved.

I used to think my mother would eventually learn something from these men. Maybe that hanging out in bars was not a great place to meet someone; or maybe that she needed to change her standards. Her standards usually hovered between 'breathing' and 'not completely repulsive.' Usually.

But this never did happen. In fact, as Mickey got older she selected even less appealing men, if that were possible. She brought home bald, fat, belching men; Short, greasy, groping men. And having these kinds of men around when I was a teenager—well, let's just say it was confusing and a little bit scary.

One more reason to be glad to be out of that house. If I didn't get out of there when I did, I imagined myself slowly turning into my mother. Slowly taking up drinking. Slowly letting life's disappointments erode me.

Slowly.

Until the years were gone, and I was alone and miserable.

And where was my father in all this mess?

What father? Ha, ha. That is what Mickey would say.

The most I ever got out of her was that I was the result of a brief affair that ended before I was born. She never explained to me where or who my father was, why he never came to see me. And after a few years, I quit asking. It only made her angry and caused her to grab that first bottle of beer out of the fridge.

Then, right after my eleventh birthday, a thick envelope arrived in the mail. It had the name of some attorney as the return address, and my name in all capital letters: SABRINA FULLER. I walked into the house with the mail when I noticed the strange envelope in the stack of overdue bills and advertisements

Curiously, I flipped the envelope over to open it. But before I could, my mother snatched the envelope out of my hands and tore open the sealed flap.

"What the hell is this?" Mickey spat out with the ever-present cigarette dangling from the corner of her mouth. She wore a faded pink slip and a bathrobe, untied and hanging open, and her bony feet were covered by a pair of dirty and worn white slippers. Mickey shuffled toward the small, cluttered kitchen table.

"What is it, Mom?" I asked, following her to the table. I was upset she'd taken that interesting envelope from me.

It was addressed to me. Not her.

But I had learned long ago to keep my mouth shut. Complaining only made things worse.

"Shut up, let me read this."

I stood behind my mother while she sat at the table, hoping to read some of the contents over her shoulder.

"Sit down! That's goddamn irritating, you hovering over me like that." Mickey put out her cigarette in one of the overflowing ashtrays on the table.

I sat across the table from her.

For a minute, an odd expression crossed my mother's face. Her lips pulled tight, as if she were a dam trying to hold the water back. Then, unexpectedly, a smile came over my mother's thin face "At least that loser was good for something. That will come in handy."

The words burst out of me, "What? What is it?"

"Your father. He's dead." My mother stated this fact with a bit of satisfaction. "Some kind of cancer thing or something it says here. Left us some insurance money."

"He did?"

I figured it out, years later, when I was old enough to know better, that the insurance money was never meant for my mother.

The envelope was addressed solely to me. But at eleven, I took my mother's word for truth. And hoped it meant something good was about to happen to both of us.

How naive I'd been. I'd trusted my mother, believed she was

doing what was best for both of us. Even now, I wondered how much of my father's insurance money had been squandered by Mickey on lottery tickets, cheap clothes, and beer. Not to mention the failing business venture she bought the following year, the sandwich shop.

———

But I really didn't want to reflect anymore on the past. Not right now. I wanted to finish my list of rooms and go back to changing my life, not reliving it.

At close to two o'clock, I finished cleaning my last room. A bit of a smile played on my lips—for once I was done early. I had plenty of time to get to my two-thirty class. Absentmindedly, I pushed my cart toward the lobby.

As I moved down the hall, I noticed the door to room 111, one of Conchita's assigned rooms, stood open. Conchita leaned in the doorway, one hand on her plump hip, the other clutching her yellow rubber gloves. Her dark eyes were hidden behind half-closed lids, and her lips curled into a sardonic grin. "Eh, *guera*, all done?"

I, a bit wary of her sudden friendliness and odd expression, answered coolly, "Yeah. Gotta make it to class on time.

"Oh," Conchita laughed, "that's right. You so smart. You gonna study yourself outta this place, eh? Leave us *estupidas* here to pick up your slack someday. You just so much better than the rest of us, I forgot."

Before I could respond, Conchita turned and closed the door to 111. I heard her laughing behind it.

Odd. What was that all about?

Conchita rarely, if ever, directly spoke to me. And usually it was to complain about how good I had it at the motel; how I probably had the easiest rooms. Alluding to some sort of sex-for-work arrangement between me and Bob. I'm not sure why she disliked me, but today? Today was something completely different. More sinister.

I pushed my cart to the storage room and unhooked the large garbage bag off the back of the cart. With my back to the door, I dragged the heavy load out toward the lobby and backed right into a warm body.

"Where are you going, honey?" Bob asked, grabbing me by the elbow. "Why would you be in such a hurry to leave, huh? You think I don't know what you've been up to?"

I wrested my elbow out of his grasp. *What in the hell?* "Um...I was taking out the trash. Is that okay with you?"

"Are you sure all you have in there is trash?" He tried to look past me at the garbage bag sitting on the floor.

"Yeah," I glared at him. "Would you like a few cigarette butts or beer bottles? Plenty of those today."

"Let me just take a look there." He pushed past me, making sure to place one of his fat, stubby hands on my rear to help himself by.

Gross.

He lifted up the extra clean towels and bottles of spray cleaner on my cart.

"What are you doing?"

"I heard something about you, and I'm here to check it out."

My heart dropped into my stomach. "Heard something?" That didn't sound good. "Like what? What are you looking for?"

Pawing to the very bottom of my towel pile, Bob pulled something out with a dramatic flourish. "You damned bitch! You think I haven't been watching you since day one?" He showed me what was in his hands: a watch, a few gold rings, and what looked like a hearing aid.

"You think I took that stuff?" It dawned on me why Conchita had that nasty smile on her face. "God! It was Conchita I saw her yesterday. I was going to tell you, but..."

"But, but, but? But what, Sabrina, honey?"

Why in hell would Conchita set me up like that? What did I ever do to her? I was so angry I could barely focus on what Bob was saying to me.

"Conchita saw you steal this stuff from one of the rooms yesterday. At first, I didn't believe her, 'cause you never gave me no trouble. But she told me right where you hid the stuff. And here it is!"

"No! It was her...Conchita! She's a liar! I wouldn't steal anything, most of the creeps that stay here don't have anything worth taking anyway!" I could feel what little control I had over my emotions slipping away.

"So, you admit you've been going through people's stuff?"

Before I could protest, he launched me out the door of the storage closet with a huge shove. "Get outta here! I don't wanna see you around here no more. Piece a white trash! Stealing behind my back! You ungrateful bitch!"

Grabbing me by the sleeve, he dragged me out to the parking lot. I felt numb. When we got outside, he pushed me. Hard. I stumbled and fell to the pavement, scraping the palm of my hand. The scrape stung and tears instantly welled up in my eyes. I was determined, however, not to let that overweight idiot see me humiliated and crying. I sniffed hard once, tucked a strand of hair behind my ear, stood, and walked to my car without looking back.

"If you think I need this loser-ass job, you've got to be kidding!" I yelled over my shoulder with more bravado than I felt. "I'll be back to pick up my check tomorrow, and it better be here!" I wrenched open the door of my Festiva and climbed in.

When I backed out of the parking space, I could see most of the cleaning girls standing outside in front of the lobby, watching me. Conchita was there, right in front, laughing and making comments to her friends. Something derogatory and in Spanish, I was sure.

Trying to keep my eyes trained on the road in front of me,

instead of on the group of sniggering Hispanic women, I flicked on my turning signal and prepared to turn out of the driveway and onto the main road. When the way was clear, I put my car in first gear and stepped on the gas. My touch on the gas pedal was a little too light, and the car sputtered and died. *Gotta love a stick shift.* The Festiva continued to roll forward into the street, and I quickly pushed on the brake and tried to restart the car.

Behind me, I knew those girls were laughing even harder. Mortified, I tried starting up the car again. It wouldn't turn over. I tried again. Finally, the Festiva sputtered to life. I put my foot on the gas, and, without looking ahead into the street, took off.

BAM!

My car slammed right into an expensive black Mercedes. "Dammit!"

five

· · ·

I DIDN'T SWEAR TOO OFTEN, but I felt the epithet was an appropriate response to my worsening situation. The driver of the Mercedes was already out of his car, a well-dressed man in his early thirties. He came around the front of his sleek, black car to inspect the damage.

I opened my door and rushed over to apologize, mortified "Oh, my God, I am so sorry!" A large dent marred the passenger's side door of his car, and a big chunk of paint had been scraped off.

"Geez, why don't you look where you are going?" The dark-haired man asked, angry. "God, I hate frickin' Seaside!" He banged the flat of his hand on the hood of his car. Then, he lifted up his wire-rimmed glasses to rub his nose with his fingers, as if a headache was coming on.

Shamefaced, I climbed back into my car to get out my insurance information. Through my rolled down window, I tried to reassure the man, obviously a businessman of some sort with his pleated slacks, button-down shirt, and tie, "I'm fully insured. I shouldn't be a big deal, really."

The man said nothing and opened the passenger's side door of his Mercedes,

Knowing that my ex-co-workers were watching the whole exchange in delight, I kept my back to the motel. The man pulled a yellow legal pad out of his car and waited for me to share my insurance information with him.

"Uh, here's my insurance card."

He snatched it out of my trembling hand.

"My name's Sabrina Fuller. Do you want my home phone number?

He nodded with a jerk. As I recited my phone number, another car approached the back of the Mercedes. Looking up, I saw a cop exiting his vehicle and head over in our direction. Guess I was going to miss class.

Dammit!

"So, did we have a little accident here?" the police officer asked, as he yanked up his slouching uniform pants and pulled out a small pad of paper.

"Yes, officer, we sure did." The businessman seemed irate with the whole sequence of events, and I didn't blame him one bit. "This idiot just pulled right out of the parking lot and smashed into my car." He gestured at me with the ball point pen in his hand and then finished writing down my insurance information.

My stomach roiled. The gray-haired officer shook his head, turned toward me, and seemed to be waiting for me to say something.

"I really am sorry. I had a bad day, and I guess I was a little emotional..." my voice trailed off. I didn't really want to share my personal horror stories with complete strangers.

"A little emotional?" the businessman raved. "I'll say! And you took it out on my Mercedes."

"Now, now," the office interrupted. "The girl's got insurance, it looks like. This shouldn't be much of a problem. And it looks like her car got the worst of it."

I hadn't even glanced at *my* car yet. And the policeman was right, the cheap Festiva didn't fare too well in crashes. The entire left front side of my car was pushed in, like the nose of a pug dog. Some sort of fluid formed a large pool under my left front tire, and the hood was crumpled like a discarded wad of paper. I silently prayed my insurance would cover a rental car for all the days my car would be in the shop.

My emotions caught up with me. "Damn! That's just great. Just great." I kicked one of the tires.

The Mercedes owner looked up from his legal pad and leaned back casually against his car. It was hard to tell, but I think a bit of sympathy chipped away at his angry expression. Maybe.

Once I signed the accident report, I made my way up the street to a coffee shop to call a tow truck.

My next class was at six-thirty, so maybe I would have a shot at making it to campus on time if I got my car taken care of and a rental worked out with my insurance carrier.

Glancing back at the motel parking lot, I noticed the girls had long since gone back to work, or left for home. I felt a little less self-conscious. It would be difficult stopping by the next day for my final check.

The businessman's car was still running after our small accident, so as soon as we were done with the report, he climbed into his car. The businessman called through the open window, "Hey, do you need a ride or something?"

I was surprised he would even talk to me. "What? Don't you hate my guts?"

He laughed a bit, "I'm not mad at *you*, really, just the situation. You kind of messed up my schedule for the day. I missed a meeting in Monterey after having lunch with my wife. Look, do you want a ride or what?"

After a few moments contemplating how long it would take to hunt down a rental car, I replied, "Yeah, I could really use the ride, but I need to call for a tow first."

"You can use my cell, if you want." He reached across the passenger seat to hand his cell phone to me through the open window. I gingerly took it out of his hand.

"Thanks. I'm really sorry. This is my first accident. I'm usually a very good driver."

"It's all right. An inconvenience, and my car...well, that's bad, but you seem like a nice kid."

Kid? Did I look like a kid?

I was twenty-four years old, and I hadn't felt like a kid in years. Maybe it was my hair in a ponytail, or my face, which was blank of make-up.

Fiddling with the buttons on the cell phone, I gave up and asked, "Um, how do you use this thing?"

He put his car in park, "Come on, get it. I'll show you." He pulled on the door handle and popped the passenger's side door open.

I hesitated for a second, and then slid into the black leather seat. He seemed safe enough, and it was broad daylight on a busy street. Sheepishly, I handed the compact phone to my new acquaintance.

"Do you have Triple A?"

I shook my head. I could barely afford the insurance on my car much less afford a membership in Triple A.

"Well, I do. You don't have some tow place that you want to call, do you?"

Honestly, I was going to call the first tow company in the phone book when I got to the coffee shop. Not like a girl needs a tow truck every day. "No, I..."

Before I could finish my sentence, he whipped out his wallet and pulled out a card. "I'll call Triple A, and they can get a truck over here. I'll wait with you until they come, and then you can tell me where you need to go."

His friendliness startled me.

"Oh, let's call your insurance people, too, to let 'em know what's up." He took the phone from my hand and pressed buttons. "You said your name was Sabrina, right? I'm David. David Carris."

"Uh, yeah, Sabrina. That's me." Feeling self-conscious sitting in this strange man's car, I snorted a laugh. Then, immediately wishing I hadn't, I stared out the window at the sidewalk while David made the phone calls.

This was weird. I wasn't used to having anyone help me. It was an uncomfortable feeling, giving up my independence, my determination to do things all on my own. Asking for help was not something I was good at.

David hung up the phone. "The tow truck should be here in about fifteen minutes, and the insurance company will be sending you some forms to fill out." Indicating the tiny coffee shop with a nod of his head, he asked, "Should we grab a cup of coffee?" He must've noticed my raised eyebrows. "I know it seems a bit odd, we didn't meet under the best of circumstances, but you look as if you could use it."

Not as if anyone couldn't notice my cheap, run-down car or the ratty belongings I clutched in the front seat of the Mercedes. Yes, I was a hard-luck case, that's for sure. No way to deny that.

"I guess a cup of coffee would be all right." I had missed my morning caffeine fix, so it did sound like a good idea.

We both climbed out of his car and entered the coffee shop. David held the door open for me, which I thought was a gallant gesture, considering. It was empty inside, since it was between lunch and dinner. Even during the lunch rush this place didn't get a lot of business—worn linoleum covered the floor, Naugahyde booths sported duct-tape-fixed rips, and a fading hand-painted sign adorned the dusty front window. I automatically headed away from the cozy booths and sat at the counter instead. I barely knew the guy, so it would be smart to keep my distance. David followed suit, picking up a menu stuck between the creamer and sugar containers.

"Are you hungry?" David perused the short list of dishes on the menu. "Do you want something to go with that coffee?

I was famished, having skipped breakfast to be on time for my job. Make that my former job. That sounded awful. How was I going to cover the rent for the next month, if I only had one more paycheck coming?

"No, I'm fine," I answered brightly. I didn't have to look *that* pathetic. "Coffee's fine with me." My stomach chose that particular moment to growl loudly. I was a pretty bad liar.

When the waitress came over to us, David ordered two cups of coffee and two pieces of apple pie.

I protested, "But I said I wasn't—"

"Hungry. I know. But I don't want to look like a hog. I'm sure you can manage a couple of bites, right?"

I knew I would most likely *finish* my pie in a couple of bites. "If you don't mind, I'm going to change clothes in the ladies' room." I slid off my stool.

"You mean, those aren't your regular clothes?" David smirked.

I couldn't help but smile back at his joke.

He continued, "Yeah, go ahead. I'll make sure no one steals your pie."

I headed to the restroom and quickly donned my jeans and sweatshirt. I wished I had enough time that morning to throw some fresh clothes into my bag, but at least this would look better than my uniform. I pulled my hair out of its ponytail and then paused for a second, thinking of how else to improve my appearance. I unzipped a small pocket on the side of my backpack to access an emergency tube of lipstick. It wasn't a bright color, but it would make me look a bit older and less pale than I felt at the moment. Or, at least, I hoped it would.

When I returned to my swivel seat at the counter a steaming mug of coffee waited for me along with a huge chunk of mediocre-looking pie. It didn't matter, though, I was hungry enough even a sad-looking piece of canned-apple pie would taste good.

David gave me the quick once-over, "Feeling more like yourself?"

"Yes." I sighed happily. "That uniform is dreadful." Then, I realized something, "But that'll be the last time I have to wear it." No more nasty uniform was one reason to be happy today. I would definitely be looking for a job tomorrow that didn't require polyester pants.

"Oh? Why is that?"

"I was fired today." How utterly mortifying! But I couldn't think of anything better to say. Like I said, I was a bad liar.

His hand touched my shoulder, "I'm sorry."

I hadn't been asking for his pity. I always shouldered my own burdens. To lighten the moment, I laughed a little too loudly and said to him, "Hey, you wouldn't happen to know someone who has a job opening, would you?" I smiled and took a large bit of my apple pie.

He stared at me hard. "Now that you mention it..."

"You've got to be kidding." How embarrassing he took my off-the-cuff remark as genuine. "You know I wasn't really asking, right? It was just a joke."

"No, wait." He held up his hands. "We need help at my office. We were going to hire a temp, but..."

My face heated. "Really, I wasn't asking seriously. I don't expect you to find me a job." I sipped my coffee. "I crunched your car for heaven's sake. *I* should be doing something for *you*."

"I'm not doing this to be nice." My face must have reflected my skepticism. "Well, maybe I am just a little," he admitted. "But we need someone to help the receptionist with mailing, answering the phones, some filing. Stuff like that." He took a bite of his pie, then chased it with some coffee. "We end up hiring temps on occasion when the work backs up and end up with these idiots most of the time. And we have to pay the temp agency an arm and a leg. I could hire you permanently for a lot less than what we would have to pay the temp firm."

"Are you serious?" I brushed a strand of hair away from my eyes. "You would do that for me? A complete stranger?" No way did I have luck this good. "Don't you even want to know why I was fired? What if I can't type?"

"Are you looking for a reason for me *not* to hire you?" He sighed. "You need a job, obviously. I need some help in the office. What's the big deal? You can't be any worse than some of the people we've had. Believe me." He folded his napkin into perfect thirds. "So, you can't type, huh?"

"What?" I balked. "Of course I can type."

He gave me a sideways grin. "Besides common sense, that's about the only skill requirement. There's your tow truck." He gestured with his empty coffee cup at the large tow truck that was barely visible through the dusty window. His gaze landed back on me. "Just think about it for a minute before you say anything."

"All right, I'll think about it." But already I knew I would take the job. Regardless of the pay, it couldn't be any worse than the seven dollars an hour at the Seaside Motel. And my future boss was much nicer than disgusting Bob.

After taking a last, large bite of my apple pie I accepted his offer. "I'll take it. No uniforms, right?"

"Well..." he kidded.

"Wait a minute!" I gasped in mock outrage.

"No, there's nothing like a uniform, per se, but there is a

dress code. You know, business-type clothes." He eyed my outfit, "You *do* have something like that to wear, right?"

I smiled, "So, then, this would be completely appropriate." I waved my hand at my jeans and sweatshirt like a game show model.

David gave me a look; my attempt at humor had fallen flat.

"Yeah. I have some things I could wear." I had maybe a couple of outfits that could pass. Looks like I would be pulling out the emergency credit card.

David had a pleased look on his face. "Good." He left ten dollars for the waitress. "Let's get out of here. And then I can take you where you need to go."

I followed him outside. An overweight man in an ill-fitting pair of coveralls stained with oil climbed down from the cab of the tow truck parked by my dented car. With a toothpick sticking out from between his crooked teeth he asked, "Are you the ones that called for a tow?"

David answered before I had a chance to speak, "Yeah. It's the red car there." He pointed at my pathetic little Festiva with its crumpled hood and broken headlight. He whipped a business card out of his wallet and handed it to the tow truck driver. "You can take it here."

"All right." The foul-looking and foul-smelling driver glanced at the card. "You gonna follow me or will she need a ride?" He gave me a leering look and a yellow-toothed smile.

"No, no ride needed," David declared, saving me from what probably would have been the most disgusting ride of my life. "We'll be right behind you. Come on, Sabrina, *dear*." He emphasized the last word, looked the tow truck driver straight in the eye, and pulled my elbow toward his Mercedes.

I followed him wordlessly.

He started up the car and watched as the driver hooked up my Festiva. "So aren't you curious?"

"Curious? Curious about what?" David made me curious

about million things. But he was just a nice guy. A nice *married* guy. And nothing else.

"What you'll be paid, your hours, what sort of business you're getting yourself into?"

Feeling pretty stupid for not asking all of those questions before accepting the job, I said, "Yeah, I guess I should ask about that." What if he wanted me to work nine to five?

I had classes in the afternoon, and it was halfway through the semester I couldn't very well drop out.

"We really don't have full-time work. So, it won't be forty hours a week. I guess I was thinking something like four or five hours a day, no benefits, of course."

"Of course." As if I would expect this complete stranger to give me a job *and* health insurance? Me, with a 401(k)? It was a laughable thought. My whole life was living paycheck to paycheck, but he didn't need to know that.

"Why don't you start at eight tomorrow? Would that work for you?" He checked the tow truck in his rearview mirror to see how far along the driver was. "Would eleven dollars an hour be okay?"

Eleven dollars? I would be working less hours and be making the same amount of money. It was hard to believe. "That sounds perfect."

"I don't usually get into the office until nine, so why don't you meet me at the office then? Since no one knows I hired you yet, it might be a good idea for me to get there first." He looked over his shoulder. "Looks like we're ready to go."

six

. . .

THE NEXT MORNING, I woke up automatically at five-thirty, even though my alarm had been reset for a later time. I rolled over on my futon couch and snuggled further under my blankets. Watching the sun creep up into the sky through the curtained window, I relaxed and enjoyed the early morning quietness.

After a half-an-hour, I yanked one of my blankets around my body and shuffled to the kitchenette of my small studio. One hand clutched the blanket closed, and my other hand prepped the coffee maker. While the coffee brewed, I stripped off my long t-shirt and put on one of the few acceptable outfits I owned: a pair of khaki pants, a white button-up blouse, and some brown leather mules that were scuffed but comfortable. Not the most fashionable outfit, but it was somewhat professional and ironed for my first day as an assistant at Ergo Technology.

I still couldn't get over my luck—bad and good from yesterday. After leaving my car at the body shop, David had insisted I borrow one of his cars—a banged up VW Bug—instead of bother with a rental car.

"This is one of my project cars...my wife hates it," David had explained. "I've probably bought three or four cars in the past year for parts or for future tinkering, and she thinks they're junk."

Handing me the keys to a white Bug, he reassured me, "This one runs well enough, and my wife will be happy to see one of them gone when she gets home...even if it's just temporary."

I felt strange taking this man's car, no matter how beat up it was. Why was he trusting me? Why was he helping me? It was easier not to think there must be some ulterior motive. Couldn't someone be a Good Samaritan? The men my mother brought home had taught me a few things about the opposite sex, and this was not one of them. I pushed the thought out of my mind.

Along with the keys, he had handed me a business card after he wrote something on the back of it. "The company I work for is called Ergo Technology. It's downtown. You can't miss it."

I tucked it in my jeans pocket, "Guess I'll see you tomorrow then."

As I hopped into the Bug and backed out of his curved driveway, I gave a quick wave to my new boss. He waved back and gave an odd half-smile.

———

The coffee was done, and I was in no hurry to get dressed. That first sip was always the best, so I took a moment to enjoy it.

What a change not to rush around in the morning, stuffing books in my car and my hair in that horrid ponytail. No more polyester! A little coffee celebration ensued. I cranked up my clock radio and did a little dance around my studio. With an hour-and-a-half of time on my hands, I listened to the news (I didn't have a TV), drank some more coffee, and carefully collected my books and notes for class.

Spanish—ugh—and American History. As my new place of work was very close to campus, I would have no trouble making it to Spanish 200 on time. Professor Aguilera would have nothing to complain about this time.

At seven-thirty I headed downstairs.

I passed by the VW twice before I remembered the accident. What a bizarre day yesterday had been.

And now I was off to a new job, new people, new responsibilities. Nervous energy zinged through me. No longer would I be on my feet all day, picking up after messy strangers. Working in an office sounded very appealing after three months as a maid. This was one job I didn't want to lose—no matter what.

I pulled into the small parking lot behind the Ergo building and took in my new place of work. It was a small software company with only about ten employees, as David had explained to me yesterday on the way to his house: some product developers, one technical writer, an Ops person, a receptionist (whom I would be assisting), David, the manager/salesperson, and the owner/president. I couldn't quite remember what kind of software they produced, but I didn't care.

I had a new job!

I leaped out of the Bug and sailed through the front door of the building with a smile on my face.

"Good morning! May I help you?" The receptionist behind the desk greeted me almost too brightly. The woman stood up, which revealed how petite she was. Bright red, obviously dyed, hair sat on her head in a very blunt bob cut with a thick set of bangs curled above her over-plucked brows. Brows that were clearly a different color than her hair. She was in her late 40s or early 50s, an aging artistic type with lots of bangle bracelets on her wrists and too much make-up to hide her wrinkles. I towered over her and probably outweighed her by at least fifty pounds.

The receptionist stretched out her hand to give a vigorous shake, and I got a whiff of my new coworker: heavy perfume with a floral scent. Not very pleasant. The odor clung to her, and I backed away slightly to allow some air to circulate between us.

"My name is Alicia. Alicia Grant." She very distinctly emoted each syllable of her name: A-Lee-Cee-Ah.

I would have to remember that.

"I'm Sabrina Fuller." Before I continued, the fact dawned on me that David had asked me to come late this morning.

Chagrined, I quickly added, "I just realized I'm early. I'm supposed to meet Mr. Carris this morning and forgot he won't be in until nine."

"Oh, dear. Would you like to wait?" Alicia pointed at the on chair in their very small reception area. A *Wall Street Journal* and an array of golfing magazines lay on the tiny coffee table squeezed into the space. Not a place I would like to spend an hour in, especially with that overpowering perfume surrounding me.

"Um." Boy, how was I going to do this politely? "I think I'll go grab some breakfast and come back when Mr. Carris is sure to be here. Thanks." I turned, pushed through the entrance door, and took a deep breath of fresh air. I hoped I wouldn't have to work exceedingly close to Alicia for long period of time. Did she know how powerful her perfume was?

I walked downtown. The Ergo office was only a few blocks from some of my favorite study spots.

Perhaps I could try a muffin at Papa Java's, another coffee-house like Morgan's, but this one was right in the middle of Alvarado Street. If I sat outside, I could do some people-watching before I had to be back at the office.

As I approached the coffeehouse, I recognized a familiar figure in black with blond hair seated at an outside table.

Patrick watched me approach him, and put up his hand in a salutatory gesture. I thought about the wadded up piece of paper at my studio. Would he have been waving at me had I called him the other night?

"Hey, how's it going?" Patrick pulled out the chair next to him with his foot.

Maybe the other night wasn't a fluke. Maybe there was something between us.

I was looking for a friend, but the butterflies in my stomach told me he could be something more than that. Kind of like Beauty and the Beast—me being the Beast, of course.

I wasn't classically pretty with dainty features and a ballerina figure. I was tall and had been since a fairly young age. My features were strong and quasi-masculine, I thought. Large mouth, a slightly long nose, deep-set eyes. My hair was probably my best feature. It was thick and shiny and hung below my shoulders. Guys generally have a thing for long hair, my mother often confided in me.

Patrick was the Beauty. Golden hair, the bluest of blue eyes, high cheekbones, and a perfect chin. He looked like the All-American quarterback. Well, maybe a little too thin to play the quarterback. But All-American, for sure. And the dark clothes? The vampire book? That added a big heap of mystery into the mix which piqued my interest even more. He was different.

Could a guy like this be interested in a girl like me?

I sat down at Patrick's wordless invitation and asked, "What are you up to? Don't you have Korean class or something?"

"Normally, yeah, but we're going on a field trip today, so we get to wear civilian clothes. The bus doesn't leave until nine, and since base is right up the hill—" He gestured at the slope that started only a few blocks over. "I thought I could dash down here for a few shots of espresso to get me going."

"A field trip?" I thought the military was all strict rules and orders. It was hard for me to imagine a bunch of soldiers being paid to skip a day of class and not wear a uniform. "They let you take field trips? Where are you going?"

"Yeah, they let us take field trips. 'All work and no play,' you know the slogan." He gave a half-grin. "We're going to San Francisco. They have a pretty good Asian scene up there. The teachers tell us that we'll have the chance to speak Korean while we are there...you know, with 'real' Koreans."

"Mmmm...sounds interesting." With his cool blue gaze sliding over me, I was having a hard time listening to everything he was saying. I felt as if I wore a bikini rather than a conservative white blouse.

"Thanks for the enthusiasm," he chided, bringing his wandering gaze back up to my eyes. "Hey, for us it's a big deal. You have no idea what class is like. Six hours a day of straight Korean. No English spoken in class from day one, wearing a uniform that you hate. Spending one day in my own clothes and out of the classroom? It's like my first day out of Boot Camp." He paused and nodded in her direction. "I should be asking what you're doing here. Are you working at The Gap today?"

I flushed at his sarcasm, the last thing I wanted was him thinking of me as some preppy. "No, but I did get a new job. I'm little early, so I'm wasting some time."

"Does 'wasting time' included imbibing a beverage?" he quipped.

"Yes, that was part of the plan." I smiled nervously and fiddled with a napkin that had been left on the table. Was he flirting with me, or did I just want to believe that he was?

God, he was hard to read.

Honestly, any man was hard for me to read.

"So, what would you like?"

I looked at him stupidly, "Huh?"

"Um, let's see, I would like to buy you a drink, if that's okay." He spoke this very precisely, teasing me for missing his first attempt at a drink offer. I think he was positively amused at my nervous reaction to him. "What would you like?"

"Oh." God, what an idiot I could be. "I guess I'll take a latte."

"You aren't one of those girly-girls, are you?"

"What?"

"You know, the kind that wants nonfat milk, decaf espresso, and fake sugar?"

Although I did prefer the nonfat milk variety of latte, I wouldn't dare admit to it now. "No, I want the whole cow and the whole coffee bean in there, please."

He smiled this sexy, crooked smile at me. "You got it. I'll be right back." He stood up and entered the shop to order my latte.

While he was inside, I took the opportunity to look at what he had spread out on the table. This time there weren't any vampire books or literary masterpieces; only Korean texts. Big books. One labeled as a workbook and another just as "Korean, Level I." There were also a couple of CD cases marked with "Lesson 15" and "Lesson 16" and a CD player with headphones. I picked up the book marked as the workbook and flipped through the first few pages.

"Interested in learning some Korean?" He startled me, and I quickly closed the workbook. "I could teach you, if you'd like." He sat at the table, one paper cup in each hand.

"No, no, Spanish is hard enough for me right now. This looks really difficult," I pointed at the large *Korean, Level I* text in front of him. "I mean, six hours a day? It would take me year to get to that level with only a few hours of tutoring a week, wouldn't it?"

He handed me my full-fat latte and a couple of packets of sugar, "You would be surprised how much you could pick up."

More curious about Patrick than about Korean, I changed the subject abruptly, "So, where are you from?" Just because I didn't want him asking me about my personal life, didn't mean I couldn't find out more about his.

"Ah...now we're getting to something that interests you, I see." Again, he smiled with a smile that seemed to say he could see right through me.

Immediately embarrassed, I answered, "No..." Then, realizing how that sounded, corrected myself. "Yes. Well, more interesting to me than Korean."

"Why don't you go first?" He took a long sip of his coffee drink and sat back in his chair, staring at me intently.

Not expecting that response, I stalled, "Uh, well...I wanted to hear something about you. My life's pretty boring, really."

Oh, no, please tell me he isn't going to be the kind of guy that pries. And I was so beginning to like him.

seven

. . .

"SO YOU'RE the shy type, huh?" Was it possible for someone to stir a latte erotically? If not, he was awfully close to mastering the technique. The stir stick swirled and dipped into the foam with a gentle motion. He looked up at me as he stirred, "I think I like that."

Okie-dokie. That was a little more information than I could handle. His gaze was penetrating. To break eye contact, I forced myself to lean down and fish something, anything, out of my purse. I grabbed the first thing my fingers touched: my wallet.

He quickly snatched it out of my hands, "All right. Now I can find out everything about you." He dramatically unsnapped it and pulled out my driver's license. "Birth date—Oh, you're a Taurus. Stubborn, right? And you're really five foot nine?"

Before he could disclose my weight to the passersby, I grabbed back my wallet, "Excuse me."

"There's nothing in there that can scare me, if that's what you're worried about."

"No, I'm not worried about anything you might find in my wallet," I bluffed. Having him look at such personal information made me feel as if he could see right through me. As if he could figure out from a bad driver's license photo that I was poor, alone, and very much wanted him to find me attractive.

"Okay." He backed off. "I guess I can tell you one thing about me."

"Thank you." My nerves ratcheted down a little. The flirtatious banter was difficult for me to keep up. I didn't have much practice at it. My mother's idea of flirting was wearing a short skirt, a low-cut top, and downing a few drinks to 'loosen up.' And I had seen what type of men that kind of flirting brought home.

"I'm from Indiana."

"Indiana?" I mocked. I couldn't imagine this black-clad, esoteric figure living somewhere as mundane as Indiana.

"OK, that's enough."

I had touched a nerve.

"Hey, I didn't mean...look, it surprised me. You don't look like someone who came from a corn field."

"Is that some sort of compliment?"

"Yes," I said quietly. Internally, I berated myself for blurting out such an insult. Sometimes—no, most of the time—my mouth was faster than my brain.

He looked at me with some doubt.

"I meant you seemed more like someone who'd grown up in LA or Chicago or something."

He seemed to accept that explanation. After taking a quick sip of his drink, he gave me a few more details, "I dropped out of college about a year ago."

When I gave him a quizzical look, he said, "Long story."

"Oh." I stopped right there, worried if I said more I would insult him yet again.

"I moved back home, but my stepfather...well, he and I don't see eye to eye. I had to get out of there. Not a lot for a guy like me"—he indicated the black skull t-shirt he was wearing—"in a small town. So, I got on the first bus out of there, and ended up talking to a guy about this language school."

"DLI?"

"Right. He was in the Army and was on leave. I never would have guessed he was in the military, if he hadn't told me." He put his hands in the pockets of his leather jacket and tilted his chair back to lean against the stucco wall behind him. "I had been an Asian Studies major in college, but the school only had one course in basic Chinese. If I could get into DLI and learn it fluently..."

"But you said you were studying Korean," I interrupted.

"I didn't have a lot of choice when I got here. There happened to be a spot in Korean, so I took it."

"Isn't it hard, though? It seems like it would be so difficult. A whole different alphabet, and the writing. I don't know if I could ever learn that." Hard to believe a guy who had quit school could dedicate himself to something as complex as learning Korean.

"You'd be surprised how easy it is to learn when you're doing it every day, all day. And if you have an interest in it, even better. Some of the guys in my class never even wanted to come here, and, surprise, surprise, they are barely above failing in class."

I leaned my elbows on the table, took a long drink of my latte, and asked him, "So what got you so interested in all things Asian in the first place?"

He enjoyed talking about himself, so it made it easy for me to keep my background to myself.

"Well, I took some Tae Kwon Do classes when I was in high school. It's like the language and the philosophy behind martial arts sort of work together. I wanted to learn more."

Then, he looked pointedly at me, "Have you ever taken any marital arts?"

I practically choked on my latte. "What? Me?" I laughed a bit.

The idea of someone as ungraceful and tall as me attempting to do something so coordinated sounded ridiculous. "No way. I'm a complete klutz...and I don't get that meditation stuff. You know, finding your 'chi' and all that."

He bristled at my reaction to his question, but accepted my response. "I think you could really get something out of it. I'm trying to find a class here. I haven't taken lessons in a few years and wanted to get back into it."

He reached out his hand to touch my wrist, "You should come with me."

I was about to dismiss the idea, but what was I thinking? Here is an attractive guy, flirting with me—at least, I thought so—and I was going to turn down his offer? Who cares if I wasn't interested in Tae Kwon whatever.

"Sure, why not? I mean, I shouldn't automatically reject something I've never experienced, right?"

He smiled. "Yeah, that's it. Be adventurous. Watch a class; you might find that you really like it. Why don't we meet up on Saturday sometime? Most places are busy on the weekends."

"Okay." I made a mental note to be more open-minded in the future.

Patrick glanced at his watch. "Look, I gotta go. It's about ten to nine now, and I would get in serious trouble if I missed the bus." He stuffed his stack of Korean materials in a canvas bag.

"Where should we meet?"

"Here's my number." He wrote on a small index card he pulled from the bag. "Why don't you give me a call on Saturday morning, and we'll set something up then." He handed it to me. "When you call, ask for Patrick McKinnon. It's a pay phone in the hall. They don't have phones in the barracks rooms, and I didn't want to spend the money on a cell. Military doesn't pay much, you know? Anyway, everyone knows who I am."

I tucked the card in my purse, glad I had gotten his number legitimately this time. "I'll see you Saturday."

He headed down the street, waved at me, and then he was gone.

A date of sorts for Saturday. That was good news. I would rather go to a movie or out to dinner, but I would try this Tae Kwon Do thing. Patrick seemed intense and driven. Quite different than I. Oh, I wasn't a slacker with no plans, but I was much more laid back and less certain of exactly how I would reach my goals in life. He seemed to have everything planned out—a few years in the military, master Korean, then...yeah? Then what?

Hmm...that would be something I would have to ask when we met again.

I picked up my purse and set off in the direction of the Ergo office. Hopefully, David would already be there, so I wouldn't have to sit in the waiting area with over-perfumed Alicia.

Ick. It really was overpowering.

"Hey, Sabrina!" David put down the Wall Street Journal he had been reading to greet me. "Alicia, she's here."

When I entered the office, my heart did a little flutter. David was cuter than I remembered from yesterday...but very married. Today, he wore a dark gray suit that was tailored perfectly to fit his athletic body and a pair of wire-rimmed glasses. How lucky was the wife that got to kiss this man goodbye every morning?

Alicia emerged from what looked like the restroom. I heard the telltale sound of a flushing toilet. Hopefully, she had washed away some of the excess perfume while in there.

She recognized me. "Oh, you're the girl from earlier this morning."

I cleared my throat and explained to David with a sheepish smile, "I forgot you were meeting me here at nine, and showed up an hour too early."

"So, did you feel stupid or what?" David chuckled and

clapped me on the back. "What a great way to start your first day at work."

Alicia's mouth flattened into a line.

"This," David began, "is our new admin assistant, Sabrina Fuller."

With a slight frown, Alicia asked, "What kind of experience do you have, dear?"

Before I could answer and list my limited skills, David interrupted, "She'll be fine. Not much to it—a glorified mail clerk. Anyone can do the job who has a head on her shoulders."

Alicia didn't seem to take kindly to anyone calling any part of her job simple. "I just don't want to spend a lot of time training, David. I sure hope you made the right decision." She took a closer look at me, sniffing a bit and judging my choice in work wear.

David didn't notice the tension between us or the fact Alicia had challenged someone higher on the job ladder than she. Instead, he continued on blithely, "I'll give her the tour. I know how busy you are. She'll be back in a flash to learn more about her duties."

He twirled me around by the elbow and pointed me in the direction of the hallway that lead off the reception area. "All right, there are the restrooms. My office is back there," he pointed at a door further down the hall.

"So, you have an office all to yourself?" I asked, impressed.

"Yep. Pretty nifty, huh? Thirty-something, good-looking, *and* I have my own office." David teased, "I've got babes around me all the time."

I snorted a laugh. "Yeah, between work and your wife, I am sure you have all sorts of free time for the ladies, right?" Boy, it was so much easier joking around with this good-looking man than with Patrick. I guess David seemed safe, he was married after all.

"Okay, you got me," he winked. "Let's continue our five-star tour of the facilities." He showed me where everyone else sat: the developers and writer in their cubes, the president in the only other office with a door. Introducing me around, he built me up as the greatest thing since cheese in a can.

He walked me back to the front desk and handed me over to Alicia, "Here's your little helper."

"Oh," Alicia looked up from a stack of CD-ROMs and FedEx boxes. "Great, I could really use her help packing this stuff."

Before he turned to head back to his office, he asked "Hey, newbie, how about we meet up for lunch? Tina's going to be out this way for a doctor's appointment, and you are more than welcome to tag along."

"Tina?"

"My wife. Thought you might like to meet her, and she mentioned to me last night she was curious to see who took one of those 'awful' cars out of our driveway. I think you are her new hero."

My stomach twisted in knots at the prospect of sitting between a married couple during what might be a rare lunch out together. I barely knew David and didn't quite understand why he wanted me along—although he *did* have a great sense of humor and seemed to think I was pretty competent for a recently-fired maid. That was definitely something in his favor. Not to mention his attitude toward me even after I crashed into his beautiful car.

"I don't want to intrude."

"Intrude? I've been married for seven years. You wouldn't be intruding, you would be a—"

"—third wheel?"

He laughed, "I'll come and get you at noon, okay?" He headed for his office before I even had a chance to try and turn him down.

"Is he always so friendly?" I asked Alicia who was buried behind a stack of CD-ROMs, a bit of a smile still on my face.

"I don't know," she said in a distracted rush. "What I really need right now is some help and not chatter, if you don't mind."

"Uh, sure." I put on my serious work face and stepped behind the counter of the reception area.

————

Beautiful women in my mind were usually small-boned and feminine with dainty jewelry and nicely-manicured nails. That described Tina Carris to a tee. Sitting at lunch with David and his wife was an agonizing experience. I was out-of-place, like a boyfriend in a lingerie store.

When David introduced me at the restaurant, Tina had coolly greeted me. It was obvious he had not called his wife to tell her I was tagging along.

Tina had carefully dressed in a crisp, cream pantsuit and a pale pink camisole-style top. Her blonde hair was twisted up into a smart chignon, a few wisps of hair artfully placed around her face.

"So, Sabrina, how do you know my husband again?" Tina's gaze took in my now-wrinkled khaki pants and scuffed fake leather shoes.

"Well, to tell you the truth," I nervously began.

Tina pulled a compact and lipstick out of her tiny clasp purse and began to freshen her lipstick, "Uh-huh?"

David saved me from the slow conversational torture. "Oh, one of those friend-of-a-friend things, honey."

I, expecting him to remind his wife that I was the person driving around town in one of his beat-up, rescued-from-the-verge-of-the-car-crushing-machine project cars, was dumbstruck. Mouth slightly open, I listened mutely as he smoothly laid out one lie after another.

"We needed someone more permanent at work, and Bill...you remember Bill? My racquetball partner?"

Tina nodded distractedly as she completed putting on her lipstick and returned it to her purse.

"Well, his neighbor's daughter goes to the community college, and she's in class with Sabrina."

"And you thought you could help her out?" Tina finished for him, smiling a bit too widely at me. "How nice. Isn't David just the kindest man?" Tina reached out, squeezed David's hand, then dropped it as if it was a dead fish.

I didn't know quite how to answer that question. It felt as if Tina was trying to bait me. Before I could say anything, David saved me once again from his wife. He was obviously very practiced in this art.

"Why don't we order?" He handed a menu to his wife. "They have really good seafood here."

Now it was clear to me why he had wanted me to come along on the husband-and-wife intimate lunch. I wasn't a third wheel, as I had earlier predicted, but was, instead, the distraction.

Tina didn't even look at the lunch selections. Instead, she glanced cattily at me, "What are you studying, Sabrina? Business? Or maybe Computer Science?" She took a delicate sip from her water glass.

"Well, I really haven't decided on a major yet." I cleared my throat. How did she manage to catch me off guard with her questions? She was the cat, and I was the mouse. "I've been working on my Gen Ed classes hoping something will grow on me."

"Oh, I see, so you don't know much about computers, do you? But somehow the idea of working for a software company just started to 'grow on you,' too?"

David, who had been reading his menu, interrupted Tina's thread of conversation before she could do any further damage. "Tina, leave her alone for godsakes. She's just stuffing envelopes. Not like you need a college degree for that."

Tina smiled cruelly across the table at me, her pink lips

stretched across her face. She had forced her husband to insult me, and she was loving every minute of it.

Before he could muster some sort of an apology, I spoke up. I wanted to show Tina I could stand up for myself. "I've done a little bit of everything the past few months to make ends meet. You would be surprised how quickly I can pick things up." Tina's pitiless smile faded slightly. "Besides, working at Ergo might give me some inspiration as to which major I should tackle."

I had parried her verbal thrust.

David glared across the table at his wife.

The waiter, thankfully, appeared at our table at the very moment I thought he might explode.

I ordered first, "I'll take the halibut steak with rice, and a Diet Pepsi." Then, feeling a dire need to escape from the tension at the table, I grabbed my purse and excused myself, heading in the direction of the restroom.

Behind me, I heard whispered, harsh voices arguing, very little of which I could understand. But I did catch "that little slut" and "aren't you a bit old" coming from Tina, and "shut up" and "no idea what you are talking about" coming from David. Beyond that I heard little else and was glad for the restroom door whooshing shut behind me.

I sat in the stall for quite a while. My heart pounded as the conversation I overheard repeated itself over and over in my head. I dreaded going back to the table, but knew I couldn't be gone much longer without it appearing weird.

I exited the stall and stood in front of the mirror. I looked at my reflection, smoothed down the flyaway bits of my brown hair, and tucked one stubborn portion behind my ear.

I had a square jaw that, luckily, was softened by two dimples, one in each cheek. But I still hated that angular, hard jaw line that reminded me of Arnold Schwartzeneggar in *The Terminator*. Not very womanly. Tina, on the other hand, was very soft and slight, very painted and perfect. I reached into my purse and pulled out some eye make-up and a lipstick. Might as well try to look a little bit better. A stroke of eyeliner here, a brush of lipstick there...at least now I appeared more my age and less pale.

I returned to the table, and right away I noticed Tina was missing. Relief washed over me. "Where's Tina?"

"Something came up. She had to be back in Marina for an appointment." David seemed distracted; he kept nervously looking beyond me, over my shoulder.

"For work?"

"No," David said weakly. He hesitated, as if he couldn't find the words. "Tina doesn't work. She's a—"

"—A housewife?"

He laughed at that, his nervousness gone. "Oh, I don't think Tina would call it that. But, yes, I guess that's what she is. She was an interior decorator for a while. Then I got this job in Monterey, and she had to leave her position at the design firm in San Francisco." He placed his fingers on his temples, as if he had the beginnings of a headache. "I think she's still punishing me for it."

"Oh."

"Dave!" A female voice called out cheerily from across the restaurant. "Is that you?"

eight

. . .

"LUCY. HI," David responded without much enthusiasm. "How've you been?"

A woman in her mid-30s, dark and slender, approached our table from the bar. She was another beautiful woman, dressed to the nines in a tailored jacket, short skirt, and slingback heels.

"How have *I* been? Where have *you* been, I should be asking." Lucy played with a string of what I knew was real pearls. This kind of woman would wear nothing less. "And who's your dining companion this afternoon?" Lucy looked pointedly at me.

"Oh, I'm sorry."David stood up and put his hand on my shoulder, "This is our new assistant at Ergo, Sabrina Fuller."

Lucy gave me one of those wimpy, womanly handshakes I hated. "Lovely to meet you dear," she stated patronizingly, as if talking to a child.

David took his seat.

"Yes. Nice to meet you, too." I felt overly-scrutinized by this well-dressed woman, so when the waiter appeared at our table with a tray full of food I bit my lip to keep from smiling at the interruption.

Before David was forced to be polite and invite her to join us, Lucy interceded, "Well, I'll leave you two to your lunch. I'm meeting someone. Nice to see you, Dave." She gave him a quick kiss on the cheek.

"Yes, nice to see you."

Lucy returned to the bar, sashaying around the maze of tables, her long legs attracting attention from the male restaurant patrons.

David leaned closer to me and whispered, "Do I have any lipstick on me?"

I picked up my napkin and wiped off the slightest hint of bright red lipstick that Lucy had left behind. A quiver in my stomach warned me against being that close to him, doing something so intimate. I could smell the spice of his cologne.

"Thanks."

That brought me back to my senses. Was I so lonely I'd allow myself to be attracted to my married boss?

My mother had never brought home a man like David. Her boyfriends usually smelled of cigarette smoke and stale beer, never had one smelled so clean, so masculine. But the only relationship I would ever have with this man would be a professional one, I would make sure of it.

It would be just like my mother to horn in on another woman's territory. To swipe a husband away from right underneath the wife's nose. But that wasn't me; I swore to be different. To not make the same mistakes my mother had.

To return my focus to the present, I directed the conversation at our recent visitor. "Who was that?"

David took a bite of his Mahi-Mahi and raised his eyebrows. "Lucy? Oh, nobody. Just an old friend."

Lunch continued on in a very lighthearted fashion. I asked him about everyone I could remember at Ergo, and he gave me all the gossip. Including a few very good impersonations of some of the more memorable characters at the office.

"And what do you think of A-LEE-CEE-AH?" He mimicked the receptionist's precise pronunciation.

I couldn't help but giggle a bit at his dead-on impression. "Oh, I guess she's all right. I can't complain too much; my last boss was a real winner." It was then I remembered I told Bob the Lecher I would be back today to pick up my check. And I wouldn't have time to stop there before class that afternoon. Heaven knows I needed the money. Rent was due soon. "Hey, David, can I ask a favor?"

"Sure, what is it?"

"I need to go to Seaside to pick up my last check from my old job. Do you think we can swing by there after lunch?"

"No problem." He seemed eager to help. "We might have to eat and run, so I can get back to the office in time for my afternoon meeting, but I don't mind."

He grew more and more likable by the second. "Great. I want to be done with that place and forget I ever worked there. I wouldn't be surprised if my old boss told me my check got mysteriously 'lost' somewhere in his office, if I waited until tomorrow."

"Oh, I don't think he would be that stupid." He gave me the impression he knew how to handle such creeps as Bob. "If he gives you a hard time, I'll be there to back you up, okay?"

"Thanks, David, I really appreciate it." Without thinking, I reached across the table and grabbed his hand. Then, suddenly aware of the warmth and solidity of that hand, I pulled away.

What happened to my silent pledge to not repeat my mother's mistakes? This was going to be harder than I thought.

Treating David like a boss rather than as a friend with romantic possibilities was the right thing to do. As much as I might dislike Tina, I had to respect that she was David's wife. And just because someone is kind to me, is no reason to believe he feels anything more than friendship.

He fiddled with his wedding band, clearly bothered by the

intimacy of that one moment. I resolved then and there to try harder.

He cleared his throat. "You ready to go?"

I took one last bite of my meal and nodded.

As we left the restaurant together, I caught sight of Lucy at the bar. She was still alone; either she had been stood up, or she was lying. I guessed the former, as Lucy, attractive as she was, could most certainly find a date for any meal. Or maybe she had been watching David with his wife, saw Tina leave, and I showed up before Lucy could make her move. Some odd tension cropped up when Lucy visited our table. As if she was sizing me up, wondering exactly what kind of 'friend' I was.

On the drive to Seaside, David explained his wife's sudden departure. "If you couldn't tell, Tina and I are having problems."

I feigned innocence to hide my curiosity. I had resolved to be a good friend, and that meant being supportive when necessary. He didn't need me prying into his personal life. "Oh?" I tried to sound concerned but not overly interested.

Like a dam that had burst, David poured out his life to me. "It's been bad for a while now. Ever since the move down here a couple of years ago. I guess when we were both busy and working in San Francisco, we really didn't see the problems we had. I think I thought it was stress or something."

I slowed my breathing. I had only met the man yesterday, was driving one of his cars, and now he was telling me his personal problems? "Whoa, David. Wait a minute. Do you really think you should be telling me this?"

Good, Sabrina. Excellent job at playing supportive friend with a conscience.

He ran a hand through his thick hair, "Yeah, I guess you're right. I shouldn't dump all this on you." He sighed heavily. "You must think I'm a nut. We should be talking about the office. I'm sorry."

It worked. I diverted him from an intimate, detailed conversation about his marriage.

"It's all right. I'm not sure I should know any of that." *That's it, distance yourself some more, Sabrina.* "Why don't you tell me about that Lucy person. She was an interesting character." There, a nice, safe topic.

"Lucy?" David uncomfortably pulled at the knot of his tie. "She's a friend. She was around a lot when Tina and I were—well, when Tina kicked me out, basically."

Whoops. This was not part of the plan. The plan was to stay off the marriage. Yes, and I had been doing such a good job. How did we end up back here?

David cleared his throat, He seemed desperate to confide in someone about it. Why did it have to be me? "Lucy was kind enough to let me sleep on her couch for a few weeks until things cooled down. She's Sidney's ex."

"Sidney? You mean, Mr. Campos?

"Yep. The one and only president of Ergo Software."

I vividly remembered Mr. Campos from the office tour: a 65-year-old, short, overweight man with a bad haircut. Why would someone like Lucy marry a middle-aged fashion don't? I thought about it for a second. Then, I started to think of every successful businessman with more money than looks; they usually had beautiful, younger wives. Or, at the very least, beautiful, younger *second* wives.

David continued, "Lucy is the one that told me about the job opening down here."

"So you knew her before you moved here?"

He didn't seem to like what I was implying, "Look, it's a long story, my history with her. But let's just keep it at 'we're friends.'"

Anxious to end the conversation, I had obviously hit a sore spot, I nodded in agreement. Then, I saw the sign for the motel, thank God. "Here we are."

He pulled the car into the parking lot. "I'll wait for you here. If he gives you a hard time, just come out and let me know." There was a grim determination on his face, his jaw was set, his eyes sparkled—as if he might enjoy a confrontation.

I smiled warily and climbed out of the Mercedes, "I'll be right back." I prayed Bob would cooperate; I didn't want David to get involved. I should be able to handle this on my own.

But I dreaded the encounter. Mustering up my courage, I talked to myself on the walk up to the entrance.

Don't let him bug you, Sabrina. Ask for the check and then get out of there.

I opened one of the double glass doors to the lobby.

"So, you couldn't stay away, eh?"

With his gut hanging over his manager's uniform pants, Bob waited for me in the lobby. He'd spread his lunch out on the coffee table, the TV tuned to ESPN. Taking another bite of his sandwich, he spoke, chewing, "Wanna bite, toots?"

He thrust the foot-long sandwich at me and then laughed, spewing lettuce on the floor.

"I'm here for my check." I stood my ground and looked Bob directly in the eye, hoping I was intimidating.

He laughed even harder. So hard, he began to choke on his sandwich. Thumping himself in the chest a couple of times, he swallowed and answered my request. "You're hilarious, honey, fucking hilarious. You think I'm the magic check-writin' man that can just whip a check out any time he feels like it?" He grabbed a paper cup and took a swig of soda. "I wish, baby, I wish."

I took a deep breath to steady my voice, "Then, you can pay me in cash. I'll wait."

He plopped his sloppy sandwich down on a paper bag and stood. "Are you crazy, bitch?" He moved threateningly toward me. "You want me to just walk behind the counter and hand you some bills? Get outta here."

I stepped back, not wanted to be manhandled out the door again. "I'm warning you, Bob. I'm warning you—" I backed up to the glass doors and pushed them open slightly.

"Oh, 'you're warning me, you're warning me'?" He mocked in a falsetto voice. "What're you gonna do? Call the cops on me? I don't think that would be a wise idea."

The weight of the door behind me gave, and I felt a presence. David stepped into the lobby.

"Hey, uh, 'Bob'?" He read the name tag pinned to Bob's wrinkled shirt, the sparkle I had seen in the car returning to his eyes. "I think you're going to get this lady her money right now or I'm going to get the tire iron out of my car and *help* you find the money. Got it?"

Bob scowled, irritated I had brought along male company, but he dropped his menacing stance and backed up a few steps, "Hey, I didn't mean nothin' man." He put his hands up in a surrender pose and backed into his small office. Grabbing his phone, he punched in an extension, "Hilda? Can you print out a check for me? Huh? Yeah, I know it's before payday, but I need it now."

Bob glanced up at David who was leaning in the doorway. He raised his hand signaling for David to be patient and wait. "Hilda, I need a check for Sabrina—right now—for, uh," Bob eyed his computer screen, "seventy-two hours, regular wage. Yep. Thanks."

Bob hung up the phone and growled at David, "Go back to the accounting office. They'll have the check ready in a few minutes.

David's steely eyes narrowed, and then he headed down the hall. I followed. When I passed by Bob's office, Bob whispered to me, "I don't wanna see you back in here ever again, ya hear? Stay outta my way, bitch."

I ignored his threat and continued down the hall. When Bob could no longer see me, I felt my knees tremble. So much for being tough and standing my ground—even a short little man like Bob could scare me.

David had already reached the accounting office and held a check in his hand. "Thank you, Hilda. Sabrina appreciates this. You really helped out." Gone was the intimidating, hardened eyes. Instead, the handsome, charming David had returned. He smiled his pleasant, toothy smile, which probably made ancient Hilda melt into her support hose.

"Come on, Sabrina, let's get out of here."

We were out the door before I could sneak a peek at Bob.

Before I knew it, I was securely ensconced in the Mercedes and on my way back to work a few hundred dollars richer.

"David." I wanted to let him know that although his tough guy act worked on Bob, I really didn't appreciate the tactic.

He interrupted me, "Ah, you don't have to thank me...yet." He smiled at me disarmingly and squeezed my hand as it rested on top of my purse.

It was hard to be mad at David when he smiled like that. But the hand? Uncomfortable, I pulled away, "Well, thank you anyway. You've been very nice to me in the past twenty-four hours." I thought back to the moment in the lobby when I first approached my former boss, "Bob is such a—"

"Disgusting slob? Lecherous creep?" David smiled at me, "Would you like me to continue?"

I laughed and enjoyed the rest of the ride back to the office. Why make a big deal out of nothing? David had helped me out, maybe not in the way I would have liked, but it *did* work. I had to give him credit for that.

nine

. . .

I WAS SITTING on my futon Saturday morning, wrapped in a blanket with a small index card in my hand. Patrick's phone number.

Today we were supposed to meet—a date of sorts. But I had to make the call. Why didn't I think to give him *my* number? My stomach twisted up inside me. If he had shown up for Advanced Spanish class on Wednesday or Friday, maybe I would have gotten up the courage to do that. But he must have dropped the class like he said he might.

Sabrina, you wimp! Call him.

Tuesday seemed so long ago.

What if he had forgotten our plans?

I fingered the phone receiver sitting in its base on the floor in front of me. Before I could change my mind, I punched in the numbers on the card and waited for a ring.

Ring. Ring. Ring.

No one was answering.

Should I hang up?

Ring. Ring.

Okay, that was six rings—that's enough. No one's there.

Then, a click and a sleepy, "Barracks, 2nd floor."

"Hi, I'm looking for Patrick McKinnon?" The words came thick and slow out of my mouth.

Suddenly, a loud bang exploded on the other end of the phone. Then, in the background, I heard a faint voice calling, "McKinnon. Some chick for you on the phone."

A few long moments passed. My heart raced, and my hands grew sweaty. I almost hung up the phone. Then, a scraping sound.

"Hello?" Patrick sounded groggy.

Damn!

I looked at the clock. I called too early—it was eight-thirty. Was that early for a Saturday morning in the Army? I guess even the military got a break on Saturdays.

"It's me, Sabrina?" My voice quavered. What if he forgot I was going to call? "We were going to meet this morning and check out some, uh—" Why couldn't I put two words together? I sounded like a fourteen-year-old calling my junior high crush.

Patrick finished my sentence for me, thank goodness. "Martial Arts classes? Yeah, I remember. Kinda early, don't you think?"

"Well, I thought maybe you military types got up at the crack of dawn or something."

"Maybe Monday through Friday, but the weekend is when I can play civilian." I heard him try to stifle a yawn.

"I'm sorry. I could call back in a couple of hours." I paced around my small apartment, twisting and untwisting the cord around my wrist.

"No, no, that's okay. I'm pretty much awake now." He cleared his throat, "Look, let's say you give me about half-an-hour, and you can meet me outside the barracks."

My stomach flip-flopped. We had a date. Talking on the phone was one thing, but meeting him purposefully for a date? I was nervous and delighted all at the same time. I stopped mid-pace and found that I needed to sit down. Now.

"Sure." *Come on, Sabrina, sound calm. As if you make dates with hot guys every day.* "That sounds all right. But I've never been up the hill before. Where are the barracks?"

As Patrick gave me directions, I started to worry. What did I know about martial arts? What was I getting myself into? Hanging up the phone with directions scribbled on the reverse side of the index card, I reassured myself I was doing the right thing.

Being a wimp got you nowhere, remember? For twenty-four years you lived with your mother and listened to her, let her talk you down...and what did that get you? Nothing. You had a lousy job with a lousy life, hardly any friends, and no happiness.

The minute I had walked out my mother's door and driven away I had been making a decision to change my life, live it differently. Take risks. Make my own decisions. Avoid her mistakes.

Checking out the Tae Kwon whatever classes with Patrick? What could be the big deal? He's cute, appears to be pretty smart, and he seems, for some unknown reason, to be interested in me.

I wished I could kick my nervous stomach out the door. I was making something very easy, very straightforward into a complicated tangle of emotions: fear, desire, apprehension. Taking a deep breath, I dug through my clean laundry, looking for something to wear.

I could do this.

———

Thirty minutes later, I was coaxing the small, four-cylinder VW Bug up the steep hill to DLI. Following the curving main road, I passed the Air Force barracks to my left: a gray depressing building with crumbling foundations and peeling paint. The second depressing gray building was the Army barracks.

But before I could park, I caught sight of Patrick. He stood outside the building in his black clothes and leather jacket, a backpack slung casually over his shoulder.

He didn't know what kind of car I was driving, so I honked my pathetic little horn. He perked up at the sound and, catching my eye, smiled and waved at me from the sidewalk on the other side of the street. I pulled up to the curb, and he crossed the street to meet me.

"Hey," he greeted me through my open window.

"Hi," I responded, trying to sound casual and calm. "So, you live there?" I pointed at the ancient building in front of us.

"Yeah. Nice, huh? Thank God I'll be moving up the hill next month."

"Up the hill?"

"The newer barracks—see, the side road?" He pointed at a narrow alley that ran along the south side of the barracks. On a small hill behind the building prettier, Mediterranean-styled buildings had been built.

"Oh, those look nice."

But he looked nicer. He was leaning his body down, so he could talk to me through the window.

Although he was thin, he looked strong and sinewy. I could see a well-sculpted chest beneath his Grim Reaper t-shirt. Staying calm was becoming harder and harder. I could feel the heat rising from his body.

"Yeah. It'll be nice to have my own bathroom." He interrupted my thoughts, which was a good thing. I wanted to stay in control of myself. After all, I barely knew this guy. Sexual attraction was not that hard to come by, as evidenced my own mother's behavior.

"What's it like now?"

"Oh, you'd love it: two bathrooms on each floor, open showers. Just like Boot Camp." He winked at me and walked around the front of my car, so he could climb in the passenger's side.

Having no idea what the Boot Camp hygiene experience was like, I changed the subject, "So, where are we headed?"

Patrick placed his backpack between his feet, "Have you had any breakfast yet?"

"Just some coffee." Little did he know I would have eaten breakfast if my stomach hadn't been a mess of nerves after calling him.

"Well, then, let's go grab some food."

The main road that wound past the barracks also led to the other side of the hill and to Pacific Grove, another small town that made up the Central Coast of California.

I pushed on the gas pedal and asked, "Where should we go?" I was genuinely confused. I didn't make it to Pacific Grove very much. More of a drive from my place. And I surely didn't eat breakfast at restaurants on a regular basis. Cheaper to make Folger's and eat a Pop-Tart at home.

He suggested a place called the Island Cafe which was only a short drive down the hill. "Hope you like pancakes. They've got every kind you can think of—and they're huge."

I found it difficult to have any kind of meaningful conversation in the car. To concentrate on my driving was hard enough, adding a sparkling conversation to the mix was too much to ask from my nerve-addled brain.

Patrick didn't seem to mind my quietness. I hadn't had many first dates in my life, so I was still learning the whole 'small talk' thing. Not that easy to be working all those hours, going to school, and still have time for a love life. My experience had been very limited. One boyfriend in high school, another couple of guys after that.

My boyfriend from high school, Donny, to put it mildly, was mess. He was more like my mother than I wanted to admit. A foul-mouthed bastard, pretty much. But, at first, he had seemed like the perfect guy. He was attentive, even sweet. Leaving little notes in my locker by pushing them through the ventilation slats at the top. He walked me to all my classes and waited outside the door when I was finished.

I thought he was very caring and chivalrous, but eventually realized his behavior for what it was—jealousy. Donny couldn't stand to have anyone else around me, not even the few girlfriends I had. After we had dated for two or three months, he became angrier and angrier. I thought at the beginning it was something I had done to make him act like he did. Eventually, I discovered Donny was just a jerk and would always be one.

In the end, *he* ended up dropping me. It didn't make a lot of sense, reflecting on it. Why didn't I dump him much earlier? Why did I stick around with him for so long?

Donny broke up with me after school one day. He told me it wasn't working out, and he never looked at me again.

I thought it was maybe something about sex, or the lack of it. Donny was my first boyfriend, and, at seventeen, I was pretty behind the curve, never having kissed a boy before. I was naive and inexperienced. When confronted with Donny's groping hands, I was unsure what to do. I only knew for certain I wasn't ready for sex.

A few days later, I saw Donny around school with another girl. Someone who seemed about as shy and insecure as I was. Rumor was they married right after graduation.

The other two men in my life had been sexual experiments. I was tired of being alone, of watching my mother come home night after night with a different guy. It got me thinking. At least she was with *someone*. At least she didn't sit in front of the TV on Saturday nights fantasizing about men who never came along.

In my college courses there were guys, guys who had been interested. I wouldn't call them handsome. They were passable. Passable nerds who had as little experience as I did.

Jim had been my first. He was more nervous than I was,

sweating and ham-handed. He couldn't even face taking my clothes off, so I kept my sweater on the whole time. It was quick, relatively pain-free, and strangely void of any real emotion.

Perfunctory would best describe it. As if I was reading it out of a medical textbook.

I think it wasn't the sex I was interested in, but the physical closeness. As long as I had that touch on my body, erotic or not, it satisfied something in me. It made me feel I wasn't alone in the world and that there was someone else out there who needed physical closeness as much as I did. It provided me comfort, and a serenity that was rare in my crazy life with Mickey.

"Here it is." Patrick pointed to a small storefront on Ocean Avenue.

My wandering thoughts returned to the present and the handsome male sitting next to me.

The Island Cafe was empty so early on a Saturday morning.

The town of Pacific Grove relied very heavily on the tourism industry to keep its restaurants and gift shops open. Lunch would probably yield a bigger crowd from the Aquarium and Cannery Row, only a few blocks away.

For now, it would be just me, Patrick, and an older couple sitting at a table by the window.

A mural spanned the back wall depicting an ocean and a beach with brightly-colored umbrellas and sandcastles, but not the kind you'd find on the cool Central Coast. There were warm, sunny days in Monterey, and Carmel had a large and lovely beach, but nothing like the tropical climate in the mural.

A large sign encouraged us to seat ourselves. Grabbing me by the hand and lacing his fingers with mine, he led me directly to a booth in the back.

I was startled by the intimacy, my first instinct was to pull away. But his warm, smooth hand in mine felt so right. I guess that meant it really *was* a date.

"How's this?" he asked me as if we had been holding hands for weeks.

"This is fine." I kept my voice neutral, not wanting to give away the fact his touch affected me so strongly. "I'm not too particular."

He let go of my hand so we could sit down, and I instantly missed the warmth. My hand was empty. Alone.

"Is that supposed to be a compliment?"

Staring at him blankly, I realized the unintended meaning behind my statement. "Oh, I didn't mean—"

That sideways smile appeared. "I'm just teasing you." He was good at fooling me. Maybe he was trying to make me let my guard down. Then, he looked at me with those ocean blue eyes, "I have to say, I was a little surprised you called this morning."

I absent-mindedly fingered the silverware sitting on the napkin in front of me, nervous and overwhelmed by the intensity in his eyes. "Why were you surprised?"

"A cute girl like you, interested in someone like me. You know, the freak."

At first, I was mute because he called me 'cute.' Did I mishear him? But then I was totally confused by the reference to 'freak.' "What do you mean, freak?" He wasn't deformed or wild-looking. In fact, his looks could cause heads to turn, if it weren't for the industrial clothing and the stomp-your-ass boots.

"I'm the loser with no job who had to join the Army. Not quite my style, if you couldn't tell." He looked down at his black clothes.

It was then I noticed the gold hoop in his ear had been augmented with multiple studs up the edge of his earlobe. "The Army lets you do that?" I reached out across the table to gently touch the curve of his ear. It was a soft touch, but a zing ran through my fingers.

"The piercings?" Before I could pull away my hand, he reached up to touch that same curve. Our fingers brushed together, and, as if a static shock had jumped between us, I quickly dropped my hand.

His eyes were cool and searching. I had to look away. My heart pounded in my chest. Was I the only one who felt the attraction between us? My fingers went back to fiddling with the silverware, and then they started unconsciously shredding the napkin.

"As long as I don't wear any earrings on base or in uniform, I'm OK. I kind of sneaked out this morning, through the side door. If I had gone out the main entrance, they would've nailed me." His gaze was less intense now, and my heart slowed.

I regained control of my emotions.

I wanted to go back to the 'loser' comment. "What makes you so sure you're a loser?"

"Well, I don't know. Most people think I am." For a moment, he seemed proud of that fact. As if he enjoyed being the outsider.

"Who are 'most people'?" I pressed.

"Everyone," he said impatiently. "I'm a geek in goth clothes. Doesn't quite fit, you know?"

I took a good look at him. He was thin, pale, average height and did look somewhat like the boy next door. A dangerous boy next door. One that could sweet-talk parents into a date with their daughter, and then take her on the ride of her life. His physical characteristics certainly didn't fit my image of some goth weirdo. "So what?" I was determined to show him I didn't judge people based on outer appearances. That I understood him. That I didn't fall into the 'most people' group.

He smiled at my answer; I had pleased him.

A warmth flooded my stomach, and I shyly smiled back at him. He could have me if he wanted me. He had to know that by now. I would love to take that wild ride with him; do something crazy, something dangerous. To find out what I had been missing all these years. My mother didn't have the sole rights to adventure in life. She made many mistakes, but I had watched her, and I was smarter than she.

Taking that first step toward Patrick was so easy and felt so good.

And if it was a mistake, it was my mistake to make.

ten

. . .

"I SAW this one martial arts studio a few blocks from downtown," Patrick began after we had finished breakfast. "I thought we could start there first."

I really had no interest in checking out martial arts classes, but I wanted to get to know more about him. If that mean I had to be bored for an hour or two, then so be it.

I gave a noncommittal answer, "Whatever you want to do is fine with me."

Perhaps I was a little too noncommittal, he appeared miffed I didn't return his enthusiasm for our plans that Saturday morning.

As we waited for the waitress to bring our bill, Patrick's blue gaze fell on me.

"Do you know how beautiful you are?" His voice was low and sexy.

"Yeah, right," I scoffed. I wasn't so good at taking compliments. They were hard to believe after years of being told I was a clod or a good-for-nothing or worse by my mother. Taking another sip of coffee, I tried to settle my nerves, but I the heat rose in my body. I liked that he found me beautiful. Why couldn't I just say 'thanks'?

"Hey," he reached forward and grabbed my chin. "You are."

The touch of his hand made my nervousness dissolve.

The waitress chose that very moment to deliver our bill. He let go. I took a deep, deliberate breath to slow down my heart. All I could think about was that touch on my face, the gentleness.

On the way to the car, Patrick talked more about his martial arts experience. I didn't understand most of what he was talking about, but I nodded my head and made comments when it seemed appropriate. To stay grounded in the conversation required a lot of effort on my part.

After so many months alone, it felt good to have a warm, male body next to me. I could suffer through a few martial arts classes for that.

———

"So, what did you think?" Patrick asked me as we exited the Red Dragon Martial Arts Center.

After sitting on a hard bench for an hour watching sidekicks and defensive moves, I was spent and bored. But I mustered up a smile, not wanting to let on to Patrick how uninterested I was in one of his passions. "Pretty powerful. Looks like it takes a lot of discipline."

A gleam appeared in his eye, "Years of training, discipline. You have to learn to clear your mind of extraneous thoughts. Just think of the motion, your body." He stopped walking on the sidewalk outside the studio, took a stance similar to one we had seen inside, and lifted his hands in a defensive pose. "Your breathing controlled. Your thoughts, controlled."

I couldn't believe he was doing this outside on the sidewalk

A little embarrassed at the stares coming from people outside, I grabbed his arm, "Let's go somewhere."

Yes, let's get back to that date we started in the restaurant this morning. I had followed him around for several hours, because I wanted to please him. Now I hoped he would want to do something that would please me.

I didn't get the answer I was hoping for.

"Huh?"

"Let's go to the beach—or Big Sur." I pulled urgently on his arm.

See, it's a date, right?

He let his arm fall to his side. "The beach?" he scoffed, as if no guy wearing black leather had ever considered going to the beach. "There were a couple more places I wanted to check out."

"Oh." I dreaded sitting through another class on another hard bench. Why did he invite me along? Was this a date? Or was I just imagining things? It seemed now as if I was just company; company for something he didn't want to do alone. "Well, I have a lot of studying to do. Maybe we could meet later?"

"All right," he said quietly.

Was he disappointed my interest in martial arts was not as rabid as his?

I dug out a pen and a scrap of paper from the bottom of my purse. "Here's my number. Give me a call."

He tucked the bit of paper into his back pocket. "You can leave me here. I'll just walk back to base."

"Okay." I suddenly felt badly, as if I had let him down. But he had let me down. His comment in the Island Cafe led me to believe this whole meeting was something more than two acquaintances hanging out. Maybe I wasn't his type, which wouldn't surprise me at all. But I could hope.

I waved at him as I walked across the street to where the Bug was parked. He gave me a quick salute before he ducked back inside the Martial Arts Center.

Downhearted I was back to being alone, but glad that I didn't have to tag along on Patrick's search for the perfect Tae Kwon Do instructor, I returned to my apartment. Time to grab some books and do some studying.

The end of the summer semester was approaching, and I had lots of papers and finals to worry about.

The memory of his hand on my chin returned to me for a moment, and I knew I'd probably spend more time wondering when he would call than working on my homework.

———

"So, do you have a boyfriend?" David asked me in the midst of a game of Tetris.

I was sitting in his office, waiting for my turn to beat his high score. Alicia thought I was helping him with a presentation for an upcoming sales meeting, but, instead we were goofing off. I couldn't believe he would ask me such a personal question after only knowing me for a few days.

I cleared my throat, unsettled, "Um, I don't know."

He laughed, "You don't know? Or do you mean the guy doesn't know—are you one of those stalkers?"

"David!" I shrieked with laughter at the absurdity of his statement, "Of course not. It's just this guy. I don't know if—" I didn't know how to explain my relationship with Patrick.

"What?" He stopped laughing and sat in one of the extra chairs in his office. "Tell me. I'm a guy. Is there something you're confused about?"

He tilted his head and pushed up his glasses.

Why did he care about my practically non-existent love life?

"Well, sort of." Maybe he could help me figure Patrick out. David was right, he *was* a guy—perhaps he could shed some light on my strange date on Saturday. I dove in and hoped I wasn't making a mistake talking about my personal life with my boss. "We sort of had a weird date last weekend, and I gave him my number. I thought we were supposed to meet later that night, but he never called."

"Hmm...dis is a veddy zerious zituation," he said using a Dr. Freud voice. "Perhaps he has a problem vith vomen, a complex of zome zort...veddy interezting." He tapped his fingers together, as if he were thinking very hard. "Does he vet zee bed?"

"Oh, David," I laughed. "You're such a goofball."

A loud knock at the door let us both know the fun was over. I opened the door to the curious face of Alicia, her red hair flaming in tufts around her face while her black-rimmed eyes scrutinized both David and me. Trying to be part of the joke, Alicia piped up, "Well, sounds like you two are having a lot of fun in here."

Dr. Freud disappeared, and David returned, "More work than fun, I would say." He cleared his throat, attempting to mask the grin on his face. "Talk to you later, Sabrina?" He stood, and as I exited his office he said, "By the way, why don't *you* give *him* a call?"

Then, he shut the door, leaving Alicia and me in the hallway "Give who a call?" Alicia asked me curiously.

"Oh, just someone—" I slipped the mailroom to finish sorting the day's mail.

———

After class that evening, I took David's advice: I picked up the phone and dialed Patrick's number at the barracks. It was Friday, and I really didn't want to spend another weekend by myself. My stomach churned as I thought about making the call, but I wanted another chance to find out if there was anything between the two of us. Even if it was just friendship.

Several rings echoed in my ear and then a gruff voice, "Second floor."

"I'm looking for Patrick?" I managed to squeak out.

"Who?" The gruff voice sounded annoyed.

"Patrick McKinnon?"

"Oh, McKinnon...yeah, hold on."

A loud clunk. Yelling. Footsteps. Then, a familiar voice, "Yeah?"

"Patrick?" Winding the phone cord around my arm, I bit my lip. The rest of the words came out of my mouth in a flood. "Hi, It's me. Sabrina."

"Hey, Sabrina. Glad you called. You wanna go out somewhere tonight?"

My worries all week had been for nothing. He sounded friendly and still interested. Who cares if he never called me? At least I wouldn't be home alone on a Saturday night. "Sure. Where do you want to go?"

"Well, I already made plans, but you can tag along. We're going to San Francisco to a goth club we heard about. Still interested?" It almost sounded like a challenge.

A goth club? What the heck was that?

My imagination conjured up an adult version of a Halloween costume party. It might be fun; or it might be scary. I took a deep breath to slow down my wildly beating heart. What am I doing? "Yeah, that sound cool. When should I meet you?"

Too late to take it back. I was going whether the logical side of me liked it or not. Without taking a risk, I never would have ended up here. And without taking a risk tonight, I would never know if there could be anything more than friendship between Patrick and me.

"An hour? Do you mind driving?"

I thought that was an odd request. How had he planned on getting to San Francisco without a car before I happened to call? Maybe my car was in better shape or something. "No, I guess I don't mind. But my car's pretty small. I can only fit three other people."

"That's perfect." Patrick sounded excited. "It's just be me and Eric."

"Eric?" I asked.

"He's an old friend. We joined the Army together. He's in my Korean class with me, and he's my roommate. You'll like him."

I had been hoping for an intimate drive up to the city. With the introduction of Eric, it was hard not to sound disappointed. "Okay, an hour then."

"Oh, and Sabrina? Can you wear something—?"

"Black?" I finished for him.

"Yeah. You would blend in a little better."

"I think I can find something that'll work."

"Cool. See you in an hour."

I hung up the phone and frantically dug through my small pile of clothes.

Something black? What did I have to wear to some goth club in the city? I didn't want to look like an idiot.

Jeans?

Yuck.

Khaki pants?

No way.

I had nothing.

Maybe I could make a quick trip to the mall to find something. In an hour? I had to chance it. Either that or dress like somebody's mom. Then, I remembered a dress I had at the bottom of my pile. It was long-sleeved, velvet, and sort of Victorian—and very black. That might work. A little Morticia Addams, but that would be a good thing, right?

I put it on and yanked on a pair of clunky black boots. I brushed my hair straight down, no curling iron tonight. What to do about make-up? Pale and pasty, right? I found some very red lipstick and a black eyeliner. That would do. After applying a heavy coat of the liner and the lipstick, I threw both into my purse.

Assessing myself in the mirror, I laughed. I looked like I was trying a little too hard. Style never came naturally to me. In high school I was never the type to have the latest fashions. I bought whatever I could afford, which wasn't what everyone else was wearing.

Oh, well. It was the best I could do on short notice. Hopping into my borrowed car, I took off for Monterey and the hill.

———

Eric was not what I had imagined. He was short with a shaved head, dark eyes under heavy brows. His frame was small and slight, and he had very feminine fingers that were long and well-manicured.

"This is Sabrina." Patrick put his hand on my shoulder and squeezed it affectionately.

"Hey, how's it going?" When Eric first spoke, I noticed he had strangely-pointed teeth and a bit of a lisp. Something didn't seem quite right, but I didn't get a good enough look at him to notice what.

Eric wore a long, black trench coat over black jeans and a black t-shirt. Very similar to what Patrick was wearing, except Patrick, once again, was sporting his black leather jacket. They both had on the same heavy-looking black boots.

"Are you ready?" Patrick asked us eagerly, slipping his arm around my waist as I leaned against the hood of my car. Under the anemic glow of the street lamp outside, his blue eyes burned with excitement. Eric was already climbing into the back seat of my car.

Eric grinned, flashing his unnaturally-sharp teeth, "Yeah, I've been waiting a long time to check out San Francisco. I've heard it's got a pretty hot goth scene."

"So, where exactly are we going?" I jingled my ring of keys.

Patrick grabbed them from me and got behind the wheel. When I hesitated, he spoke softly to me seductively, "Get in. Trust me."

It was like a caress, that voice, when he spoke so softly. Before he shut the door, he took in my appearance, the dark make-up, black dress. He liked it. His eyes were hot on my skin, and I shivered under his gaze.

"Nice." he said appreciatively.

I smiled, self-conscious, "I wasn't really sure if I got it right."

Eric added his own opinion, "Do you have a black eyeliner with you? You know what would look hot?"

I dug through my purse until I found the eyeliner I brought along.

Patrick seemed to know where Eric was headed, "Yeah, that would be perfect. You gotta do it."

"Do what?" The black eyeliner dangled in my hand.

"Use the eyeliner on your lips."

I wasn't so sure, but wiped off the red lipstick with the back of my hand. Who was the goth expert here? Certainly not me. I crossed in front of the car, slid into the passenger seat, and tilted the rearview mirror toward me. Around my mouth was a blood-red smear. I rubbed at it with the back of my sleeve, then lined my lips with the eyeliner. When I finished, I turned to face Patrick for his approval.

"Oh, yeah. That's perfect," he intimated, putting his right hand firmly on my knee. "You look incredible."

I blushed at his praise and at his hand. That was definitely more than a friendly gesture. Right?

He started up the car.

Curious about our destination, I couldn't help but ask, "Do you guys know where you are going? Or do we need to buy a map?"

"I know where to go," Eric asserted. "Should take us about

an hour-and-a-half." He was now just a small, dark shape in the back seat, but his thin, effeminate fingers rested on his knees in a spot of street lamp light.

Something told me we wouldn't be home until very late that night.

"Let's go, man," Eric said impatiently.

As the car headed off base, I mused about what The Goth Pit would be like. Guess it was too late to back out now. I touched a finger to my lips and pulled it away, looking at the oily, black smear of eyeliner. Rubbing it away with my thumb, I felt an urge to tell Patrick to stop, to let me out, to let me go home. Who was I trying to fool?

But I didn't.

Instead, I leaned back in my seat, and let the darkness wash over me.

eleven

. . .

AFTER A FEW WRONG TURNS, Eric guided us onto a deserted street in the warehouse district, not too far from San Francisco Bay. It was ten o'clock, and I was tired of driving around. Abandoned buildings surrounded us, no loud music, no people dressed in black. I couldn't believe a goth club existed only a few steps away from where we finally parked.

Patrick handed me my keys and got out of the car first. Eric followed, his black trench coat engulfing his slight body.

"It should be right around the corner from here," Eric said.

"Come on, Sabrina," Patrick urged me.

Hesitantly, I exited the car. I didn't like the idea of leaving David's car on some empty street in a deserted part of San Francisco. But as I got a better look at the street around us, I noticed more empty cars parked nearby—many much nicer than mine. There must be something around here besides rats, garbage, and decaying buildings.

Patrick grabbed my hand and led me down the street.

As we turned the corner, I noticed a knot of people hovering outside a doorway lit by a purple light bulb. I also the night pulsed with music—a loud, death knell of a beat. Industrial, dark and rhythmic, like no music I had heard before.

I wanted to turn around; I didn't belong in a place like this. What was I thinking? My hands were clammy, my heart was racing. I should be back in Monterey, studying, drinking a latte, sitting alone.

At that moment, Patrick squeezed my hand in excitement, "I've been waiting months for something like this. You are too cool, Sabrina."

If it weren't for that hand, I would have already been halfway down the block—too cool?

It was apparent to me now neither Patrick nor Eric had a car of their own. I was cool because I was their source of a car for the evening. I suspected I was the assumed designated driver as well. Why, oh, why did I leave my apartment? How could I possibly fit in here?

I was a fraud. As if I was dressed up for Halloween, instead of a night of clubbing.

The hesitation and worry grew in me like a thunderhead cloud right before a pounding rainstorm, right before the rain crashes down on everything. I had to leave. Someone was sure to figure me out, call my bluff.

A black sign with glow-in-the-dark writing read "Cover $10."

There, I just wouldn't take the money out of my purse. No money, no entrance, no freaks surrounding me, questioning my credibility.

I couldn't pull this off.

Patrick slapped down a twenty dollar bill in front of a very large and imposing man in black with a spiky dog collar around his neck. Still clutching my hand, he pulled me forward into the smoky purple-lit entrance of The Goth Pit. I felt my heart drop into my stomach.

Crap.

———

I was expecting something weird, something different than any other club I had been to. Maybe something like the raves I had seen on made-for-TV movies where partygoers did drugs on the tables or carried around knives in plain view.

I was wrong, very, wrong.

The Goth Pit was pretty much like any other club: dim lights, a bar against one wall, small tables circling a dance floor and a stage. What made it unique were the patrons. Men led women by leashes and dog collars. Women led men around in the same fashion. Lots of boots, black, and piercings.

Eric immediately dissolved into the crowd. Patrick stood by me for a moment, lit up a cigarette, and asked, "Wanna get a drink?"

"Sure, but just one. Aren't I driving us back?" Even in this bizarre atmosphere, I could only think of doing the responsible, boring thing. Why couldn't I let loose? Get bombed off my ass and dance as if I had heard this music before?

To have a mother who was willing to explore her wild side, made me more than timid when it came to letting loose. Most of my life, doing the responsible thing had kept us from losing the house on more than one occasion. It was scary to contemplate putting my instincts aside and follow Patrick's lead.

He pointed to a table by the entrance and, trying to be heard over the music, said loudly, "Why don't you sit there, and I'll be back in a minute."

If I never tried anything different, how would I know who I really was? What I wanted to be? What I really enjoyed? This was my chance to explore a completely different way of life.

"What would you like to drink?" he asked in that same, loud voice, as I sat at the empty table.

Never having tried many alcoholic beverages, I chose the most familiar, "A screwdriver, I guess." I wasn't planning on getting totally drunk, but I did wonder what kind of person I would be if I did. What would I do or say? Would I be different? Confident and brassy? Or would I be like my mother: mean and jealous?

On the rare occasion I went out to a bar, I stuck to the least complicated of drinks. Never any beer. Beer was my mother's drink of choice, well, beer and whiskey. The odor of beer sickened me, its fermented pungency reminding me of my mother's every insult, every verbal attack. A bottle in her hand when I came home from school meant I should steer clear of her for several hours, unless I wanted to become the target of her anger.

Patrick left me at the table, working his way toward the bar. I looked forward to having that glass in my hand. The stir stick and napkin should keep my hands busy and my nervousness at bay for a while.

Our minuscule table was covered with empty plastic drink cups and damp napkins. While I waited for my drink, I indulged in a favorite pastime of mine: people-watching. And this was a prime spot for it.

Women dominated the scene. Many danced in groups of two or three, undulating to the loud beat of the music, their pale faces and dark make-up giving them an ethereal appearance under the purple lighting. A few guys on the stage danced wildly, bouncing around like balls in a pinball machine. The male mode of dance wasn't smooth and sexual like the female. It was jerky and violent; arms flailed, heads bobbed.

I caught sight of Eric, still shrouded in his trench coat, jaggedly making his way across the dance floor. He seemed unconcerned and unaware of the bunches of oscillating bodies around him. His hooded eyes focused on some point in front of him up on the stage. Focused on somewhere or someone that I couldn't pinpoint from my seat at the table. Eric's shaved head disappeared into the rippling crowd.

"Here you go," Patrick startled me.

My ears had adjusted to the blaring background noise, but we both had to speak at the top of our lungs to be heard.

"Thanks," I answered, taking a sip from my drink.

"Look, some guys I met over at the bar were telling me about another place we might want to check out after this. If you don't mind." He nodded his head in the direction of the bar, and I could see a pair of leather-clad goths watching the dance floor. "I'm gonna go back and find out what else they know."

"Go ahead. I'll just be here." I slowly stirred my drink.

"You should go out and dance."

"Maybe." I took a sip of the screwdriver. "I'll think about it."

He was right, I should try and get out there. What was there to be afraid of?

The dancing was different than what I was used to, but nothing I couldn't handle.

I think.

Maybe if I finished up my drink first. Liquid courage, so they say.

Patrick returned to the guys at the bar, leaving me alone at the small table. I watched the dancers and realized I couldn't find Eric. He was lost in the crowd somewhere. After about ten minutes of downing my drink, I tired of waiting for Patrick to return to the table. The beat of the music was throbbing, my feet were involuntarily tapping to the beat, and a warm spark of bravery flickered to life after my last sip of vodka and orange juice. It was time to ignore my fears and get out there. Better than staying at the table all night long. Maybe I would end up having some fun all by myself.

Just as I was about to make my goth dancing debut, a loud crash erupted from the stage.

Eric was kicking someone in the gut who was sprawled on the floor in front of him.

I whipped my head around to look for Patrick at the bar. He

had already seen the fight and was headed for the stage. He pushed through the clot of female dancers.

I leapt to my feet and chased after him, hoping to stop him from getting involved. But it was too late. A tall goth with a mohawk and spiked boots darted forward to grab Eric from behind. Patrick sprang onto the stage in one smooth move and intercepted the mohawk-wearer, grabbing a fistful of his ripped, black t- shirt. Mohawk Guy, caught in mid-stride, tripped over his own feet, and Patrick took the opportunity to shove him hard, propelling him to the floor. When he hit the floor, Patrick grabbed his arm, twisted it behind him, and began pushing it upward until the Mohawk Man cried out. Even in that position, he tried to thrash out of Patrick's grasp.

From my spot, I had clear view of everything. It was like watching an action movie in the theater. But this was no stunt-acting. I felt a scream die in my throat, uncertain what I should do.

Eric, meanwhile, was in an out-and-out fistfight with another goth that entered the fray. Being small turned out to be quite an advantage, he was nimble and moved quickly, sidestepping punches that would have caught a larger man. After dodging a few blows, Eric landed a hard one of his own right on his opponent's nose.

Blood flew across the stage and onto a curtain that hung on the back wall.

My legs finally unfroze, and I pushed through the crowd of stunned dancers, yelling Patrick's name. I was desperate to make myself heard above the din before someone called the cops. The next thing I knew, both Eric and Patrick were jumping off the stage.

"Come on," Patrick yelled over the loud music. "This way." He pointed at an emergency exit sign to the left of the stage.

I caught up to them at the exit. All three of us pushed through the door and escaped into the cool night air. The alarms from the emergency door blared. Both Eric and Patrick laughed, stopped outside the door in the alley, and took deep gulps of air. Patrick leaned over with his hands on his knees and wiped a stream of blood from his nose.

I was weak in the knees, sick to my stomach, and shaking all over.

When I found my voice, anger mixed with fear spilled out, "What in God's name was that all about?" I had never been so frightened in my life.

"That asshole had it coming," was all that Patrick said.

"Fucker," said Eric as he spit blood and something else out of his mouth. False teeth? Then, I realized why Eric's teeth had looked so odd to me. He had been wearing fake vampire fangs, ceramic-type caps over his incisor teeth. "Cracked one of my fucking teeth," he growled.

Neither of them seemed to want to give me an explanation of why they were involved in a brawl. Hearing sirens a good distance away, I tugged on Patrick's sleeve. "We need to get out of here. Now."

All three of us ran down the alley. We'd parked only a couple of blocks away.

"What in hell just went on in there?" I asked.

"Just let's get in the car and go home."

I grabbed the sleeve of his jacket. "Patrick, I think I have a right to know."

"Can you just fucking drop it?" he snapped at me.

I was momentarily stunned by his anger. It reminded me of my own mother's inexplicable anger at the slightest provocation.

I stopped walking. "You can find your own ride home." I turned away from them and jogging down the street. My heavy boots clomped on the sidewalk. Tears formed in my eyes. What an idiot I was. I was nothing more than a free ride into town. He was never interested in me for anything else.

I heard footsteps behind me. "Hey, baby. Hey, Sabrina. Wait."

Patrick chased after me. He grabbed me by the arm. When he saw my face, he instantly softened, "Don't cry. I didn't mean to upset you. It's just that—"

He engulfed me in a hug. The raw smell of his jacket leather was comforting somehow, and I began to cry softly. "You scared me. What was that all about? Why did you get in a fight with those guys?"

"Oh, baby," he said into my hair as he caressed my back, "They were just some jerks, that's all. Let's get out of here, huh?"

It felt good to be held. He was warm and solid; I tilted my head up. He kissed me delicately, and then touched my cheek with his fingers. His lips were gentle on mine, and I pulled him closer to me, not wanting to break from him. I was protected by his body. Warmth radiated from the pit of my stomach.

Patrick was the first to pull away. He looked into my eyes. "You really are beautiful."

Eric interrupted us. "Man, we really need to fly. The cops are coming."

The wailing sirens grew louder.

Slightly embarrassed Eric witnessed our closeness, I wiped the tears from my face, sniffed, and took off for my car again, leaving them both ten steps behind me. "Come on. The car's over here."

My nerves were jangled from that kiss. Focusing my mind on the car and escaping the scene calmed me. It also kept me from overanalyzing what had passed between Patrick and me. Right now, that was too much for me to handle.

We all managed to get into the car and out of San Francisco without being pulled over. When we reached Highway 1, the main road to Monterey, I felt much safer.

Eric was snoring in the back seat. Patrick stared at me as I drove, twirling a strand of my dark hair between his fingers.

"So, what did you think?"

Those were his first words since we'd left San Francisco some ninety minutes earlier.

"Of what? Your bloody nose?" My answer was laced with sarcasm. How could he possibly be thinking about The Goth Pit and my impressions after he had nearly been arrested for assault? This was not how I pictured our first evening out together.

He sighed loudly, "No, not my nose. I wish you could forget that." Patrick made it seem as if punching people in the face was a regular thing with him. "I want to know what you thought of the club."

The fighting had horrified me. I didn't know this pale, thin person sitting next to me was capable of such violence and anger. He was more powerful than I had imagined, more masculine. And, in a way, that made me feel more feminine. He could protect me, if need be.

I gave my honest opinion of the club itself. "It was interesting."

"That's it?"

"Well, it was my first one, so I didn't know what to expect, really. Some of the girls...where do they get clothes like that?"

"You just have to know where to look. Not at the mall, that's for fucking sure." He paused for a moment and, while I kept my eyes on the road, I could sense him appraising me. "You would look so hot in something..." he trailed off, still twirling my hair.

I found the twirling very sensual. It made me want to stop the car and kiss him much more thoroughly than we had on the street earlier. I sucked in a breath, "Something what?"

"Something bad. You could be such a hot goth chick."

I flushed at the praise. I tried to envision myself wearing a flowing dress like the ones the threesome on the dance floor wore. Tattoos swirling up my arm, my hair dyed an obvious black, make-up giving me the same pale complexion. It was hard to imagine. Jeans, sweatshirts, and ponytails were more my thing. But if I wanted to make a change, couldn't I? Surely all the girls on the dance floor could look like me, if they had the right clothes. Dressing like a goth, it was just a costume. Something to hide behind.

"You think I could?" I followed the exit to Monterey.

"Oh, yeah." He leaned toward me, kissing my neck.

For a split second I melted, the feel of his lips on my skin was electric. Then, I nudged him away with my shoulder, "Not while I'm driving, Patrick. I can't concentrate on what I'm doing." I was also worried Eric might wake up and see us.

"I just can't keep my hands off of you," he whispered huskily. He returned to twirling my hair.

Before tonight, I didn't know if Patrick was attracted to me or only interested in friendship. His actions had been hot and cold. But these last few hours his intentions were obvious. My nerves were attuned to his every movement, his every touch. My nervousness danced in the background, but I tamped it down as best I could. This was so much better than being alone.

The car climbed the hill to the base, and I pulled around to the back of the barracks where there was a large parking lot. The motor purred in neutral, and a snore from Eric rumbled from the back seat.

"So," Patrick led off, unbuckling his seat belt.

"So," I mimicked, wondering what was going to happen next. My hands were clammy, and I wiped them self-consciously on my thighs.

He picked up my hand and turned it palm up. On my palm he traced invisible lines, which caused me to shiver in anticipation. "I hope you had a good time, not including the whole fight thing. I'm really sorry you had to see that." He was concentrating on my palm, and then he looked up at me with those clear, blue eyes.

I melted a bit. "Oh, it wasn't such a big deal." Although in the back of my mind, the fight replayed over and over again in surreal slow motion. That violent, out-of-control Patrick was someone I didn't want to see again, but this one in the car, and the one that embraced me on the sidewalk? I really liked that Patrick.

"Patrick, I—"

I never got to finish what I was going to say. He covered my mouth with his. And Eric continued snoring in the back seat.

twelve

. . .

ALICIA LIKED PRECISION AT WORK, even when it came to such things as stamping envelopes with the automatic stamping machine. A bit of a blurred postage stamp would cause a frown on her overly made-up face and a comment like, "Sabrina, you have to make sure it's clear. Otherwise, we might have to stamp it again and waste postage."

She was always thinking of ways to eliminate wastefulness at the office. As if it was her own household budget she was trying to stick to.

But I learned how to create the perfect postmark on each envelope and how to create the same on the postage tape we affixed to boxes of software. I also learned how to sort the mail Alicia-style: all mail is put in alphabetical order, then mail is placed in the individual mail slots, largest items on the bottom, smallest on top. Annoying, but simple to do, and it was worth the effort to make Alicia happy. The unhappier Alicia was, the more precise she wanted things—an almost-empty garbage can emptied out and the new liner put in just so, magazines arranged on the coffee table in a perfect fan, pencils sharpened to just the right degree of sharpness. It went on and on.

And it was enough to drive most people mad. I guess that's why they had never bothered to hire anyone permanently before. No one could put up with Alicia's peculiarities for long; at least not for eleven dollars an hour.

But I could.

Her precision and drive for neatness was the polar opposite of my mother. It felt good to work in an office where neatness was appreciated. Even if it was obsessive neatness.

I needed that methodical routine on Monday after my weekend with Patrick because my mind wanted to drift back to Saturday night, to recall those last few moments before Patrick returned to his room in the barracks. Eric never did stir from his spot in the back of my car. We prodded him quite hard to wake him up. When we had parted ways, Patrick had been sweet, even tender.

A familiar voice snapped me out of my reverie. "So, did you have a good weekend?" David leaned across the receptionist's counter, watching me work. His soft brown eyes examined me carefully. He was an expert at picking up on the smallest of cues.

Was it obvious my mind was not on my work?

I stuffed padded envelopes with CD-ROMs for Ergo's latest software package, trying quickly to think of the best way to answer his question. "Oh, it was all right." I kept my gaze on the piles of envelopes in front of me.

If I didn't even know exactly what I was feeling about Patrick, how was I supposed to explain it to David? It was best to tell him as little as possible and keep his questions to a minimum. I didn't need to have an Oprah moment right in front of the whole office.

"Really?" He smiled slightly. "Just 'all right'?" he teased. He was so sure of himself.

Was it just me, or could he read all women like a book?

In an exaggerated English accent he challenged, "Methinks milady telleth a lie."

Right at that moment, Alicia entered the room. She had been gathering some things from the supply closet, and her arms were full of padded envelopes and black marking pens. "Sabrina, have you finished—" Alicia trailed off when she caught sight of David standing by the counter. "Oh, do you need something, David?"

The air had cooled considerably with Alicia's arrival. There was no love lost between these two. They were polar opposites: Alicia was formal and precise, taking her job very seriously. David was relaxed and juvenile, at times, taking just as much time out of his work day to goof off as to make a big sale.

Alicia, I had discovered, worked for Mr. Campos long before Ergo Software was on the horizon. David knew she was the one employee he couldn't touch, and it grated on him.

Before he could make what would most likely be a sarcastic reply, I interjected, "Just wishing me a good morning is all."

David had a grim look on his face. He tapped me on the top of my head with the *Wall Street Journal* he was carrying and said, "We'll talk later, kiddo."

I flashed him a quick smile as he passed by me to head to his office.

Alicia took control of the reception area once again. "How many of those do you have left to pack?" she asked, indicating the stack of envelopes and the box of CD-ROMs next to me on the floor. Without waiting for an answer, she drove ahead to the next question, "Do you think you could get to the mail? And then we need to help set up for a presentation in Mr. Campos's office."

As Alicia ticked off the tasks for the rest of the day, I drifted off, thinking of the coming Friday evening when Patrick and I planned to meet again. This time, I was hoping it would be just the two of us and no Eric. The steamy kisses we shared made me believe he would be more than willing to leave his friend behind, but, if anything, I had learned Patrick was unpredictable.

The morning was a blur of activity: packing, sorting, filing answering the phone. It wasn't until around noon I had a chance to take a breather. Walking to the kitchen area behind the mailroom to pour a cup of coffee, I heard the front door open and someone enter the reception area. The chatter of two women was all I could make out. One of the women was Alicia, but the other?

Mug in hand, I headed back to the reception desk. An attractive head of neatly-arranged blonde hair was visible. There was no mistaking Tina, David's wife.

"He's in a meeting, Tina, but you're more than welcome to wait." Alicia pointed her to the few seats in the small waiting area.

Tina, wearing designer sunglasses, tilted the lenses down to peer over them at the seats Alicia had pointed out. Clearly not satisfied with that option, Tina presented one of her own, "I think I'll wait in David's office."

"All right," Alicia responded with only a slight hesitation.

It sounded as if that was unusual behavior for Tina. "Would you like a—"

But before Alicia could finish her usual offer of coffee, Tina had breezed past the receptionist desk, opened the door to David's office, and closed it solidly behind her.

I thought I heard Alicia whisper 'bitch' under her breath, but that seemed impossible. Alicia was always formal and polite, regardless of the situation. But some part of me wished I had heard correctly. It would make Alicia seem more accessible, more human. Less office automaton.

About thirty minutes later, the meeting had ended, and potential Ergo clients spilled out into the reception area. The president, Mr. Campos, handed out business cards and packets of information about the software. David shook hands, thanked everyone for coming, and headed to his office. The visitors left with Mr. Campos to enjoy lunch at a nearby restaurant.

Silence filled the office.

Then, all hell broke loose.

Angry yelling erupted from David's office. Alicia pretended to be immersed in the latest supply catalog, but I could tell she was listening to every audible word.

It turned out Alicia straining her hearing was unnecessary.

Tina threw open David's office door with a bang. "Do you think I am making this up? Do you, David?" Tina screeched. Her earrings jangled loudly as she argued, her head bobbing up and down like an angry chicken.

David, still inside his office, was inaudible to me and Alicia down the hall.

"I'll show you the test. Do you need some sort of proof?" Tina was livid, veins popping out from her skinny neck. "I don't want this any more than you do, but I thought you should know." Tina's voice quieted to an anguished squawk.

She stepped away from the open doorway, hands clutching her expensive handbag, "I'll be at my mother's."

"Tina." A disheveled David appeared in the doorway as she headed toward the front door. "Goddammit, Tina. Come back here. Let's talk about this."

The front door slammed shut behind Tina's well-dressed figure. He stood for a moment in his doorway, looking more than a little lost. After one glance at Alicia and me, he shut the door solidly and retreated into his office.

Alicia said one thing, and one thing only, "That David's a real piece of work."

I thought the better of asking her what she meant by that statement. I didn't really feel like diving into office politics having only worked at Ergo for a short while. Better to keep everyone in my good graces, until I figured out who I could trust. Gossiping about my boss, the man who hired me and was loaning me a car, would not be a good move. Instead, I continued to sort the mail, trying hard to pretend nothing had happened.

After working in silence for a while, Alicia asked me if I could answer the phones for her while she took her lunch break. I waved my hand at her as the phone started to ring, shooing the older woman out of the building.

"I'll answer it. You go ahead," I told her.

Alicia left, and I picked up the phone. Before I could say anything, I heard David's voice on the line, "Alicia, could you send Sabrina into my office, please?" He sounded anxious and unsure.

"David, it's me." As much as I wanted to stay neutral here at work, it was hard not to react to David's obvious distress. He had been very kind to me, and it made me feel as if I owed him something. A little friendly concern never hurt anyone, right?

"Thank God." There was relief in his voice. "Could you come back here?"

I rushed to his office.

"Shut the door, please."

I did as he asked, but couldn't help blurting out, "What happened, David?" He had to know that both Alicia and I heard the arguing.

"Tina's pregnant."

Stunned, I sat down in one of the extra chairs in the office "Congratulations?" I didn't know what else to say. The yelling match with Tina clearly meant he wasn't very happy about the news. It was as if all the air had been sucked out of the room.

"She's pregnant. Eight weeks."

"Oh." Seeing his dispirited face, I felt as if I had been kicked in the stomach. David was usually happy, silly even, with me at the office. It was hard to watch such a confident, charismatic man behave as if he had just lost his best friend.

"What am I going to do, Sabrina?" He took his glasses off and ran his hands through his hair. "Our marriage has been falling apart for years. I don't want a baby. Tina has to see that."

"See what?" I didn't understand what he was getting at.

"She has to see that we can't have a baby. she's insane! What is she thinking?" His eyes were wild as he started to pace behind his desk.

"You don't mean that she—that you want her to—?" I couldn't even form the words I was thinking. It was too horrible. I thought David was a kind man, a generous man. He had given me, complete stranger, a car of his own to drive. I would think he could have some kindness for his own wife.

"I just know I can't have a baby. Not now. And especially not with her." His voice lowered to a desperate whisper.

I sat silently in the chair, wishing I had never set foot in his office. "This isn't my place, David. I need to get back to the desk." I knew David and I had developed some kind of rapport that went beyond the boss-employee relationship, but this revelation was too much for me to handle.

As I got up from the chair and grabbed the doorknob, he protested, "Sabrina, please. Don't think I'm some horrible guy. You just don't get it."

But I was already out the door heading back to the receptionist's desk. When did I go from being his friend, to being his confidante? It didn't make any sense. Didn't he have anyone else to talk to about this? I shouldn't be in the middle of two married people and their problems.

Several co-workers returned from lunch, and the phone began ringing. Gratefully, I fell back into my job, trying to put David and Tina out of my mind.

David whizzed past me out the door to the parking lot. He hopped into his now-fixed Mercedes and took off down the street. Hearing the tires squeal in the parking lot, I was glad he was gone.

When Alicia returned from lunch, I decided to take a short drive over to Morgan's to think and clear my head. I hopped into my borrowed car and couldn't help but shiver. It felt so wrong to be in that car now. That car symbolized the beginning of my relationship with David, a relationship that had soured. I wished I had never taken David up on his offer. It was one more thing to tie me to him, to make it look as if I accepted his behavior and his decisions.

That was when I decided to take the car back to David's house after I stopped for coffee and something to eat. I would leave the keys in his mailbox and...and then what? He lived far from town; no taxis that far out. No pay phones to make any calls. I parked the car in front of Morgan's and sat in it for a moment, resting my head on the steering wheel.

What was I supposed to do?

———

Tap, tap, tap!

I jumped. Someone was tapping on the driver's side window. I rolled it down slowly.

"You all right in there?"

It was a man. A young and not-all-that-bad-looking man wearing a white apron and holding a steaming Morgan's paper cup. For a moment, I thought I knew him. The brown hair and kind face. I couldn't place him. I said nothing, but shook my head grimly.

"Looks like you need a double-shot today, instead of the usual." He returned to leaning up against the faux stone wall of Morgan's and sipped his coffee.

The usual? What is this guy talking about? It was then that noticed the name tag. 'Tim,' it read.

Yes, Tim.

I vaguely remembered him being nice to me the first night I met up with Patrick. Had he been serving me regularly?

Pretending I remembered him all along, I answered, "Uh, yeah. Need something stronger than 'the usual' today for sure." I got out of the car, grabbed my purse through the open window, and quickly entered the shop to avoid any more conversation. My mind was muddled with thoughts of David and Patrick, babies and fist fights.

Behind me I heard Tim call after me, "We're out of blueberry scones."

The door clanged shut behind me. Blueberry scones? Had he been watching me? I didn't come to Morgan's every day, and I didn't remember this Tim guy working there hardly at all.

And, heck, I had only been living in Monterey since mid-May. Out of all the hundreds of people that probably pass through the doors, why would he know my eating and drinking habits so intimately?

Maybe I should start studying at one of the other coffee-houses a little more often. But now it was too late to leave. It would be awkward and obvious if I turned and left. He was still outside, not ten feet from me on the other side of the glass: his well-built, tall figure angled against the wall. Worried he would see me staring at him, I averted my gaze from the window to the line of people waiting in front of me.

When I approached the counter, I gave my order. A non-fat latte with a bran muffin to go—that would show him!

As I waited for my order, Tim came back inside. Not to work, it seemed, but to check some papers on the wall near the storage room. As much as I wanted to pretend I didn't see him I found myself watching him as he flipped through what looked like a work schedule hanging from a clipboard.

"Non-fat latte, bran...to go!" The barista on duty, a short Hispanic fellow, yelled out.

I caught Tim smirking at me, one eyebrow raised at my change of routine. Feeling my face heat, I snatched the bag out of the barista's hand and turned to leave. Even as I walked out the door, I could feel Tim's eyes on me.

My quiet retreat at Morgan's felt tainted.

I liked going there anonymously to study, and I knew the next time I went to Morgan's I would be worrying more about Tim working there and watching my behavior than about my homework.

––––––––

Before I realized what I was doing, I found myself parked at the bottom of David's driveway.

Dammit.

I didn't mean to drive there. My mind was so caught up in everything that I drove on autopilot. There were no other cars in front of his house, thank goodness.

Just as I was about to head back to work, I changed my mind.

Why not?

Why not get rid of the car now, while no one is around? No awkwardness.

I thought I remembered seeing a convenience store a mile or two away on the drive over. It would probably have a pay phone. I could call a taxi or find a way to rent a car.

Set on leaving the car, I got out and looked around for a mailbox at the curb in which to leave the keys.

No such luck.

They had, instead, one of those mail slots in the front door. So, I resolved to jam the keys through that thing instead.

Crunching up the gravel walkway to the front door, I lifted the metal door and pushed the keys through. They jangled loudly, landing on the hard wood floor below.

A feminine voice from inside the house called out, "Who's there?" Then, the clatter of high heels on tile echoed closer and closer. "Is that you, lover?"

Lover?

thirteen

· · ·

THINKING it had to be Tina, I bolted down the driveway like a rabbit running from a hawk. I barely made it around the thick wall of hedges that separated the house from the road, when I heard someone throw open the front door. I leaned against the green barrier trying to catch my breath, my heart in my throat.

Peering around the edge of the bushes, I saw not the perfectly coifed blonde hair of Tina, but a brunette.

Lucy? Lucy Campos?

The woman I had met at the restaurant not too long ago. David had obviously not been very straightforward about his claim that Lucy was an 'old friend.'

It seemed as if Lucy was expecting David any minute. So I decided to leave before I was discovered, jogging down the street clutching my Morgan's bag.

Okie-dokie. That was way more than I wanted to know about my boss, and who I had come to think of as my friend. That man led a very complicated and messy life. Marital problems, unwanted baby, an affair with the ex-wife of his boss...

I needed to get out of there and fast.

Where was that gas station I thought was nearby?

I would be mortified if David saw me.

By my watch, I had already been gone an hour from work.

Considering I usually only took half an hour for lunch, Alicia would wonder where I was. I couldn't afford to lose my job, even if seeing David on a daily basis would be an uncomfortable part of my work day.

Where was that stupid store?

I hadn't really been paying attention on the drive over, so the location of the convenience store was not too clear in my mind.

Was it this street? Or one street over? Or was it three miles down the road instead of one?

Up ahead, I noticed a wooden bench. Tired from walking in my work shoes, I sat and decided to drink my now-cold latte and eat my hopefully-filling muffin. As I took a sip of my coffee drink, a city bus pulled up in front of me.

I was sitting at a bus stop.

Thank God!

The door hissed open.

"Sorry, no food or drink allowed," the overweight driver warned. He nodded his head toward a garbage receptacle next to the bench.

Just as I was about to abandon my lunch, I saw a small sign inside the bus dictating the fees: Adults - $1.50.

Oh, God. I had spent most of my cash buying lunch.

Frantically digging through my purse, I counted the change I had left.

"Are you getting on or what, lady? I got a schedule here."

A bored-looking Asian woman sitting on one of the front seats glared at me, two plastic bags of groceries lay at her feet.

I pulled my hand out of my purse, looking hopefully at the few coins I managed to find.

Dammit.

I had two quarters and a few pennies. Not even close.

The bus driver grunted at me in disgust, the door hissed shut, and the bus pulled away from the curb. I stood there, annoyed, irate, disheartened. I threw the change angrily back in my purse and sat on the bench. Might as well eat my lunch. I wasn't going anywhere.

Honk, honk!

What the—?

"Hey, need a ride?"

It was Tim from Morgan's in a beat-up Chevy Nova. Mid-bite, bran muffin crumbs filling my mouth, I could say nothing. Could he see the look of abject horror in my eyes? Was he was following me?

Oblivious to my widened eyes and my furtive glances around for an escape route, he picked up some books from the passenger seat, as if I had already accepted his offer.

"Here, let me just move some stuff. Then, there'll be room for you," he said casually, as if giving me a free ride was a regular part of his day. "My car is a pig sty, I know."

Then I saw it. Right there on the passenger's seat.

The book.

The same Spanish book I had. Professor Aguilera's class...was he in it? Had he been in the same class with me all summer, and I never noticed?

Tim tossed the books carelessly in the back seat and scooped up some fast food wrappers and empty soda cans. These, too, got thrown into the back.

He pulled the handle on his dented, rusting car. The door opened, inviting me to enter. "Come on. Where do you need to go?"

I swallowed my bran muffin, my mouth suddenly dry. "Back downtown," I croaked out.

"Okay." He looked up at me expectantly, nothing but kindness in his brown eyes.

Hardly believing I was doing it, I climbed into the car. Tim accelerated toward the downtown streets of Monterey.

"Your name's Sabrina, right?" He asked with a smile after a few minutes of silence.

I nodded my head and kept my eyes on the road.

"You're friends with that guy with the earrings, leather jacket —? What's his name?"

"Patrick," I answered carefully.

"Mmm. Seems like an interesting guy."

Did I detect a tinge of sarcasm in his voice? He was looking straight ahead at the road, so I couldn't read the expression on his face. "I don't know him that well. We just started hanging out."

"Oh," he responded, a bit of lightness to his voice. And did I see a bit of a smile on his face? Then he immediately launched into a different topic, "So, are you ready for Aguilera's test next week?"

I took a quick sip of my very cold coffee drink, hoping that might calm me down. "I've been doing a fair amount of studying. And you?"

"It's really just review for me. I've taken the class before but Aguilera wants me to be her assistant next semester."

"Be her assistant? You mean, you're not a student?"

"No. I finished my Master's in May and want to pursue a Ph.D in Latin American Studies."

This surprised me. I thought he was your average high school graduate working for minimum wage.

He continued on, "I'm taking a year off to work and make some money. Being Aguilera's assistant will be job number three. By next summer, I should have enough saved up so I don't have to fund my entire education with student loans."

I found this discussion very interesting. Maybe he wasn't such a creep after all. Could it be he was a normal human being with actual career aspirations and not an amateur stalker?

"Where else do you work besides Morgan's?"

"I've been running errands for the DJs at KMAR. I have some connections there. They were nice enough to give me the job. Odd hours, so I work a lot of nights. It fits in pretty well with my work schedule at Morgan's." He sighed. "All right. Enough about me. What about you? What are you doing with your life?"

Suddenly, I felt as if I wanted to tell him everything about me. He was easy to talk to; a nice guy. But I had never let anyone in before. My past, my relationship with my mother—no one knew. Not even my good friends from high school. And I liked it that way—at least, I thought I did.

It would be freeing to share my secrets with someone. To unburden myself of my past and move forward. I thought leaving home and coming to Monterey would help me bury my past, so I could make my life whatever I wanted to. I could pretend I had the perfect childhood, the perfect family. Now, sitting here in the car with Tim, I yearned to tell him all the ugliness I had seen, all the sadness and loneliness that made up my childhood. To hear the words spoken aloud might rid me of that weight.

But I was afraid he would reject me as low-class or white trash before he ever got to know me. I could lie to him, but I was tired of lying.

Maybe it would be better to say nothing at all, as usual.

Keep my private life private.

When he realized I wasn't going to speak, he drew out his next attempt at conversation, "O-o-o-kay. Why don't I just turn on the radio?" He reached for the first button on the car stereo.

Great. He probably thought I was a total whacko. Couldn't I have thought of *something* to tell him?

Anything?

Even if it wasn't true?

He was supposed to be the whacko, not me.

Lord, what a nightmare this day was turning out to be.

The radio blared a commercial in rapid-fire Spanish. The announcer overemphasized the inflections of each word. As a fledgling Spanish-speaker, trying to keep up with the dialogue gave me a headache.

"Sorry." Tim punched another button on the stereo and some easy listening music poured out of the speakers. "I listen to the Spanish stations to keep my language skills sharp, but I don't think 'twenty percent off' or 'deal of the century' is going to help me get through grad school."

I couldn't help but laugh.

A small laugh. Very small. In fact, my laugh was more like a smile with an expelling of air out my nose.

But it worked—the ice had broken.

"I'm studying for my Associate's Degree," I blurted out.

"Huh?" I think I shocked him with my rapid-fire statement.

"That's what I'm doing with my life currently." And then I found myself doing exactly what I had set out *not* to do: talk about myself. "I'm trying to work my way through school. Not as easy as I thought."

"And they keep raising the tuition every semester," he added as if he understood how hard it was for me.

"I know, they think that $100 'student fee' is no big deal, but when it means I'll either get to pay rent this month or take another twelve credits—"

"You gotta pay the rent," he finished for me.

Our conversation was so normal. I never knew two people could talk so comfortably about everyday things, especially not a guy.

"Hey." He looked over at me. "You wanna get together some time and study?"

The first feeling that shot through me was guilt—I was just starting a relationship with Patrick, and here I am sitting with another guy in his car talking about a study date. But A strong desire to say yes bubbled up inside. There was something about him, a kindness and sincerity I hadn't experienced with Patrick.

I looked at him, his hair ruffling in the wind, and it felt so right to be sitting there next to him. So comfortable.

Unlike the nerves and butterflies that tangled my stomach when I saw Patrick, Tim settled me just with his presence.

"Sure, that would be great. Obviously, you would be helping me a lot more than I would be helping you."

"That's okay." He turned onto a road that would lead us right into downtown. "You never know, you might teach *me* something."

Before I could think up a verbal parry to his thrust, I saw the intersection right near the office quickly approaching.

"Oh! I need to get off here," I indicated a street corner only a block from the office.

"All right," he sounded a little bit disappointed our conversation had to end.

And, to tell the truth, my spirits deflated a bit, too. It was the most natural conversation I had ever had with a guy.

Tim pulled over to the curb. "Thanks so much. You saved me back there." A flashed a genuine smile at him.

He hadn't even questioned me once why in the heck I was car-less and sitting at a bus stop when only moments earlier I had been sitting in a perfectly fine car right in front of his very eyes. In fact, he had been pretty accepting of my odd behavior, strange circumstances, and a crumbly bran muffin making even more of a mess out of his car.

Once I slammed the door, he leaned over to the open window and smiled at me, "Really, it was my pleasure." His brown eyes sparkled, and I felt a twinge of something in my stomach— nerves? And then he was off.

And, whoops!

We had forgotten to exchange phone numbers or make any plans for our study date. Did I do that subconsciously?

Tim was pleasant and engaging, and, heck, wasn't bad to look at, but he was so easy to talk to I could imagine myself dumping my whole life story on him. He was definitely the type that would ask too many questions, wanting to get inside my head. So far he had asked me about school and studying, but how long would it be before he questioned me about my family? My background? There was nothing there for me to be proud of, nothing but the tragicomedy of the Fuller family. And what was that good for but heavy dose of pity?

Patrick, on the other hand, was satisfied with knowing very little about me. No close attachments, no questions that dug beneath my surface. Maybe physical closeness was all I needed right now, to keep the loneliness from creeping in. And Patrick could certainly provide that.

When I ran into Tim again at Morgan's and the topic of a study date came up, this time I would listen to my head, not my heart. I would find a gentle way to turn him down. Thinking about that moment, disappointment burned in my stomach.

———

The next few days passed quickly. David was 'out sick,' so it was manageable for me to be in the office and do my work without distraction. And, yes, I still had work to do. After I had arrived so late the other day, Alicia had been very understanding.

"Everyone has a late lunch every now and then. Don't give it another thought," she had said to me.

Alicia hadn't pressed me for any information I might have about the blow up between Tina and David. The rumor of what had gone on that Monday morning was making the rounds. Alicia knew I had been in the office when something had happened, but she never asked me one single question about what I might have seen or heard.

That is when I started to realize what a good woman she was.

Once I got past her anal retentive qualities, she was quite a pleasant person, to tell the truth. Rarely did she have a bad word to say about anyone, and she always worked diligently. I never remembered her goofing off or taking an extra-long coffee break.

It was during those few days when David was gone, that Alicia and I struck up an odd sort of friendship. This began most innocently with a question, as most friendships usually do.

"So, I've been wondering, what did you do before you worked here?" I had been wanting to ask Alicia this question for a while. She dressed in a bohemian fashion with lots of beaded jewelry, most of which seemed original. To me, it didn't seem that Alicia had been a receptionist her whole adult life.

"Oh, a bit of this and a little bit of that," she answered cryptically.

We were both sitting at the front desk doing tag team filing. One person filed the paper in the appropriate pulled folder, the other person put the folder away in the filing cabinet.

"No, come on. I'm curious." I pressed until she capitulated, "Tell me."

She drew in a deep breath, "Well, back in the 70s, I was a very well-known folk singer. I wrote my own music, and some of the songs were even played on the local radio station." She threw out a honking laugh at that admission, "Can you imagine that? Me, on the radio?"

I squinted my eyes and looked at her, imagining a younger woman with long, fiery hair and a guitar, "Actually, I can. That makes a lot of sense." I filed a few more papers. "Do you still write music?"

"Oh, I don't do much song-writing anymore. I went through a pretty bad divorce and ended up bankrupt. Lovely, huh?" She tightened the scarf that had loosened from around her bright red hair. "So, I had to find work to get myself back on my feet. My ex was kind of a wealthy one, you know. But he managed to cut me out of any kind of alimony. I barely got enough child support for our two kids to make rent. I spent the little bit of savings I had on a divorce lawyer. A lot of good he did me—"

"I'm sorry, Alicia. I didn't mean to pry."

To go from marrying a wealthy man to bankruptcy? That must have been hard for her to admit. Her brutal honesty about her past made me like her even more. She trusted me with these ugly details, but was I really worthy of that trust? I wouldn't share the same intimate details with her.

"Nothing to be sorry about. Don't worry yourself over that. I'm pretty used to my situation nowadays. The kids are grown; my ex is remarried. Life goes on."

I wish I could be so cavalier about my past, my history. To let go of all the hurtful things in my life would be so freeing. Maybe someday, with some distance, I would be able to do what Alicia has done. Maybe.

"Your ex sounds like a creep."

"Pretty much," Alicia agreed. "It's those attractive, well-off ones that you've gotta look out for. They see a pretty girl who they like, and then—" Alicia snapped her fingers. "It's over. They're on to someone new, and you're yesterday's news."

We both reflected on this bit of wisdom for a moment, filing things in silence.

"So, do you have yourself a boyfriend?" Alicia asked.

"Um, I guess you could say so."

"Oh?" Her ears perked up. "What's his name? What does he do?"

"Patrick. He's a linguist."

"One of those military boys from up the hill?" She clucked disapprovingly at me. "I should have included them in my list of ones to watch out for."

I was slightly annoyed by Alicia's blatant stereotyping of all military men. "He's a nice guy, really."

Alicia lifted an eyebrow at that statement; I guess I must have sounded a little defensive.

"You just be careful, all right? Make sure you know what you're getting yourself into."

"I will, Alicia. I will."

How I wished I had listened more closely to Alicia's warning come Friday night.

fourteen

. . .

"TURN HERE," Patrick pointed me in the direction of a small side road, which would take us up into the foothills surrounding Monterey Bay. "There's a really amazing turnout a few miles down the road."

"All right." I followed his directions, driving my newly-repaired Festiva. It felt good to be back in my own car and to be alone with Patrick. No Eric in sight.

When I had picked him up in front of the barracks, Eric had been standing there with him at the curb. For a moment, my heart dropped. I had hoped to spend an evening alone with Patrick. However, as he approached my car, Eric gave only a short salute to both of us. Then, he joined a small group of people that were gathered out by some picnic tables on the south side of the barracks building. A girl with jet black hair and heavy make-up turned to watch us drive away. Eric touched her on the shoulder and shook his head. The girl pulled away from him, lit a cigarette, and stared at me.

Weird.

. . .

Fifteen minutes later, the road twisted and curved in front of us like the cypress trees that grew beyond the dirt shoulder. We were quiet, the radio was off, and my thoughts were wandering, and the strange girl was forgotten.

Here was this warm, male body next to me. We weren't touching, but my nerves were hypersensitive to his presence. One minute my heart would race out of control, the next goose bumps would rise on my skin. Patrick's presence gave me the oddest sensation of attraction and anxiety, desire and agitation. It was exhilarating.

He reached for my denim-covered leg at that moment; his hand was heavy and warm on my thigh.

"So, how do you know about this road," I asked, his touch rattling my concentration. The question helped me focus on my driving.

"When I had my car, I used to drive all over the place, exploring." He rolled down his window to let the night air blow in. It was unusually warm for a coastal summer evening.

"What happened to your car?"

"Oh, it's stupid. You don't want to hear it." He set his elbow on the edge of the open window and stared outside at the trees and open sky above.

I pressed him, not willing to let him get away with a vague answer, "It can't be that stupid. Come on, tell me." As if him answering would mean something about our relationship or that he cared for me to know these details about him.

I felt his gaze taking in my profile. "I was out here driving one night with some friends."

I assumed Eric was included in that group, but who were the other 'friends' he was referring to? He never mentioned anyone else.

"We pulled off the road, right on the edge of a really steep cliff. I forgot to put on the fucking parking brake, I guess, and I had parked close to the rim." He paused here, taking time to suck in some air between his clenched teeth. His fingers tapped on the arm rest. "Anyway, I saw it out of the corner of my eye. The car started to roll. Over it went with all of our stuff. I had to climb down the hillside to get our books out. My car was totaled."

"That's awful! You're lucky no one was in the car."

He nodded. When he spoke again, his voice had picked up hard edge, "My mom got the insurance money for it and hasn't sent me any of it."

"Why wouldn't she send you the money?" I blinked rapidly. "I mean, it was your car, right? How does she expect you to get around?"

"It's more my jackass of a stepfather than anything else. Asshole." He withdrew his hand from my leg. "He was so fucking glad to get rid of me when I enlisted." He slammed his hand on the dashboard. "Fuck him! He doesn't care what happens. He's just glad I'm two thousand miles away."

I touched his arm. My mother had been more than happy the day I had left. I knew what it felt like to be despised in your own home. My mother tolerated me for twenty-three years. There was no real love there, just a relationship built out of need. I was the only person she had, the only one that would take care of her, the bills, the store. Without me, she would be lost. But even on that last day when I was about to drive away, she never thanked me, never told me she appreciated anything I had done.

The sting of loneliness returned. Just thinking about being at home with my mother was enough to bring it back. I gripped Patrick's arm tighter to reassure myself he wasn't alone. I knew what he was feeling.

Patrick pulled away. His anger was palpable in that small car, the heat rising from his body. But I understood it.

We drove along in silence for a few more miles. Then, the car burst through the heavy cover of the trees, and we were in the middle of an open space. Wide dirt shoulders flanked us on either side. Fields stretched out from the road, edged with pine and cypress trees. The night sky above was clear, cloudless, and full of stars.

"Wow. It's so beautiful," I whispered as I took in the surroundings. I parked the car on the shoulder. The gravel crunched under the tires, and crickets sang loudly in the fields.

Patrick climbed out of the Festiva and stretched himself out on top of the hood, his anger magically gone. The metal pinged and squeaked under his weight, but he pushed himself up higher on the hood until his back rested on the windshield. He put his arms behind his head, as if he was suspended in a hammock, and gazed into the sky.

I stood next to him, knowing the hood of the car couldn't manage my extra weight. After a few moments of staring up at the sky, appreciating the bright stars, my neck tired. I wanted a more comfortable viewing spot. A split rail fence divided the field from the shoulder on the other side of the road. I headed for it, across the two paved lanes.

"Hey," he called out to me, "where are you going?"

"Just over here, I want to sit down." I stepped onto the pavement.

"Wait." He stood up on my front bumper and leapt to the ground. Catching up to me, he grabbed my hand and led me the rest of the way across the street to the fence. We both climbed onto the top rail and took in the view of the field and trees framed by the starry sky above.

The gentle evening breeze blew his hair across his eyes. The planes of his face were outlined by the starlight, and I reached out to touch his jaw. He grasped my hand in his. His eyes were soft, and goose bumps rose on my skin. He stared at my mouth. Leaning toward me, slowly, he touched his lips to mine.

A slow heat built within me, and I leaned toward him, deepening the kiss. His hands grabbed my shoulders and gently pushed me back. We parted, the moistness of his kiss on my lips.

"Do you have a blanket or anything in your car?" He asked me with a quiet intensity.

"Maybe. What are you thinking?" My senses reeled from his touch and that kiss.

He jumped to the ground. Putting his hands in the pockets of his leather jacket, he smiled secretively. He backed away from me and crossed the road to the car. "Just an idea. You'll see."

For a moment, he looked like a small boy, his blond hair ruffled by the wind, a mischievous twist to his smile. His face could appear so innocent, but I knew darkness lurked behind those blue eyes. A darkness I was coming to understand.

He turned and closed the distance between himself and my car. Popping the hatch, he rummaged through the pile of my belongings still stashed in the trunk. After a few moments, he pulled out a tarp, part of my camping gear. He bundled up the tarp in his arms and lugged it back across the road. I hopped down from the fence rail as he tossed the tarp over it and into the adjoining meadow. Then, he climbed over the fence and carried the tarp further into the field.

"Come on!" he urged me.

"Where are we going?"

"It's better to look for shooting stars if you're lying on the ground." Patrick, finding a level spot in the grass, spread out the tarp.

"Shooting stars?"

One minute we are kissing, and then we are looking at shooting stars? I didn't understand.

"The Perseids."

"Huh?"

"Every year in August? The Perseid meteor shower?" He answered me patronizingly. "You know."

Not wanting to appear dense, I responded back, "Oh, yeah."

I could sense him grinning at me in the darkness; he knew I was lying. He pulled me down onto the cool tarp. The almost-complete blackness made for good viewing of the shooting stars. No houses stood nearby, and the foothills blocked the glow from the Monterey street lights.

Patrick and I lay side by side, heads touching, hands interlocked. I wanted him to touch me again, but I hesitated to move. There was a comfort there, lying under the dark blanket of the night sky. I could smell him—a slightly smoky perfumed scent of incense.

Staring wide-eyed into the night sky, I scanned the blackness for movement. I could only hear our breathing and the rush of the wind through the pine trees. My limbs relaxed. I should have been cold, but Patrick's body heat warmed me. Then, all I could see was the night sky and the edge of Patrick's silhouette. The trees disappeared, and it was only our backs against the tarp. I imagined the tarp kept us from falling into the sky, a magnet keeping us attached to the earth.

A streak of light flashed in the corner of my eye. "There! I saw one." Then, another streak, like a kite's tail, passed by. "Oh!"

Patrick tugged me toward him on the tarp. "Come here," his voice a throaty whisper.

He pulled me on top of him and kissed me. He reached under my clothes, unsnapping and unbuttoning. Skin on skin.

The cool air brushed up against my half-naked body, causing me to shiver. I pushed lightly on his chest and pulled my mouth away from his. It was all happening so quickly, before I had time to think.

Our eyes met. I took a breath. Patrick's eyes were dark and liquid, their usual clear blue masked by the night. I fell into those eyes like a meteorite falls from space in the night sky. A meteorite that burns brighter than any other object in the sky, burning out quickly, leaving the sky dark once again.

He ran his hand into my hair and pushed my head down to his, so that my lips touched his. I imagined he was the magnet keeping me from falling into space. His warm hands, his solid legs, and his chest pressing against mine.

His kisses trailed down my body, and I knew where this was leading. And I wanted it. I wanted to be as close and as intimate as two human beings could be. So I let his hands drift lower. I let him undress me completely.

As he entered my body, I watched the stars streak across the sky behind us. The last thought in my head was the stars, those brilliant, beautiful stars.

fifteen

. . .

I WOKE UP MONDAY MORNING, groggy and confused. Friday night filled my thoughts. That whole evening had been so unreal. After we had folded up the tarp and repacked it in my trunk, we had driven back to the base in an odd silence. I hadn't wanted things to move so quickly between Patrick and me, but it had felt so wonderful to be with someone. To give my body wholly over to someone. To not be alone any longer.

The sensation of his hands on me lingered days later. That dark, animal look in his eye when he entered me still made me shiver.

On the drive back to town he had said nothing, but he'd placed a hand on my thigh. As if he had marked me now, and I was his.

When I dropped him off at the barracks, he leaned over the parking brake handle and had kissed me warmly. His lips lingered over mine, his hand caressing my neck. He whispered, "I'll see you."

I spent the rest of my weekend immersed in books and papers for my classes, trying not to think about that night. Where was our relationship was going? Was it just a night of meaningless sex? His goodbye had been so casual. I didn't want to push anything on him or on myself. It was as if a thread kept us together, which could snap at any moment.

Small steps and less conversation would be best.

Anything more, and I would be afraid he'd disappear and I'd be alone with my thoughts and my books.

Now I had to face David at work. I had managed to avoid him last week. He'd gone about his business with startling efficiency. As if he barely knew me. As if he hadn't told me anything about his wife and their relationship.

I hoped Monday he would still be the same—cold and distant. That would make things less awkward for both of us.

I pushed through the glass front doors of the Ergo Software office. A rush of warm air blew my hair wildly behind me. The door shut with a loud whoosh.

Alicia greeted me, smiling, from the receptionist desk, her purple horn-rimmed reading glasses perched on her beak-like nose.

Last week, when David and I had been avoiding each other, Alicia had struck up conversation. She must have sensed something had changed between David and me. Maybe she figured I now saw David as she did: an egocentric jerk. She never said that to me in so many words, but her attitude toward him revealed she didn't respect him very much.

The only thing he was really good at was selling Ergo's software, which kept us all working. She could respect him for that, but not much else.

"How was your weekend?" she asked.

"It was all right." My feelings were muddled about my weekend, so I had difficulty with my answer.

She was nice enough not to press for details. Instead, her smile shrank a bit, and she continued filing her stack of paper work. My short answer had hurt her feelings, and at the moment, I didn't care.

I headed to the mailroom to pull out the boxes of CD-ROMs I would be shipping that day. In such a small company, the admins wore many hats: phone answerer, coffee maker, product shipper.

We worked in comfortable silence most of the morning, which was only interrupted by the phone ringing. David was nowhere in sight.

At around noon, David's office door opened.

When had he arrived?

He looked as if he was in serious thought: his suit was very wrinkled, he was unshaven and scruffy. In fact, he wore the same suit he had worn on Friday.

How strange.

He approached the front desk, as if he didn't even see me. "Alicia, I need some help with the presentation this afternoon. The PowerPoint slides aren't ready yet, and I have some other materials that need to be reviewed."

Alicia, instead of immediately offering her assistance as was her usual style, sat quietly. Perhaps she was hoping David would ask politely, she was stickler for common courtesies.

The phone rang. "Hold on a moment, David." Alicia picked up the receiver, "Ergo Software, Alicia speaking. How may I be of service?"

I busied myself with the box of CD-ROMs, checking the packing list for each order. Because I was so immersed in my task, I failed to notice Alicia had already hung up the phone and grabbed her coat and purse.

"Sabrina!" She called out to me in a thick, high-pitched voice, "Can you take over the desk for me? That was the dentist—completely forgot I had an appointment this morning."

How did overly-organized Alicia forget something like a dentist appointment? No wonder she sounded upset.

"Of course." The words were scarcely out of my mouth before she sailed out the door, purse in one hand, cardigan sweater in the other. I stopped packing the shipping boxes and, instead, sat down at the front desk to finish the filing Alicia had left behind.

David stood next to the counter. His quiet presence unnerved me, but I tried to keep calm. I was waiting for the other shoe to drop, for him to bring up the car I had left in his driveway with hardly an explanation. I wanted to pretend it never happened. But, if I hadn't taken advantage of his kindness to me the day of the accident, then where would I be right now? At another motel in an even seedier part of town? Delivering pizzas to drunk college students?

I continued to organize the files in front of me.

Out of the corner of my eye I saw him rake his hand through his hair. "Uh, Sabrina?"

My eyes back on my work, I offhandedly mumbled, "Mmm-hmm?" But underneath my indifference, my emotions were roiling.

"Are you any good with PowerPoint?" His previous hesitation had disappeared and his usual confidence returned. "I have about ten slides that need to be redone and a few more that need to be added to the presentation I'm giving this afternoon. I would really appreciate it if you could—"

I sighed. It wasn't a personal request, but something that affected Ergo, and I couldn't let Mr. Campos and Alicia down. If David needed my help, I should help.

"Sure, I can do that for you, but I don't have PowerPoint on this machine." I used my chin to indicate the computer I shared with Alicia on the receptionist's desk, as my hands were full of folders and papers. "I think Alicia deleted it by accident when she was in one of her 'cleaning' moods."

Alicia had a tendency to over-organize, simplifying and categorizing everything around her as much as possible. That included the programs on the computer; if she didn't use something on a semi-regular basis, it was a good bet she would delete it to make her computer desktop look less cluttered.

David's fingers tapped on the counter. "You could use the computer in my office, and I could work out here."

"All right." I set the files down. "If that's okay with you. Just show me what I need to do."

I didn't want to find myself liking David again. He had proven himself to be nothing but an insensitive, cheating jerk. But he could be so charming and so self-assured sometimes, that it was hard to dislike him.

As I stood, he put his hand on my shoulder. I self-consciously shrugged it off. "Please, don't."

"Don't what?"

"Don't...with your hand." I continued forward to his office, leaving him standing in the receptionist area. But before I could escape his reach, he caught me by the wrist.

I froze.

"What's wrong, Sabrina? I thought we were friends. You can talk to me, can't you?"

I kept my eyes on the floor. I couldn't stand to look in his eyes and see what I knew I would see there: sadness, loneliness maybe. I pulled my arm out of his grasp.

I took a deep, slow breath. "I thought we were friends, too. But, lately, I just don't know. There's too much going on."

I didn't want to clarify that statement by saying there was too much going on *with him*: a failing marriage, a pregnant wife, and an affair? I really didn't need to get into the middle of that mess.

He slowly let go of me. "Too much going on? You mean with Tina and me? How does that affect our friendship?"

I lifted my head. I was surprised to see sadness reflected in his eyes. His crumpled suit and days'-old beard made him appear more vulnerable. Like a little boy who had just woken up from an afternoon nap.

Darn it, I could feel my resolve crumbling. "It shouldn't, but—"

"But what? I'm still the same guy that beat you at Tetris." He gave me a wary smile.

He was so good at lightening the mood with a joke and at diverting the topic to something pleasant.

I felt touched he was so concerned about what I thought of him, so I smiled back. I wished last week had never happened. I wished we could go back to being two good friends, gossiping shamelessly about co-workers and going out for burgers at lunch. I wished we could sit in the same room while I laughed at his silly attempts at humor or his fake accents. I willed my unpleasant memories to the very back of my mind.

"I think you're mistaken," I teased, the fun me coming back. "I beat you five out of seven the last time!"

He laughed then. His full, rumbling laugh. It erupted from him like water from a geyser. And the glint reappeared in his eyes; a glint that signaled to me the old David had returned.

He was pleased I'd already forgiven him.

After rerouting the receptionist's phone to David's office number, we sat together in his office. I, at his desk, hurriedly adding changes to the PowerPoint slides; he, in the extra chair, sitting very closely to me and watching over the curve of my shoulder. I liked feeling his presence there, like a faithful dog curled at my feet.

While finishing up the slides, he gathered the rest of the materials for his presentation.

"David?"

"Yes?" He asked distractedly, stuffing handouts into an accordion folder.

"You were going to clean up before the meeting, right?"

He stroked his rough jaw and looked a bit surprised by what he felt. Closing the door to his office, he took a long look at himself in the small mirror that hung on the back of the door.

"Jesus, I look like I spent the night under a bridge. Why didn't you say anything?"

He brushed at the arm of his suit jacket, as if he could magically erase the wrinkles. He reached for a duffle bag in one corner of the office. Out of the zippered side pocket, he pulled an electric razor. He flicked it on and began to shave himself using the small mirror.

I found myself watching him, not being able to pull my eyes away. Being raised solely by my mother, I never had much exposure to the habits of men. Mostly just their sexual and drinking habits, but not the more routine things.

Shaving was such a masculine activity. I observed as each patch of his angular face became smooth. He didn't seem to mind having an audience.

"Do you think I have enough time to run off to the cleaners? I think I at least have a clean jacket there I could change into." He looked down at his watch, taking note of the hour.

I cleared my throat and my mind, tucking a strand of hair behind my ear, and offered, "I could pick it up for you, if you want."

"Really?" He was so good at manipulating me into doing what he wanted: first, I had forgiven him for his behavior last week and now, I was offering to run personal errands.

That clean-shaven, handsome face looked at me expectantly, and I couldn't resist, "Sure, I don't mind."

He already had the dry cleaner slip in his hand and a twenty dollar bill. "That should cover it; if not—"

"I have some money on me. You can owe me."

He gave me a sideways smirk, looking so earnest and kind, my heart melted a little. After shaving, his eyes seemed brighter, his teeth whiter. Almost as if he had shaved away the bad parts about David I disliked and had left behind all the good things. Here was the whole David I knew.

I grabbed the cleaner receipt from his hand and ducked out of his office.

I stopped to pick up my purse from behind the receptionist's counter. Then, as I exited the building, I caught sight of Tina making her way toward the front entrance from the parking lot. Once again, she was stylishly dressed, every blonde hair meticulously in place.

Seeing her made me nervous; I zipped around the corner to avoid eye contact.

As I dashed out to the dry cleaner's only a few blocks up the street, I wondered why Tina wanted to confront David again in such a public place—his place of employment, for God's sake. What right did she have to barge in on him while he was trying to work?

The faster I made it back to the office, the better. Maybe I could interrupt any arguments or unpleasantness by delivering his dry cleaning. Why couldn't Tina leave him alone? Let him be miserable in peace? Why did she have to nag at him, prod him, until he exploded?

How had he ever fallen in love with her in the first place? She was more interested in her perfect appearance and her designer handbags. Every time I saw her, she spent more time touching up her lipstick and fixing her hair than speaking to her husband. No wonder David was having an affair.

Tina drove him to it.

My mind imagining Tina as the devil incarnate, I entered the dry cleaner's in a daze. Handing the slip and a twenty-dollar bill to the attendant, I continued to muse on David and Tina's odd marriage.

Maybe he had to marry her? Why would either of them want to be married to the other?

———

I returned to the office, dry cleaning slung over my shoulder. Pushing open the front door of the office, I thought I would hear shouting coming from David's office, but it was quiet. Unusually quiet. I frowned, set the stack of cleaned clothes on one of the chairs in the reception area, and crept toward David's closed office door.

Nothing.

No voices, no arguing, not even whispering. What was going on?

Mr. Campos turned the corner and spied me.

"Sabrina!" He called out with an agitated growl.

I stopped in my tracks, and my heart jumped into my throat.

Sidney Campos didn't sound too happy.

"Yes, Mr. Campos?"

"What was all that yelling about? And where in the devil is David? We have a big presentation in fifteen minutes, and he has all the slides." He wrung his hands absentmindedly, large sweat stains already under each arm; he was a walking stress case.

"Yelling?" What happened while I was gone? "I can get you his slides, if that's what you're worried about. I was helping him finalize them this morning."

"Thank God. Please tell me you finished them."

"Yes, but—" I wasn't sure if I should tell him that David's wife had showed up only a few minutes ago.

"Look, get me those slides, and then start looking for David. He's got to be nearby—maybe he went to grab some coffee?" He seemed annoyed but desperate for his right-hand man, the one who landed all the big clients, to be present at the meeting. Mr. Campos might have technical knowledge and a head for numbers, but he was not the biggest people person. David filled in for that shortcoming.

"All right. I'll email you the slide presentation, and then I'll take a walk down Alvarado."

He seemed pacified by my solution. "Good. Let me know immediately if you find him."

"Of course." I zipped into David's office to email the slides on his computer. I noticed his duffle bag was missing. The desk was neat with papers carefully arranged and pens perfectly stowed in a holder. But something seemed off. It was almost *too* neatly arranged, especially if David and Tina had some sort of argument as Mr. Campos had implied.

However, I was in a hurry to email the slides, so I slipped behind David's desk and plopped into his chair. I double-clicked on the email icon.

Addressing a new email to sidney.campos@ergo.com, I then clicked on the attachment icon to search for the slides David and I had been working on. It only took a few moments to find the right file, but as it was uploading, I noticed another email window was open at the bottom of the screen.

What had David been writing? Thinking it might hold some clue as to what happened to him, I clicked once on the minimized window to expand it.

Sidney,

Forgive me for not coming to you in person, but I will be unable to attend the meeting this afternoon due to a sudden illness. Sabrina can get you the slide presentation. Hopefully, I will feel better tomorrow. I will call you from home tonight to find out how the meeting went. Sorry for the short notice.

David

Weird. He had never sent the email. It was just sitting on his computer. Why would that be? Did he maybe send Mr. Campos another version of the email?

It didn't make much sense to spend time looking for David

now. So, I picked up the phone on the desk and entered Mr. Campos's extension.

"Sidney Campos."

"Mr. Campos? It's Sabrina. I think I know where—"

"Sabrina? Never mind about looking for David. Seems his wife got in an accident, and he had to meet her at the hospital. Nothing serious. Just some bumps and bruises; Tina should be fine. I'll just have to wing it at the meeting."

Confused, I mumbled an okay, then slid the phone back into its cradle. What was going on? When did Tina get in an accident? And how? I was only at the dry cleaner's for fifteen or twenty minutes at the most. And what was with the email on David's computer?

"Where are you, dear?"

Alicia's familiar throaty voice carried down the hall from the main entrance, so I headed back to my usual spot behind the receptionist's desk.

Then, a dark thought came to my mind: what if David had hurt Tina? What if that anger I had seen last week spiraled out of control? Could it be?

David, what did you do?

sixteen

. . .

"HELLO?"

It was Saturday morning, and I had been folding a basket of clean clothes when the phone rang.

"Sabrina?"

I could barely hear the voice on the other end of the line. "Yes?" Was it Patrick?

"It's me." The voice gave a nervous sort of cough.

"Patrick?"

"Uh, no...who's Patrick? It's David."

"David?" I was perplexed. Why would he be calling me? "How's Tina?" I thought back to my suspicions that weird day at the office. David had been absent from work all week. Everyone believed he was watching over his wife as she recuperated from her 'accident.'

"Tina?" He said reluctantly. "She's okay." The nervous coughing started up again.

"So...?" Would he please get to the point of his call? I wanted believe what everyone else believed—that Tina had been involved in a minor car accident. But something happened in his office while I was gone. I knew it.

Sitting on my folded-up futon, I tucked the receiver under my chin and picked up a pair of matching socks, folding them together. Maybe I should give him the benefit of the doubt and listen to his explanation.

"Um, well, I wanted you to know—"

Usually so well-spoken, exuding charm in every syllable, why was David having such trouble making simple conversation?

I cut him off, "No, I don't know All I *do* know is that you disappeared at work, I heard there was fight, and then Tina's in the hospital."

"I know, Sabrina, I know." The regret in his voice was unmistakable.

Something *had* happened that day at work. I had a sour taste in my mouth. What kind of man would hurt his wife? A pregnant wife? Had she somehow driven him to it?

My mother could do that to a man. Get right up in his face, yelling and screaming obscenities. I had seen her slapped once or twice, which scared me, but I could understand why her boyfriend at the time did it. My mother could get under your skin that way.

Had this been what happened? My stomach flip flopped at the idea of pressing him for more information. Instead, I wanted to end the conversation. This revelation was too much to process. "So, why is it you called?" I folded my laundry, placing each item on the cardboard box that served as a coffee table. The crisp feel of the clean clothes in my hands and the scent of the detergent calmed me. This was my world, this every day routine. The rhythmic motions of flattening, creasing, and turning shirts right side out.

"I wanted to apologize. You were so helpful, and then, Tina— I didn't know what to do."

What did he want from me? Understanding? Forgiveness?

"And I also wanted to ask if you would meet me for coffee

somewhere? Maybe later today or tomorrow? It would be nice to just talk."

Abruptly, I stopped sorting and folding my clothes and switched the phone to my other ear. He had caught me off guard. "Um, I don't think so, David."

"Why not?" I could hear the disappointment in his voice.

I wanted to say yes because he had been kind to me. He had offered me a job, given me a car to drive. I wanted to return the favor, but at the same time I was disgusted with myself for giving him the time of day. That was what loneliness did to me: created a person who would find any excuse to sit beside another human being and just talk. No matter what kind of person he was. Was I really that desperate? Was I really that pathetic?

"I can't, David. I just can't." I hung up with a soft click.

I leaned against the refrigerator, and my stomach roiled. I had never seen him act violently toward anyone in the office, not even the day of the accident, when I could tell how angry he was. He had managed to get his emotions under control and ended up befriending me. But with Tina—with Tina he yelled, banged things around. He was such a different man.

I sighed. Work was becoming a very unpredictable place. I almost wished I was back working for Bob. At least I understood that kind of man. He made his intentions known right up front, no hiding behind charm or good looks.

The phone rang.

I jumped.

I hardly ever received phone calls that weren't telemarketers, and now I had two calls in less than an hour. I let it ring a few times to make sure someone hadn't dialed my number in error.

Four rings. Five.

I snatched up the phone, "Hello?"

"Hey, Sabrina. It's Patrick."

My breathing quickened. He never called me. "Hi. What's up?"

"Thought maybe we could get together tonight, around seven or seven-thirty?"

"Sure." My heart raced as I envisioned our night under the sky of raining stars. Looking up at the clock, I noted the late hour, unzipped my sweat jacket, and kicked off my shoes.

"Eric had this fantastic idea—"

My heart fell. I hoped Patrick and I could have another date alone.

"Tonight it's going to be really clear, and there's almost a full moon. Eric was thinking that we could drive down to Asilomar and hang out."

"Asilomar?"

"You know, sort of south of Pacific Grove. The beach?"

"Uh, I guess so. Yeah." I had never been so far south of Monterey before. Even though that part of Pacific Grove was only short five-minute drive from downtown, I mainly stuck to my apartment, work, and school.

"Great. Do you think you could come pick us up?"

Now that I understood why Patrick didn't have a car, it didn't bother me to be the chauffeur. He didn't have a car because his stepfather was a jerk. I got that. It made sense. I was willing to help him with his lack of vehicle even if it was for something he wanted to do.

I liked feeling needed.

"Sure, I can drive."

It was seven o'clock now, so I tucked the phone under my chin and shimmied out of my unzipped jacket.

"Cool. See you then."

I hung up and completed undressing in my minuscule kitchen, stuffing a bagel half in my mouth. That would be dinner. I had about forty-five minutes to shower and dress before I picked up Patrick—and Eric.

———

Some days in Monterey the air was crisp and clean, as would be expected of any town on the water. Tonight, however, the air was stagnant and smelled like rotting fish. I shut the vent to keep out the stench. Sometimes even driving a few miles away from a location would be enough to encounter fresher air. But for now, the scent hung heavy around me, even with the closed vents.

I cranked up the radio while listening to a local rock station, knowing as soon as Patrick and Eric got into the car, I would end up putting in one of their homemade CDs. The only thing we had in common was a mutual appreciation for The Cure. Otherwise, I was pretty uneducated in the world of Goth music. So for the ten-minute drive up to the Presidio, I listened to what I liked.

Approaching the barracks, I saw two figures waiting near the curb—most definitely Patrick and Eric. They were dressed in the same black clothes I had seen before, but this time they brought along something new.

"Hey," Patrick called to me as I got out of my car. He gave me a slow, seductive half-smile.

I touched his boyish face and smiled back at him, "Hey." That face appeared to be so good, so pure, so beautiful there in the darkness.

"Can you hand me the keys, so I can unlock the back?" Patrick asked.

"What is it?" I handed him my keys. Eric stepped from behind him with a case of beer.

"Oh." My least favorite beverage. The smell always reminded me of my mother. In my mind's eye I could still see the open beer cans in the kitchen, around the bathtub, by the TV.

"Come on, put it in the back," Patrick told Eric as he lifted the hatchback.

Eric loaded that and a black duffle bag into my trunk. While his friend was occupied with putting things in my trunk, Patrick gently picked up my hand and kissed my palm, and then the inside of my wrist. A slow warmth spread from my fingers and traveled up my arm. But, embarrassed that he displayed something so intimate in front of his friend, I pulled my hand back before he could go any further.

He chuckled a bit, probably laughing at my shyness, but he let me go back to the driver's seat to wait for them.

I gripped the steering wheel as if it was a lifeline to sanity. His lips on my palm had been intoxicating. I had wanted to let him explore, to touch more than just the merest patch of exposed skin. And that was so unlike me.

Intimate moments for me had been very controlled, almost clinical. I was not a person that cuddled and kissed. For me, it was all or nothing. Most of the time it was nothing. But with Patrick, it was as if all the nerves in my body had awakened. That night on the tarp under the stars, he had flicked a switch.

Eric took his usual spot behind the passenger seat. Awkwardly, he pulled the end of his long trench coat into the car and greeted me, "Hey, Sabrina."

Then, he opened a large, soft-cover book with a demon on the cover and flipped through the pages.

Patrick slid into the seat next to me and slammed the door. "Do you know Pacific Grove at all?"

I loosened my grasp on the steering wheel, forcing myself to think about the here and now, and not the night we spent together on the tarp. "Sort of. I know how to get downtown, if that's what you mean."

"Well, we need to pick someone up. I have an address. Let's hope we can find it."

"Who are we picking up?" A fourth person?

"Gretchen," Patrick said as if I should know who he was talking about.

"Uh-huh." When he didn't elucidate any further, I put the car in first gear and asked, "And who's that?"

"Remember? Eric's girlfriend?"

I was glad to hear the fourth person joining us would be a girl—and Eric's girlfriend to boot. She would keep him busy, and I could have more time alone with Patrick. But, unlike Patrick implied, I didn't remember any such conversation about a Gretchen. I didn't want to argue the point, though. Having her along would only improve things.

I nodded and drove in the direction where I thought this girl's house might be.

Patrick gave my knee a squeeze, making it hard for me to concentrate on my driving. Then, he and Eric started a very involved conversation about the book Eric was reading.

"So, I got my character worked out last night," explained Eric. "Man, this is going to be fan-fucking-tastic. We haven't played a game, in what, six months?" He held up a small spiral notebook and tapped it on the back of Patrick's seat.

"What's his name again? Methuselah?"

Eric kicked the back of Patrick's seat with his black-booted foot. "What the fuck? Where the fuck did you get that name? Mateo Remember? Mateo. He's 500 years old, from Tuscany."

"Yeah," said Patrick. "That's it."

Keeping half my mind on the road and half my mind on the bizarre conversation going on between the two guys, I realized we were lost. But I kept driving, hoping I would recognize a street name soon.

Patrick patted a well-worn journal in his lap, "Got my character all laid out, too. But there are a few things I need to work on. Can I borrow your book sometime tonight?"

"Yeah, that's cool."

I dared to ask a question, "What are you guys talking about? What game?" I couldn't let my curiosity lie.

Patrick tried to help. "It's an RPG."

I looked at him blankly, and he sighed. "A role-playing game

Now, don't freak out when I say this: do you remember *Dungeons and Dragons*?"

Instantly, the image of one of the nerdiest guys in my high school flashed in my head. Before I could answer, Patrick continued.

"Okay, same idea, better game. Oh, and cooler people."

I doubted that bit of trivia, but listened as he explained further.

"It's a vampire role-playing game. You create a character and then get together with a bunch of people and play. We've had games go on for days."

It was then that I noticed he was wearing vampire teeth. Although on the outside Patrick was beautiful to look at, sometimes he could be awfully bizarre. Downright weird. For a moment I felt as if I was the only one dressed in regular clothes at a masquerade party.

Patrick sat there, as if he was waiting for me to do something. As if I should be reaching into my purse for a pair of wax lips or a set of furry cat ears to put on my head. Join the party. It's freak night on the beach.

I was relieved when Eric broke the awkward moment. "Hey," he called from the back, "Aren't we supposed to turn here?"

A street sign whizzed past me. I braked hard and made a sharp left onto the narrow road. "Sorry."

I wondered what kind of girl Eric would be dating. Her house was only a few doors down; I guess I was about to find out.

seventeen

. . .

MOST HOUSES in pricey Pacific Grove were small, tiny even, compared to what passed for a home elsewhere. Victorian in design, but in doll-like proportions, each house was squeezed onto its minuscule lot. Being so valuable, most homes were well-maintained with elaborate paint jobs and expert landscaping. A few, like the house we pulled up in front of, were run-down with peeling paint and unkempt yards. Surprisingly, even a wealthy area like Pacific Grove had its share of seedy homes and equally seedy neighbors to fill them.

Gretchen's faded pink house hunched lopsided on its lot. Rusted metal curlicues framed the front stoop and held up a sagging plastic corrugated sheet that served as an overhang for the front door. The yard in front of the house was only big enough to contain two large pine trees with low-growing branches, which cast dark shadows on the stoop. Under that overhang, in the dark, I saw a shape of what appeared to be a young girl standing by the door.

The girl flicked on a lighter and lit a cigarette she already gracefully held in her lipsticked mouth. The small orange flame briefly lit up her face—square-jawed with black-rimmed eyes and a stubby nose. Taking a few puffs, she hesitated, watching us from the dark spot under the trees.

"Gretchen?" Eric leaned out the open car door from the back seat. "Let's go."

It was then that I noticed Eric, too, was smoking. My mother smoked like a chimney. There seemed to be two kinds of people who grew up around a smoker—those who would follow in their parent's footsteps and pick up the cigarette habit, and those who were so disgusted by their parents smoking habits they did everything to avoid cigarettes.

I was definitely in the latter group.

Gretchen and her cigarette approached the car, and, without saying a word, dropped it on the sidewalk and crushed it beneath her boots before sliding into the back seat next to Eric. In the rearview mirror, I watched as she tightly clutched Eric's small hand in hers and leaned her head against his shoulder. She couldn't have been more than fifteen or sixteen years old. And how old was Eric? Twenty-four? Twenty-five? What in hell was he thinking? More importantly, what were her parents thinking?

Patrick broke the silence with some bit of politeness, "Gretchen, this is Sabrina."

"Hey," came the lackluster reply from Gretchen.

"Hey." I sat in the car as it idled, waiting for someone to tell me where to go next. I gave up. "So, where are we going now?"

Patrick gave me directions through town, and we eventually ended up on a road that ran along the beach front. The shore was rocky, with very little actual beach to be found, especially since it the tide had come in.

The drive was breathtaking. Large waves exploded over the rocks and boulders. With an almost full moon shining brightly in the crisp, clear night sky, I drank in the view, oblivious to the conversations taking place around me.

Eric and Patrick continued their discussion of role-playing and vampires, the ceramic teeth they had been making and selling to other people on base, and even the quality of the food in the military dining hall.

Gretchen said nothing. All she did was light cigarette after cigarette, cling even more closely to Eric if that were possible, and pick at her long, black-painted fingernails.

Driving further south of town toward Asilomar, the houses that edged the winding coastline road became fewer. Eventually, Patrick pointed out a long picnic table perched on top of a small cliff that jutted out from the shoulder of the road. "There it is. Pull in over there."

I parked on the sandy shoulder.

The curvy road, usually packed with tourists on any given weekend, was completely empty of any other car but mine.

After I stopped, Patrick and Eric grabbed the case of beer out of the back.

Besides being the only non-smoker in the group, I was not much of a drinker either. Especially not beer. And especially not when I had to navigate winding coastal roads. Every one night stand my mother ever had, and there were many, left the lingering odor of sweat, stale cigarettes, and cheap beer throughout our small, two-bedroom house. A few sips, to keep from appearing like a buzz-kill, would be all I could tolerate. I wished I had the forethought to ask more about our plans for the evening, and then I could have brought along some soda or at least some bottled water.

Gretchen, close behind Eric, grabbed a can of beer out of the open case now sitting on the top of the picnic table. While she took a sip, I took a long look at Eric's girlfriend. Wearing a long and clinging black skirt, black cotton blouse, and black boots that blended perfectly with the guys' boot-clad feet, she was a bit on the chubby adolescent side. Gretchen was the perfect goth girlfriend, but was way too young for Eric.

In my jeans and sweater, I definitely was the odd person out.

Watching the three goths interact made me question again

why Patrick would be so interested in me. And sleeping with me, for God's sake. What is it that attracted him to me? I didn't understand it.

But then I was reminded about what my life was like before I met him. Before I was alone and empty, and that was a place I didn't want to return to. We might not have much in common, but we had an attraction between us, and for now that was good enough. His touches, his kisses, his attentions made my life a little bit better. I could wake up in the morning and have something to focus on besides work and school.

I trotted to catch up to the threesome as they sat down at the picnic table. Why else would I be here if he didn't think I could fit into his world? I was willing to change, to do whatever it took, to be what he wanted me to be. Then, I wouldn't have to think about my old self anymore—the quiet, shy, obedient doormat. I didn't want to be her anymore.

The table, gray and warped from the abuse it received sitting unprotected from the wild Pacific Ocean, had one leg chained to a rusty metal loop embedded in the rock beneath it. On top of the table, Patrick and Eric had already laid out their books, ready to discuss more role-playing stuff, I assumed.

I sat next to Patrick.

Although it was late summer, once the sun set, the cold took over quickly, especially when a strong breeze, like tonight, blew inland over the sixty-five degree ocean water. I was glad I brought my beat-up jean jacket. I shoved my hands into the pockets and huddled on the bench trying to conserve body heat.

Gretchen, who hadn't brought a jacket or sweater with her, sat stoically on the other side of the table, uncomplaining, but shivering with each new gust of cold air.

As Eric and Patrick attempted to work on their characters and discuss the finer points of vampires versus humans, I took a moment to page through another book in Eric's duffle bag. I wanted to understand their interest in playing such a game.

What was the point? Spending hours and hours acting out scenarios from a book pretending to a vampire? I thought I was missing something, a vital piece of the RPG puzzle. Otherwise, why would these two adult men spend so much of their time creating characters and discussing strategy?

In the moonlight I attempted to read the page upon page describing character traits and the details of fictitious cities and weapons. After ten minutes or so, the guys realized it would be hard to hold open a book in the fierce wind. So, instead, they put the books back in the duffle bag and drank.

Gretchen, to my dismay, was already working on her second bottle of beer. Did this girl's family have no clue as to what she was up to? She noticed me staring rather too intently at her, stood, and walked toward the edge of the precipice. With the neck of her beer bottle grasped in one hand, she puffed anxiously on her cigarette and looked out over the waves and dark water.

Eric opened his third or fourth beer with his effeminate, smooth hands. The dark, long lashes of his eyes gave him a hooded look, which complimented his ceramic vampire teeth—if Goth Dracula was what he was going for. He moved lithely as he slid off the picnic table bench to join Gretchen. The thought of Eric in the military, wearing a uniform, keeping up physically with some of the other men I had seen on base, troubled me. At least Patrick, if not mentally fitting in with the military, physically had the appearance he could keep up with the demands the Army must put upon him. But Eric? It didn't even look as if he could one push-up.

Eric slid his arm around Gretchen's waist. They were an odd couple. Two small people, but Gretchen had the more masculine features and Eric had a more fragile, leonine quality to his face.

"So, what's going on in that pretty head of yours?" Patrick spoke out of the side of his mouth as he attempted to light a cigarette in the gusting winds.

I tapped my fingernails absentmindedly against the full beer bottle in my hands and turned my head away from the couple near the edge of the rock. "My head? Oh, you don't want to know."

"Don't I?" He smiled lasciviously and scooted closer to me on the bench. His hand stroked my thigh while his arm encircled my shoulders. "I think I might have an idea already."

He turned my chin toward him, lightly kissing me. I leaned into the kiss, craving contact. Although the stale cigarette taste wasn't very appealing, the closeness felt good.

Then, kissing me more deeply, he laid his hand on my breast. At first, I leaned into his touch, but then I remembered where we were. I pulled out of the kiss and pushed at his hand, I whispered, "Patrick, they can see us!" I motioned my head in the direction of Eric and Gretchen, who were no more than twenty feet away. And if someone happened to turn around...

"Don't worry about them. It's dark here—they can't see us." He reached for me again, that sideways smile returning—devilish almost. He started to pull up on my sweater, seeming to enjoy my opposing reactions: my discomfort and my prurient response. Goose bumps rose on my stomach from the cold wind, and blood rushed to my cheeks.

I did worry, but as I tried to pull gently away, he held me tighter.

"Stop it!" I hissed.

With an angry moan, he let me go and grabbed a new bottle of beer from the cooler. "Forget it, Sabrina. I should have known Miss Goody-Two-Shoes couldn't handle it."

Before I could respond to his insult, he called out to Eric. "Hey! Let's go down on the rocks." He leapt up from the rickety picnic table, never even glancing back at me. As if I wasn't even there.

What was he talking about? A 'Goody-Two-Shoes'? My mother used to describe me like that.

. . .

"Watcha got there, Sabrina?" My mother set down a plastic cup full of ice and whiskey, plunked into one of the empty chairs at the kitchen table where I was studying, and yanked away one of my books.

"Mom, I need that. I have a test tomorrow." I grabbed at the science book my mother flipped through.

"Oh, now, lookie here." My mother had turned to a chapter on genetics and began to read, "The gene is the principle unit of inheritance." Her words began to slur and, as she gestured at the page, whiskey sloshed out of her cup onto the book. "Your good-for-nothing father...well, too bad you 'inherited' more from him. You and me, we're night and day, aren't we?"

Realizing I wouldn't get my book back until my mother was done with her drunken speech, I watched in silence.

"Yeah, night and day. You, the little Goody-Two-Shoes. Trying to make me look bad. What'd I do that was so awful, huh? You always gotta point out when I give the wrong change at the shop. Always got some excuse for your friends why I never finished high school. Are you ashamed of me? Huh?" She slammed the book shut and flung it across the room.

I winced at the crash that followed. I knew better than to respond to any of the questions she posed. The anger usually blossomed quickly. Already my mother was standing up to refill her cup, muttering to herself, as if I wasn't even there. When she'd filled it, she wandered unsteadily into the back bedroom and slammed the door. A few moments later, I heard the blare of the TV in my mother's room. I picked up the science book that had landed behind the cigarette-burned couch and went back to my studying.

My mother made me ashamed to act like a decent human being.

. . .

Patrick made me feel the same way. I pulled my jacket closer around my body and picked at the label of my beer bottle. I eyed my car keys lying on the table in front of me. Why was I still here? This was not how I imagined my next date with Patrick. I wanted to pick up the keys and drive out of there. Let *them* figure out how to get home.

Tucking my wildly-blowing hair behind each ear, I took in the surroundings once again. The dark road was empty. A few lights winked in either direction. Homes were scattered up and down the coast, but miles away from where we sat.

Just go. They'll find their way back.

I held the keys in my palm and jingled them quietly. My mouth firmly set and my eyes steely, I swung my legs out from under the picnic table and prepared to leave.

"Fuck!" Eric yelled from somewhere down on the rocks, his muffled voice barely louder than the crashing waves. The cliff edge was too steep for me to see what was going on. Gretchen was gone now, too. A wall of spray shot up from the rocks below.

eighteen

. . .

"GRAB HIM, Gretchen! For Christ's sake...get over here!" The tight, strained quality of Eric's voice instantly gave me a chill.

Racing to the edge of the large boulder, about fifteen feet below me I could make out three dark figures on the saw-toothed rocks along the seashore. As my eyes adjusted to the moon shadowed beach, I could hear a few groans coming from a prone form draped over the rocks.

"Sabrina!" Eric spied me peering down at them. "I need help! Get down here!"

"What happened?" I cried out, trying to be heard above the wind and the waves.

Gretchen, reticent for almost the entire evening, finally found her voice, "He climbed that big rock." She pointed to an impossibly steep and slimy boulder that was surrounded by more water than sand.

I hunted for a way to climb down to the beach safely. I spied a sloped, sandy portion of the boulder that would put me within a few feet of everyone. I quickly scrambled down.

"How did he fall?" I looked, disbelieving, at Patrick's lifeless body battered by wind and the crashing surf.

"A wave came and knocked him off," Eric said, tension thick in his voice.

On the few feet of sand that made up the beach, Patrick had slipped and fallen directly onto another jagged rock. His leg was twisted awkwardly underneath him, and he was completely soaked. When the tide pulled back, Eric rushed to his friend and attempted to drag him over the pointed rocks, away from the wild, pounding waves. Gretchen passively smoked a cigarette and stuck close to the embankment.

I stumbled into the surf that eddied around the patchwork of rocks on the shore and grabbed Patrick under one arm while Eric grabbed the other. Then we pulled. The water was bitingly cold. It might be California, but the water could cause hypothermia in a matter of minutes. Together, we managed to drag him onto a small patch of sand next to Gretchen.

"Is he conscious?" I panted, shivering as the wind hit my damp clothing.

Eric knelt down and slapped Patrick in the face several times, "McKinnon! Hey, are you with us, man?"

Patrick shook his head and tried sit up. Falling back onto his elbow, he lifted one sandy hand to the back of his head and groaned. When he pulled his hand away, it was covered in blood. A stain, which appeared black in the darkness of the moonlit night, spread over his shirt. He fell back onto the sand, his eyes rolling back into his head.

"Shit!" Eric said with quiet desperation.

"We need to call an ambulance." I shuddered at the sight of all the blood. Feeling dizzy, I sat down hard on a flat rock. "He needs help."

Gretchen handed Eric her cell phone.

Eric thrust it back into her hands. "No way." He backed away from me and Gretchen. "You know how much trouble we'd get in? If he goes to the emergency clinic on base, and they have to report it as alcohol-related—" He stumbled and pointed at Gretchen. "And she's only sixteen. We'd be busted."

Gretchen looked unfazed by Eric's admission she was under-age. She shrugged and slipped the cell phone back into her bag. Still smoking a cigarette, she trudged up the rocky incline and disappeared from view after only a few moments.

Eric didn't even notice his girlfriend had enigmatically left the scene. "We've gotta help him out of here." He crouched down and attempted to pull Patrick into a full stand.

"You're crazy. He needs a doctor, not a ride home." I helped Eric with Patrick's dead weight.

"Shut up!" He grunted under the strain. "Dammit, just help me out."

Groggily, Patrick came to, finding himself standing up with Eric and I playing the roles of crutches under his arms. "Where are we going?"

"We're going to get you some help," I replied and gave Eric a hard glare.

Eric opened his mouth, but said nothing. Instead, he continued toward my car.

Gretchen was already inside smoking cigarettes and tapping the ashes through the cracked-open window.

Breathing hard from the exertion, Eric gasped, "Get in front, Gretch."

She opened the door and pushed the passenger seat forward to climb out. Eric and I laid Patrick down on the back seat, then helped him sit up so Eric could climb in next to him.

"Come on, let's go." Eric pulled the seat back to allow Gretchen to sit in the front. As I started up the car, Gretchen tapped another cigarette out of the pack sitting in her lap.

"Do you mind?" I growled. My patience was gone, and, along with it, my tolerance for Gretchen and her chain-smoking.

She looked at me wide-eyed, then slipped the cigarettes into her bag. Instead of smoking, she picked at her fingernails again and somehow ignored the chaos going on in the back seat.

I pushed hard on the gas, and the car fishtailed on the gravel shoulder.

Patrick needed a doctor. Now.

I straightened the car out and sped back into town. The cute Victorian homes I had admired on our trip to Asilomar passed by me in a blur of colors. I focused instead on the street signs, trying to figure out how to get back to base as quickly as possible.

A groan came from the back.

"Jesus!" Eric exclaimed in a panic. "He's bleeding all over the place. Do you have a towel or anything? Fuck!"

Keeping one hand on the steering wheel, I wriggled out of my jean jacket, switching hands to get the other sleeve off. Once the jacket was free, I shifted to the next gear and flung it into Eric's lap. "Here. Direct pressure. Direct pressure is supposed to stop bleeding."

"I know that, for Christ's sake! Just drive the fucking car." Eric folded up the jacket and pressed it to the back of Patrick's head.

I felt sick to my stomach. In my rearview mirror, I could see Eric's shirt covered with bright red splotches of blood. How in the hell had I gotten myself in this mess? What kind of nut case was I dating—no—sleeping with? I imagined myself back at home in my claustrophobic studio apartment, lonely but safe. Doing homework sounded very good to me at the moment.

"Turn here," instructed Eric, one of his blood-covered hands pointed to a smaller, secondary entrance to the base. "The clinic is right down this road."

Unfamiliar with the other parts of the Presidio, I followed Eric's directions. I drove past what looked like old, abandoned buildings. Skirting a large, grassy parade field that overlooked Monterey Bay, I wondered if Eric knew where he was going. It was dark here, and I saw not one human being or car. But then, up ahead, I saw some bright, fluorescent street lights rimming a large, newer-looking building.

"That's the clinic. Drop us off here."

We were at least a hundred yards away from the entrance. "Drop you off? Here? I'm coming with you."

"Fuck, Sabrina! *Drop us off.* You have to take Gretchen back home; no one can see her here. *No one.*" I knew from the seriousness in his voice his military career would be on the line if any of his superiors caught him with a drunk, underage townie girl. The Presidio was a small base, and news traveled fast.

I stopped the car.

Gretchen climbed out and stood, arms crossed, on the curb. Tipping the passenger seat forward, Eric hauled semi-conscious Patrick out of the car. He stumbled along, which proved to me they could make it to the clinic together. Eric was his best friend, after all. He wouldn't let anything happen to him. He would make sure he got some help. I was positive.

After watching them limp toward the clinic entrance, I waited for Gretchen. Then, I headed back toward Pacific Grove and the dark little house where she lived. What else could I do?

When we pulled up in front of her house, surprisingly Gretchen spoke to me, "He'll be all right." She lit up one last cigarette, slipped around the back of her house, and the darkness swallowed her.

I sat there for a moment, and then the tears came. Tears of worry, tears of anger, tears of despair. Everything had fallen apart. That day in Morgan's when I had spoken with Patrick for the first time, something had come alive inside of me. For months I had been working and studying without friends, without someone to keep me going, give me encouragement or a shoulder to cry on. When I had left home, I thought leaving my troubled past and starting over in a new place would be easy, would be freeing. I thought my mother was the main source of my problems and frustrations, and that once some distance was between her and me, things would get better. But, instead, almost nothing had changed.

Maybe it wasn't my mother who was the problem.

Maybe all along it had been me.

I was weak. I made stupid decisions.

Patrick kept the loneliness at bay for a while. But tonight, I'd seen his true nature. He wasn't much different than the mother I had left behind. He was self-centered, brooding, and thought everyone in the world was against him. Even me. When I didn't want to play along with him at the picnic table, he had been angry. My feelings didn't matter to him like I thought they had.

I felt badly he was injured, but sitting here in the dark, I realized that was all I felt for him.

That discovery left me feeling hollow inside. All that wasted emotion, all that time spent cultivating a relationship that really never was. I had been just another female body to him.

Emotionally drained, I started up the car. An overwhelming tiredness settled into my body. I didn't want to think about it anymore. It took great effort to shift the gears and make the turns that would take me home.

After I opened the door to my apartment, I crumpled on top of the futon. Closing my eyes, I fell into a restless sleep.

———

I was awakened the next morning by the insistent ring of my phone. Groggily, I sat up trying to clear my head. Then, the events from the night before came back to me all in a rush.

I felt nauseated. All that blood—it was so horrible.

I grabbed the receiver. "Hello?"

"It's Eric." His voice sounded dull and devoid of emotion.

"How's Patrick? Is he all right?" I should at least ask about his injury, even if I never wanted to talk to him again.

"He's in a coma."

My ears started to ring. I sat down hard on the floor, feeling weak. "A coma?" All the bitterness toward Patrick dissipated like smoke. "But you took him to the clinic. We got him help. He's okay."

"I woke up this morning. He was there in his bunk—unconscious. I couldn't wake him up."

I was confused. "In his bunk? Wasn't he in the clinic? Why wasn't he there? Eric, what happened?"

"I gotta go. Just thought you'd want to know. He's in the hospital now." Eric's voice cracked. I could hear him taking deep breaths.

"Eric? Eric!" I demanded, wanting to know what exactly had happened last night. But the dial tone beeped in my ear. He'd hung up on me.

I might have decided last night that our relationship was over, but I had never wanted him to be seriously injured. *In a coma.*

He was in his bunk.

Eric never had taken him to the clinic. He had walked him back to the barracks, sneaked him in somehow, and then left him there to slip into unconsciousness. All to cover up for his own problems, to keep himself out of trouble.

My God.

These two weren't friends; they fed off of each other. Each justifying the other's actions all for their own selfish reasons.

My stomach was in knots. For the moment, my state of shock kept the tears at bay. What was I supposed to do now?

I should go and visit him in the hospital, but I didn't want to. He had hurt me badly. I wanted a chance to sort out my feelings before I went running off to be at his bedside.

I stood up slowly, shakily. There was only one person I knew that might be able to help me sort out my feelings. But I had told myself I wouldn't be friends with someone like that any longer.

He had wanted my forgiveness, my understanding, which I couldn't give. But he was the one person I had left that could help me think this through.

My own personal problems pushing to the forefront of my mind, I snatched my purse off the counter in the kitchen and pawed through the contents. I found what I was looking for: a slightly wrinkled business card. Flattening it out on the counter, I put my index finger under the cell phone number listed on it and dialed.

Breathing deeply, I listened to the ring on the other end, trying to keep my emotions in check. Four rings, then five.

God, I hoped I didn't get voicemail. Then, a click.

"Hello?" David's voice rumbled out.

"David, it's me."

"Sabrina?" He sounded relieved, glad. He joked, "Isn't it kind of early to be making social calls?" It sounded as if everything was back to normal between us. As if nothing had happened.

His voice was soothing to my ears. I thought back to the first few days after I had met him, how charming he was, how kind. If I could use that little part of David to help me through this crisis, I wouldn't be a bad person, would I? I wouldn't be condoning what he did to his wife, would I?

All my sadness, all my despair came pouring out, "David, I need to see you."

nineteen

. . .

"WHAT'S WRONG? WHAT HAPPENED?" The concern in David's voice brought my tears closer to the surface.

"Can we meet today after all?" I cleared my throat, hoping to keep the tears from coming.

"Of course. When? Where?" He sounded so worried for me. "In an hour? At Morgan's?"

I heard muted voices, as if he had put his hand over the receiver. Had he and Tina made up? Or was that Lucy? I pushed these thoughts from my mind. It really was none of my concern. I needed David for a little while, and then—

"David?"

"Sorry, Sabrina. Yes, I can meet you in an hour."

"Thank you." Relief flooded my body like high tide fills a tide pool.

"See you in an hour."

I hung up the phone bolstered by the knowledge I would have someone to talk to soon, and then everything would be better.

David would help me think things through, get a clear perspective.

I sat on my bed staring at the sunlight angling in through the half-closed blinds of my one small window. I wanted the sunshine to pour in and warm my skin. I had been surrounded by darkness for too long.

I pulled the cord to raise the blinds. It was a beautiful day. Even from my apartment window, which looked out onto the traffic of Fremont Boulevard, the hills gleamed under the early morning light, and the sky was as blue as a robin's egg. I stood there for a long while, clearing my head and thinking about absolutely nothing but the warmth of the morning sun.

———

When I entered Morgan's I hoped to slip into the small back room and wait until David arrived to order anything. Music with a Latin beat poured out from the speakers. The chatter of early-rising coffee addicts filled the main seating area.

I ducked my head, but got a quick peek at the counter. No Tim. Guess he wasn't working today.

I slammed into a hard object in front of me. Strong hands grabbed my shoulders.

"Whoa, are you okay?"

It was Tim. He had been wiping down tables in the back room.

I knew I didn't look right. My eyes were red-rimmed and puffy. I had been staring so long out my window at the apartment I hadn't had time to take a shower. My hair was messily tucked into a bun. I had no make-up on. For sure I looked a fright.

"I'm fine," I answered tightly, knowing there was no way he would believe me.

"Right." He removed his hands from my shoulders, but still stood tall in front of me, as if he was waiting for an explanation.

"Excuse me," I said gently, having no energy to explain myself to a guy I barely knew.

He blocked the doorway to the small alcove.

"Of course." His voice had softened a bit. He stepped aside and allowed me to pass. He watched as I entered the room, and I thought I saw a look of concern in his eyes. But he said nothing more, returning to the main room to leave me in peace.

I sat down at a table near the window. The isolation from the customers chatting in the other part of the coffeehouse allowed my thoughts to wander. Just what I didn't want. I wanted to forget. I wished I had never met Patrick.

I held my breath to get my emotions in check. Not a good place for a breakdown. I steeled myself with the thought that David would be here soon. David would know what to do, what to say. He would know how to make me laugh again and forget my troubles.

"Here. I thought you could use this."

I jumped. I had been staring out the window so intently I hadn't noticed Tim enter. He stood next to my table with a steaming paper cup and a blueberry scone wrapped in a napkin.

When I hesitated, he said softly, "Take it. It's on me."

My stomach turned at the thought of eating anything, but the coffee smelled good. I took the offered cup delicately and set it down on the small table. Tim placed the scone next to the cup. "Let me know if you need anything else. I'm a pretty good listener."

I wasn't expecting that. I barely knew him. What gave him the idea I would want to divulge my thoughts to a stranger? Well an almost-stranger. He had driven me back into town the other day, and we were in the same class. But still, David was coming.

"Thanks," I said with a small smile. "But I'm waiting for someone."

A troubled look crossed his face. "Oh, I see. Well, I better get back to work." He started to walk away from me, but then stopped, turned, and looked at me as if he wanted to say something more. He seemed to think the better of it, shaking his head, and left.

Where was David? He was fifteen minutes late so far. Not as if he was one for punctuality, though.

I got up to grab the newspaper from the rack near the entrance. Tim watched me from the counter. He probably thought I was lying when I said I was meeting someone. As if I had said that just to get him off my back

A well-read copy of the *Monterey Herald*, the sports section missing, was hanging over the wooden dowel of the reading rack. I grabbed it and darted back to my table, not giving Tim another thought. But I could feel his eyes following me.

After twenty minutes of reading and re-reading the newspaper Tim appeared in the doorway.

"So, did he stand you up?" he asked.

Tim grabbed a chair, turned it around backwards, and sat across from me. He folded his hands and rested them on the back of it, giving the impression he would wait all day for a satisfactory answer.

What the heck did this guy think he was doing?

"What business is it of yours?" I attempted to fold up the newspaper, snapping and cracking it right in his face.

"I'm just tired of it all. Tired of nice girls always choosing the jerks."

"The jerks?" At first I was confused, then I realized he must be talking about Patrick. I quieted. "Oh, yeah."

"That *is* who you're waiting for, right? Your boyfriend? Black leather jacket, threw up in the hallway after class a few weeks back?"

Without warning, tears filled my eyes. Patrick was lying in coma on some hospital bed right now. A fractured skull or something worse. God, what a mess I had gotten myself into. I covered my mouth to hold back a sob that threatened to escape.

Tim's eyes widened. "Hey, it's all right. I'm sorry. I shouldn't have been so harsh." He slid his chair next to mine, reached over, and tucked a loose strand of hair over my ear.

The gentle touch calmed me. I looked up at him, my eyes brimming with unshed tears. He looked straight into me, his brown eyes full of concern.

And that's when I did it.

I threw my arms around him. I couldn't help myself. The comfort of a warm, solid, human body helped more than words ever could.

For a moment, he sat there stiffly, as if he didn't know what to do with me. But then he must have realized there was something more to my tears than a broken date, and he pulled me closer. He murmured in my ear, "Hey, hey. It's okay. Everything's going to be all right. I'm not going anywhere."

I pulled back, and he tipped my chin upwards. The depth of emotion I saw in his eyes startled me. A mix of worry and something else.

I took a quick breath, opening my mouth to speak. That was when he kissed me. Just ever so softly.

This was not what I had intended. He was sweet, he was kind, and he was attractive in that academic, studious sort of way. But my boyfriend—ex-boyfriend—well, whatever Patrick was to me—was in the hospital. And to be kissing another man —well, it just felt wrong.

I pushed at Tim's chest to break us apart.

"Please...don't." His lips on mine had affected me more than I thought.

David came sailing into the back room, "Sabrina, I'm so sorry that—"

Clearly misunderstanding what he saw, he growled at Tim,

"What do you think you are doing?" Grabbing his arm, David wrenched it away from my waist. "Get off of her!"

Tim stood up, and his face darkened.

I tried to intervene, "David, stop it! He was just—"

"Attacking you?" David glared at Tim, pulled back his fist and prepared to swing.

I was frozen to my chair.

Tim, at least four inches taller than David, moved forward threateningly at that accusation and spat out, "I was only trying to help."

"Help?" David echoed, his voice laced with anger. "Get the hell out of here before I break your nose."

Horrified at the direction they were headed, I stepped between them. Where did my friend, David, go? He should be jovial happy, making jokes. He should be lifting my spirits and making my troubles go away, not adding to them.

I had made a serious mistake, calling him.

"Leave him alone." I pleaded with David. Sensing the warm presence of Tim directly behind me somehow helped, made me less afraid to tell David exactly how I felt.

"Get out of the way, Sabrina," David spoke quietly, his anger boiling just beneath the surface.

So, what I had suspected earlier was true. David could be a charming man at first, but then, when he felt slighted, all hell broke loose. I had seen a smidgen of this unpredictable anger at the accident, but he had been so smooth about covering it up. He could turn the charm on and off whenever he felt it would be to his advantage.

"I said, stop it, David." My face had hardened. His charm was gone and, without it, he could no longer affect me. "Leave *him* alone. Leave *me* alone. I never should have called you. Just go."

David's jaw tightened almost imperceptibly. Clenching and unclenching his fists several times, he took a deep breath and glared hard at Tim. He looked as if he wanted to say something, but instead he smoothed back his hair and straightened his glasses. Backing slowly out of the room, he stated darkly to David, "This isn't over." And then he was gone.

Tim's eyebrows came together. "Who in hell was that psycho?" He watched intently as David exited the coffeehouse, climbed into his Mercedes, and zoomed off down the street.

I had already grabbed my wallet and keys off the table. I had come into Morgan's looking a sympathetic ear and, instead, ended up proving that the one friend I thought I could confide in really was an abusive crazy man. On top of that, I had somehow managed to find myself in an uncomfortable romantic entanglement. It was time to leave.

Tim caught me before I headed out the door. "Hey, where do you think you are going?" His hand gently grasped my elbow.

My mind was racing—what should I do next? My first impulse was to flee. Not only flee Morgan's, but to flee from Monterey. Start over again somewhere else. Away from the craziness that followed me from my mother's house.

Tim was too kind. He didn't deserve all of the confusion and chaos that clung to me like the stench of rotten fish.

I yanked my elbow out of his grasp and mumbled, "I have to go."

As I pulled open the front door to exit onto the street, Tim called my name. I blinked at the strain in his voice.

I never asked for his concern.

I continued down the street and blocking out his calls for me to come back.

———

My cardboard boxes were no longer stand-ins for a coffee table and bureau. Now, they were packed full of my meager belongings. Not much more had been accumulated since I arrived in

Monterey four months earlier: a set of Corelle dinnerware I discovered at the local Salvation Army, a plastic trash can which was much sturdier than the paper grocery bag I had been using, an a maroon bath towel purchased at Wal-Mart my first day in town.

My mother wouldn't let me take anything from the house—only my clothes, shoes, and a toothbrush. I hoped I could smuggle out a few necessities, such as a pillow or lamp, but the minute my mother had discovered my plan to leave, she had watched me like a hawk.

In fact, Mickey even had the audacity to paw through my bag right before I walked out the door. Maybe to make sure I wasn't taking anything too valuable. As if there was anything of value in my mother's run-down house. Before I could snatch my tattered duffle bag from my mother's searching hands, Mickey grabbed a black cardigan sweater from the tangle of clothes, declaring it to be hers.

Both of us very well knew it belonged to me. Considering my mother was as bony as a skeleton and five inches shorter than me, it wouldn't make sense that this size extra-small woman would buy a size medium sweater. Mickey clutched that sweater to her chest and then practically pushed me out the front door.

Leaving this new place was a totally different experience. No scowling mother. No dilapidated house. This time, I felt hollowed out like an apple without its core. My sparse pile of belongings huddled near the door, a dejected lump of well-worn clothing and dented, sagging cardboard boxes. The only pieces of real furniture I had worth saving were my futon and a small bistro table that functioned as my kitchen table. The table would fit in my Festiva, but the futon would have to be left behind.

I sat on the arm of my futon, falling backwards onto it. A deep sigh. A welling of tears. All too familiar sensations. Sensations I thought I would never feel again. I longed for a sense of place, but for some reason I had found only emptiness here.

For days after Patrick's accident I had tried to build up enough courage to visit him. I had called the hospital to find out about his condition once, but was told only family members had access to that kind of personal information. What if he were still unconscious? Hooked up to tubes and wires? It scared me to think about it.

It had been over a week since he went into the hospital, making it difficult for me to concentrate on my studies or at work. For the past few days, I had been preparing for and taking my final exams. The summer semester had ended. My last final had been this morning, and I had needed to be on my game, but it was hard. It was my Spanish final. As I walked into the lecture hall for the last time, memories of Patrick filled my mind. To focus on my exam was near to impossible.

The encounter with David at Morgan's made work no haven for me either. Although his hours had been sporadic since he flew off the handle with Tim, when I did see him at the office, he ignored me, walking determinedly into his office and keeping the door closed all day long. He only came out for coffee and the bathroom

Alicia seemed secretly pleased at David's new office personality. With David locked up in his office all day, she could do her job without interruption, without him asking for this and that, without him making fun of her work habits. It was as if Alicia was queen of her kingdom again.

Alicia, though, was probably worrying about me right now.

I had to ask for a day off from work due to my finals schedule. The redheaded receptionist had become more motherly than friend-like in the last couple of weeks. And Alicia knew what kind of strain I had been under since the accident. Add to that the stress of studying for my exams, and she'd probably show up at work tomorrow with a batch of chocolate chip cookies to cheer me up.

At that thought, a small smile formed. I would leave one

good friend behind. The night of the accident, I wish had thought to call her instead of David. If things had been different, if things hadn't become so messy and complicated...

Well, why think about ifs? There was no way to fix what had happened. Time to work on my plan: leaving would be the best thing. Then, I could start to forget. Start to build a life again. Away from these draining, emotional tugs-of-war that consumed me here in Monterey. My mother drained enough of my life away in her bitterness, her selfishness. I couldn't waste any more of myself here.

I swung my legs around to the front of the futon and slowly forced myself to sit up. Arms crossed over my lap, I took one last look at my apartment. My first true home. And how sorry a home it had been. Bare white walls I never had bothered to cover with anything except menus from the Chinese place down the block and pizza coupons. Small, dingy windows that barely let in the morning light, much less any fresh air. But it had been my place.

I grabbed my purse off the floor. I intended to have my last paycheck and my exam results sent to General Delivery in Morro Bay, my next destination. It was another seaside town a few hours' drive from Monterey. A smaller, foggier one with fewer tourists and more unpopulated coastline. Maybe I would try waitressing there.

My hand reached for the doorknob, but I hesitated for a moment, deciding which box I would manage down to the car first. I chose one of the larger boxes, pulling it out of the group. Then, I turned the knob.

"Hey."

I jumped. But then I recognized the figure in the doorway.

twenty

. . .

"TIM?" I said, shocked. "What in the heck? How did you—? Who—?" Seeing him there in front of me, my thoughts returned to that gentle kiss in Morgan's, and I felt my color rise slightly.

"Look, this wasn't my idea. I came here to—" But before he could finish, he noticed the stack of boxes and clothes next to the door. "What's all this? Are you going somewhere?"

I defensively blocked the open doorway with my body, as if that would somehow keep him from asking more questions. "That's really none of your business." I redirected the questioning, "How did you know where I live? Did you follow me?" I had a few conversations with him, a quick kiss, and now he shows up at my door? I was more than a little freaked out.

"Follow you?" He said as if he was offended at my question. "I told you that this wasn't my idea—" He ran a hand through his hair. "Look, my mom thought—"

"Your mom? What does your mom have to do with anything?" This man made no sense. I wanted to leave, and he stood in my way. I picked up one of my cardboard boxes and pushed past him to reach the stairwell. "Why in hell would she give a damn about someone she doesn't even know?"

He put his hands up in a conciliatory fashion, allowing me to pass unimpeded, but he tramped down the stairs after me.

"Yes, my mom. Didn't she tell you?"

"Tell me? Tell me what?" God, he was irritating as hell. Just get to the point, please. I continued to my car, lifted the hatchback, and plopped the box inside.

"I thought you knew."

Now I was getting very, very annoyed with him. He was talking in complete riddles. "What am I supposed to know?"

Before he could answer, I headed back up the stairs to grab another box out of my apartment. No reason to delay my departure because he couldn't explain himself better. Selecting a medium-sized box filled with my iron and some toiletry items from the bathroom, I grasped the cardboard edges for a good grip.

The phone rang.

Tim continued, "I thought you knew that—"

I propped the box on one hip, picked up the receiver, and waved a hand at him, urging him to be quiet.

His voice trailed off. "Hello?" I tucked the phone receiver under my chin so I could pack the few things left out on the kitchen counter into the half-filled box.

"Sabrina?" a hoarse voice croaked out.

"Who is this?"

"It's me. Patrick."

Shock and relief filled me, and I forgot about my packing and leaving. Even forgot about Tim standing right behind me.

"Oh my God. How are you doing?" I dropped the box to the floor and plunked down on my futon. Quickly processing the turn of events, I put my head in my hands.

Patrick was okay. He was going to be okay.

"I'm all right," he said. "I can't talk very long. This one bitch of a nurse has been watching me like a hawk since I woke up a couple of days ago."

Same old Patrick. It was almost as if nothing had happened.

He sounded weak, though.

My heart beat rapidly, my hands turned clammy. He was going to be all right. "When can I come visit you?"

There was a pause on the line. "Actually," Patrick rasped, "I need you to do me a favor."

"A favor? What kind of favor?"

"Could you go see Eric for me? I've been trying to call him, and you know what it's like."

With only two phones for one wing of the barracks, I knew too well how frustrating it was to call for Patrick and hope the person who answered the phone tried to find him. A few times I had been left hanging, listening to the noises in the hallway, until someone saw the phone off the hook and hung it up.

"How do I find him?"

"Go inside the barracks to the desk, and you can have him paged. I can't miss finals."

While I prattled on with Patrick, Tim tried desperately to get my attention. He waved his hands in my face; I brushed him off. He whistled; I shushed him. As a final attempt, he ran down the stairs and returned after a few minutes with one of the boxes I had just packed in my car. Before I could react, he hurried off most likely with the idea of bringing back another box.

Exasperated, I asked Patrick, "Could you hold on a sec? There's someone here I need to get rid of." I put my hand over the receiver to mute it.

Tim walked in the door with another box just as I ended my sentence.

Whoops.

He dropped my box full of dishes to the floor. "I'm sorry. Did you just say you need to get rid of me?" he said, tension rising in his voice.

"Hey! You're lucky that Corelle stuff isn't breakable!" There was no way for me to salvage what he had overheard, so I might as well go for broke.

Tim shoved the box out of the way with his tennis-shoe clad foot. "Do you want me to leave? Am I that irritating?"

I thought I saw anger lurking in his eyes...or was it a hurtful look?

"Look, it may not be much, but it *is* my stuff. Could you be a little more careful?"

The tinny echo of Patrick's voice interrupted me, "Sabrina? Are you there?"

To my surprise, Tim swept the phone receiver out of my hand and barked, "Look, bozo, I was here first. Call back later." He slammed the phone down on the hook.

No longer worried about Tim's feelings, I fumed, "What in God's name do you think you're doing? That phone call was absolutely none of your business!"

"I came here to ask about your finals, and I find you packing. Where are you going?" To me he seemed awfully distraught for a mere acquaintance. That kiss in the coffeehouse meant much more to him than I knew.

How could he possibly be attracted to a mess like me? And at the moment, I was treating him pretty badly.

I had to shut down any feelings he might be harboring for me. On that car ride back to town, he had been curious about me, had wanted to learn more than I was willing to tell. Any more time spent in his company, and he would probably pepper me with personal questions, dig into my background, and find out about my drunk of a mother. A guy with aspirations like his didn't need a girl like me weighing him down. I wasn't worth his time, and if he couldn't see it, I would have to show him.

"Why do you care if I go anywhere? You barely even know me." I stepped past him and yanked the nearest box further into the apartment. "Anyway, I changed my mind."

"You did?" I thought I detected a small sound of relief in his voice.

Now that Patrick needed my help, I couldn't take off.

But once he was better, once he was back on his feet, then I could reconsider the move. I owed Patrick that much for trusting his friend to take care of him that night. I never should have left him bleeding there in the dark, so helpless.

"Thanks for bringing up my stuff." Pulling out my dishes, I quickly stacked them on the bare shelves in my tiny kitchen.

Tim had an unreadable expression on his face. When I crossed in front of him to grab another box, he gently stopped me by the arm. "I'm glad you're staying, no matter what convinced you."

I couldn't think of how to respond. My thoughts were mainly on Patrick. This Tim thing was too confusing, too hard to handle. He needed to find someone more like himself.

"Thanks."

Tim smiled, not one of those on-top-of-the-world smiles, but a strained, tight smile. "Well, I guess I'll see you around, then."

"Yeah, I guess so." I felt guilty having him leave like that. I never did find out how he knew where I lived and what all that nonsense about his mother was. For a second, I felt as if should ask him to sit down and talk awhile.

But as he walked out the door and gently closed it, my mouth couldn't form the words.

Patrick needed me, and I didn't have the time or energy to think about Tim and his feelings. The way I left things after the accident with Patrick, well, now I could reconnect with him. Make up for leaving him there with Eric and not making sure he was taken care of.

I went over the conversation with Patrick in my head. He couldn't get a hold of Eric. He needed me to go to the barracks and see Eric in person.

In my heart, I didn't see how Patrick could be ready to take a final exam in a week after his accident.

Maybe I should visit Patrick in the hospital. But what would I say to him when I finally saw him in person?

———

"Uh, hi, my name's Sabrina Fuller. I'm here to see Eric..." I was nervous standing in the lobby of the Army barracks.

Patrick had always come *out* of the barracks; I had never gone in.

The private behind the counter at the end opposite the entrance looked at me blankly. "Eric? Eric who?"

Crap!

I didn't know Eric's last name. All those nights spent with him seated in the back of my car, and I had no clue what his last name was. I felt like a fool.

Trying to save my dignity, I made up something, hoping this serious-looking, uniformed person would believe me. "Well, I met this guy the other night downtown, and he said I could find him here. I know his name is Eric, and he's taking Chinese—"

The Army man looked embarrassed for me. I sounded like such loser, trying to track down some poor guy that let me down easy.

Oh, God. Please let this man help me so I can get out of here!

"Eric?" The man seemed to be giving my question a lot of thought. I was hopeful that there would only be one Eric in the Chinese classes.

Then, a flash of semi-genius hit me. "Um, he's a friend of Patrick McKinnon?"

That bit of information seemed to do the trick. "Oh, I know who you're looking for. Edwards." Before I could say anything, he began to scribble on a piece of note paper in front of him.

Folding the paper in half, he handed it to a private behind

him. "VanKamp, take this up to Edwards. Second floor. Last room on the right."

He opened a side door and slipped out from behind the counter, taking off down a long hallway. I stood awkwardly, not really sure what to do next.

The man in camouflage behind the counter cleared his throat, "You can have a seat over there, miss." He pointed at the rows of seats behind me.

I smiled and nodded, then dashed for the closest chair. I felt like such an idiot. Hoping Eric would be in his room, I tapped my feet nervously on the tile floor then fiddled with the contents of my purse when I felt the eyes of the private behind the counter on me. I found an open roll of mints and popped one in my mouth, hands trembling. After a few minutes, Eric's slight figure entered the lobby from the hall. I briefly closed my eyes.

"Eric!" I was a little too enthusiastic in my greeting. He shrank back instinctively from my wide smile and loud voice.

"What's up, Sabrina?" he asked. "Didn't think I would see you around here again."

I was shocked to see him in his Army uniform. He wore a light olive shirt and tie under a darker olive jacket decorated with a couple of medals and a name tag, which made him look almost respectable. Nothing like the heavy-lidded person I had seen that night at the rocky beach. No vampire teeth and cigarettes today. His shaved head, which gave him a malevolent appearance off base, blended in well with the other military-style cuts that the privates sported.

"Patrick asked me to come." I stood from the hard plastic chair.

"Oh?" he responded warily.

"Why haven't you been answering his calls?" I chided him. "You're his best friend, Eric."

He remained standing in front of me, arms clasped behind his back. "It's complicated."

"Complicated? What's so complicated?" I was outraged he would dismiss his behavior so simply. "He's your friend. He's in the hospital. He wants to talk to you, see you. For God's sake, Eric, he almost died because of you." My voice had started to rise and, in that tile-floored room, it echoed for all to hear.

In a harsh whisper Eric swore at me, "Shut the hell up. Are you trying to get me in trouble?" He rubbed his hands nervously together. "Look, I'm taking my exams in two days. Then I'm out of here. Off to Hawaii. I don't need Patrick fucking up my life."

I couldn't believe what I was hearing. "*He's* fucking up *your* life? As far as I can see it, Eric, *you're* the one who fucked up *his* life!" But before I could continue on my tirade against his betrayal, I picked up on something he had said. "Wait a minute...you're taking your exams *this* week?"

"Yeah. So?"

"Patrick told me the exams were at the end of *next* week."

"The man was in a coma for forty-eight hours, does he even know what day it is?"

"Look, he wanted me to come to you for help," I explained. "He wants—"

"What does he think I can do for him?" Eric said. "Does he think he's going to take the exams with the rest of the class? He's gotta be nuts. They rolled him already."

"Rolled him?"

"Right after the accident. They put him in the class behind me."

"What? What does that mean? When can he take the exams?"

"The class he rolled into is three months behind. I guess he'll take the exams in December or maybe November."

"No, he wants to take the exams with you."

Eric laughed derisively. "There's no way he can do that." He straightened his tie. "Look, I gotta get going. I only have a couple of days to study, and I need to practice my orals. Tell McKinnon I'll see him in Hawaii."

At that, Eric turned and left me in the lobby. He headed straight for the long hallway that would take him back to his room and his studying.

Bastard.

What was I going to tell Patrick? I couldn't delay visiting him now, no matter how nervous the idea made me. I didn't want him to blame me for not making sure he got to the clinic. Even if he didn't remember any of what had happened, I still felt guilty about the whole thing. And who knows what he would look like, bruised and battered? Bandaged and helpless?

He needed my help, now more than ever.

I strode purposefully over to the counter and cleared my throat.

"Yes? Can I help you with something else?" the private behind the counter asked me.

In front of him on the counter was a thick, red book with what looked like Cyrillic lettering inside. He also had a Russian-English dictionary sitting off to the side. He was a language student, too.

"Yes," I tried to sound confident, in charge. "I need to bring Patrick McKinnon his books, so he can study."

"Um, I don't understand. You want me to give you all his study materials?" He didn't sound too convinced.

"Yes," my voice beginning to falter.

"Well, I can't do that, miss. Those books are government-issue." He gave me the once-over, probably noting my lack of military uniform. "I don't know you from Adam. You could walk out of here with some very valuable language materials."

"So, what do I need to do to get him his books?" Wouldn't the Army *want* him to study? Wouldn't they want him to do well in his class?

"To tell you the truth, miss, I think someone has already been in touch with McKinnon about that. And I am not at liberty to discuss it with you," he said bluntly, looking away from me and concentrating on writing in the large workbook in front of him.

Rebuffed and discouraged, I left. But I knew what I had to do next: Visit Patrick in the hospital. I should explain to him in person what had happened and find out if he really did get his books from someone else. And since I didn't know where the hospital was—

I turned back to the private behind the counter, "Um...can I ask you one more thing?"

He looked up from his book, irritation glittering in his eyes, "I'm listening."

"You wouldn't happen to know where the hospital is, would you?" Coughing nervously, I reached for a pen sitting in a metal pen holder on the counter. Scrap pieces of paper sat stacked in a small box, and I grabbed one, ready to write an address or directions.

The sailor sighed and then droned, "You know Highway 68?"

I scribbled furiously, worried that if I didn't get it all the first time around, that he wouldn't take the time to explain it to me again. Once he had finished his short, matter-of-fact description, he picked up his pen and wrote something in Cyrillic in his workbook.

I folded the paper and stick it in my purse. "Thank you." I headed toward the entrance doors.

The private grunted a welcome without even looking up from his work.

I wanted to see Patrick and tell him what happened in person, I had to get over my fears about what he might think of me for abandoning him. I concentrated, instead, on my driving, pulling away from the curb and heading toward the southern exit. The trip to the hospital should be a short one if the directions were correct.

After a few minutes, I turned onto Highway 68. A small sign for Pacific Grove Coffee & Tea caught my eye. Although I had never been much of a tea drinker, a cup of hot, herbal tea seemed like the perfect thing to calm my nerves. Quickly flicking on my turning signal, I pulled into the small parking lot.

The line inside was short, but it was a tiny place, so it still felt crowded. After ordering my tea, I sat at one of the tables for two lining the front windows. With such a small amount of interior space, a table any larger wouldn't have fit.

I chose the last table in the row, sitting in a corner with my back was to the wall so that I could look out at the customers and the street at the same time.

I took a deep sip of my tea, breathing in the herbal steam that emanated from the mug. It was rather peaceful, even in that cramped, crowded shop. People tramped in and out. Murmurs of voices mixed with the jazz music.

Then, I saw them come in. Together. Holding hands.

twenty-one

. . .

LUCY AND DAVID entered the coffee and tea shop, but didn't notice me in the corner. I ducked my head behind a freebie magazine someone had left behind advertising real estate. David was the last person I wanted to see. His reaction at Morgan's had been so out of control, so crazy. I learned how unpredictable his behavior could be.

But Lucy hadn't.

My heart beat rapidly. It was time someone called him out for his behavior. Confrontations were not my thing, but in this particular situation, I had to do something. I may not like Lucy, but she deserved to know what kind of man she was involved with. If I managed to make him angry enough, maybe...

Screwing up my courage, I lowered the magazine and called out, "Hey, David, how's it going?"

He abruptly turned at my greeting, and I waved brightly at them, a smile plastered on my face.

David, for a moment, appeared dumbstruck—his mouth agape. Lucy looked blankly at me, but once she recognized me her face clouded.

"Hi there, Sabrina," David remarked woodenly. He must

have sensed his usual jocularity and charm would no longer be effective with me after his outburst the other day.

Keeping a wide smile, I looked pointedly at his companion, "You're Lucy, right?" I stood up and held out my hand, waiting for the well-dressed woman to accept my handshake.

Lucy dropped David's hand and, like Tina, shook my hand limply.

"I'm sorry; I don't remember your name," Lucy said apologetically, but the steely glint in her eye said otherwise.

"Sabrina Fuller. I work for David." My earlier fear turned into confidence as I saw David's face pale for a moment. He knew something was up. "We met at that restaurant awhile back? I was having lunch with David and his wife."

I wonder if she knew anything at all about the last argument David and Tina had at work.

Lucy flipped her hair over her shoulder. "Yes, I think I remember now. David's new little project. Working hard for your five dollars an hour?" She arched a perfectly-plucked eyebrow to accompany her insult.

I ignored the comment completely, turning my attention to David, "So, how's Tina feeling?"

Lucy looked warily from me to David. I could see the curiosity growing, her eyes snapping. David loosened his tie and wiped a bead of perspiration off his forehead.

"Tina?" he said slowly, as if he wasn't quite sure where I was going with this line of conversation. "Uh, she's doing great."

"Well, that's good to hear. I haven't seen her around the office since the 'accident.'"

His eyes narrowed. He set his mouth in a firm line and gripped Lucy's elbow more tightly. As if he was thinking, *don't fuck this up for me, Sabrina, or you'll regret it.*

But I was past the point of caring, he had taken it too far yesterday at Morgan's and with his own pregnant wife. He deserved it.

Before David could say anything, Lucy flinched at the clamp of his hand on her elbow, and asked him with a growing confusion, "What accident? You said she was at her mother's."

"Really?" I directed my words at Lucy. "Was that before or after you put her in the hospital, David?"

The stillness could be cut with a knife. David's eyes widened. I think he looked so surprised, because he never thought I had it in me, the courage to call him on his lies. For that was what his charm had been all along, lies. He was the best goddamn liar I had ever met.

"I don't need this," David growled, his anger barely concealed. "Let's go, Lucy, she's crazy. She doesn't know what she's talking about." He yanked on her elbow.

Lucy had a questioning look on her face. Maybe David's tug on her elbow got a little too hard or maybe something I said got her thinking, because she stopped in her tracks and pulled herself out of David's grasp.

Lucy's voice shook, "You have *some* nerve." She didn't believe me. Or she didn't want to.

"I'm just telling you what I know," I told her calmly. "Why don't you ask him yourself? I'd like to see if he has the guts to lie to your face again." I couldn't believe the words that were coming out of my mouth; it was as if I was a completely different person. Maybe somewhere deep in my brain the new Sabrina was taking shape, the stronger, bolder Sabrina I had always wanted to be.

"Goddammit, Lucy, get in the car. Now," David's voice was like ice, his green eyes filled with fury. If there hadn't been a roomful of tea drinkers, I wonder what he might have done to me.

He dragged her out the door. Lucy, who wore fragile spiked heels, tumbled to the sidewalk at the force of his pull.

The patrons of the tea shop stared at the attractive couple. Their low murmurs of conversation stopping abruptly.

"David!" Lucy screeched, as if she was shocked he would have treated her so roughly.

"Get in the fucking car," David raged, arms flailing.

Lucy struggled up from her undignified position on the sidewalk and took a few steps away from him. She violently shook her head, tears spilling down her face. As she backed even farther away, she reached into her tiny handbag and drew out a cell phone.

David, knowing a small crowd was watching his every action, quieted his voice, "Get in the car, Lucy."

Lucy ignored him and kept pressing buttons on her cell phone

"Fuck it," David roared and climbed into his Mercedes. He pealed out of the parking lot and barely missed hitting a minivan.

Lucy stumbled toward the curb.

A weight of dread lifted from my chest. David had been angrier than I had ever seen him, and it was frightening. It was not the reaction I had anticipated. But if that's what it took to make Lucy see what kind of man he was, then I was relieved I had pushed him so far.

Before, I might have worried about what David would think of me, as crazy as that sounds. But my mother had the same tendencies, to yell and curse and even throw things, when she was angry.

Over the years, I had learned to keep my mouth shut because it kept Mickey's mood swings to a minimum. But how different would things have been at home if I had stood up to my mother every once in a while? Let her know exactly what I thought of her?

The confrontation, instead of sapping my strength, gave me the motivation to see Patrick. I wanted to tell him what happened that night and why I left him with Eric. No more guilt, just honesty. And if he couldn't forgive me, well, then, I guess I could live with that.

Sipping the last dregs of my tea, I slung my purse over my shoulder and exited the shop. The sun sparkled in the bright September sky, and I felt recharged, energized. The only thing that brought my spirits down one small degree was the wish I could have confronted my mother as honestly. But regret was not going to get me anywhere. This was the life I had now, and I wanted to keep it.

Who would have guessed only a few hours earlier I had been on the verge of moving away to avoid all of these emotions? Leaving had seemed the only option, and now I was discovering I was a lot stronger than I had given myself credit for. Standing up to David was only the beginning.

———

I covered the few miles to the hospital in no time. After finding out Patrick's room number from the receptionist, I easily found his room on the fourth floor.

The door to Patrick's room stood slightly ajar. I heard a drone of voices, a bit of laughter.

Who else would be visiting? Could it be his mother? Or maybe it was a nurse?

I pushed gently on the door, knocking as I opened it, so as not to surprise anyone.

"Hello?" I called out. "Is it okay if I come in?"

A slender figure in white was perched daintily on the bed next to Patrick, book in hand, back to me. Definitely not his mother. Who was this? And what was she doing sitting so cozily next to Patrick?

"Hey, Sabrina, come on in," Patrick cheerily announced. He was looking at me over the mysterious person's shoulder. As if it was nothing special and strange women sat on his bed every day.

The young woman turned to see who had interrupted their conversation. Her dyed jet-black hair and dark make-up hinted at her goth interests, while her white Navy uniform explained where she and Patrick had made their acquaintance.

Internally, my mind was reeling, trying to process what I was seeing.

Wait. She looked familiar. The girl from the picnic tables who'd stared at me. Why was she sitting so closely to *my* boyfriend?

I tried to appear cool and pleasant, not wanting to reveal my surprise for fear of looking like a fool. "Hey, Patrick," I said, trying to sound as detached as possible. "I stopped by to let you know that I managed to find Eric."

"Oh, yeah." He looked right at me as if there was nothing odd going on, "Doesn't matter anymore." He nodded in the pretty woman's direction. "Kate here already brought me everything I need." He lifted up one of his Chinese books from class for me to see.

Kate, huh? And where did this Kate come from? I wanted to ask. *Who is she? Why is she here? Why is she sitting on your bed and not me?*

He looked good. Although he was lying back on his angled mattress, his eyes looked their usual gorgeous blue. I had expected him to be tired, perhaps weak and groggy. He had a huge bandage wrapped around his head, which had been shaven on one side, and he was a bit paler than usual. I almost felt silly for worrying so much about his injury.

"Oh." I fiddled with the privacy curtain that hung on metal loops from a track in the ceiling.

Patrick nodded to a chair on the other side of his bed. "Have a seat. Kate and I were just 'talking shop.'"

I clutched the curtain as if it was a lifeline and silently

rejected his invitation to take a seat. In a dazed voice, I echoed, "Talking shop?"

Maybe it wasn't as bad as it looked. Maybe she was just a student in his class.

But then a smile twitched on pretty Kate's red lips, "Yeah. Didn't Patrick tell you? We're in class together." At the word 'together' she placed a hand possessively on the stack of his Chinese books that lay between them on the bed.

It was a cruel dig. Kate looked as if she knew exactly who I was; maybe she even knew Patrick had never mentioned her name to me. I was an outsider. I had been dating Patrick for weeks now, why wouldn't he have mentioned her to me? Maybe I wasn't the only one he had been dating. Maybe that is why he told me so few details about himself here in Monterey.

I kept the details of my life quiet because hiding my past from everyone was the only way I could pretend to be normal. Burying the memories of years of loneliness, the words my mother used to hurt me, the death of an unknown father was the only way could cope. There was no point in airing my dirty laundry for everyone to see; they were my private hurts, my private humiliations.

But Patrick held back information for selfish reasons. And I was deeply hurt by that.

Trying to maintain my dignity, I answered as though I had a vague recollection, "Kate? I think I remember you telling me something about some of the people in your class." I knew she wanted to me leave. She wanted to hurt me and then watch me go, defeated. But I wasn't ready to give in. I decided to take the proffered seat and scooted it closer to Patrick.

Unfortunately, Patrick didn't allow me to keep my dignity very long, "I never told you about Kate."

A malicious twinkle appeared in Kate's eyes; she knew she had won this round. And she was determined to win the next.

Ignoring me, Kate turned to Patrick. "Funny isn't it? Last

time *you* were the one to visit *me*." She turned her attention fully on him as if I wasn't even in the room.

Patrick rolled his eyes and groaned, "You're never going to let me live that down."

She laughed a tinkly laugh and tucked her chin length hair behind one ear, "Nope. Choosing your car over me? Why would I ever let you forget that?"

Kate must have noticed the look of confusion on my face, because she asked me, "What would you have done, Sabrina?"

"Done?"

"Didn't he tell you about wrecking his car?" Kate gave the impression that if I didn't know about the accident I was somehow no friend of Patrick's.

"Yes, he told me about his car. It went over a cliff." If there was something he had left out, I wanted to hear about it.

"Did he mention the car ran over my foot on the way down?"

He attempted to divert the story, "I didn't think she would be interested in—"

"In what? Hearing you practically shoved me out of your way to get to your goddamn car?" Kate's bell-like laugh filled the small hospital room.

I was glued to my chair, my mouth suddenly dry. All I could do was watch the interaction between the two of them.

"Kate, I told you I was sorry. I didn't even know you hurt your foot until—"

"Forget it, Patrick." She leaned over and kissed him quickly on the cheek. "I forgave you the first time you came to visit me in the recovery room after surgery."

There was an easiness between them. He looked pleased with himself, happy.

I was flabbergasted. Here was a man I had spent a considerable amount of time with, had slept with, goddammit, and *now* I was finding out about this other woman? She was obviously very important to him. I wondered for a fleeting moment which of us he had called first today. And I had come here to apologize for leaving him the other night? I don't think so.

There I was, sitting next to someone I *thought* was my boyfriend, someone I *thought* I had wronged, and all the while he had been hanging out with someone else? My blood began to boil. I could feel the words coming to the surface, waiting to burst out of me. I was ready to lay him low. Make him feel like crap and leave him quivering in his hospital bed.

"Time to take your vitals, Mr. McKinnon!" A bright, cheerful voice interrupted my plans.

A nurse, dressed in white scrubs scattered with little puppy dogs, bustled into the room—all three hundred pounds of her.

Noting Kate's and my presence, she suggested, "If you would like, you can wait in the hall. It should only take a few minutes."

Before we could decide, the nurse whisked the privacy curtain around Patrick's bed, making it clear she had a job to do whether we were done visiting her patient or not.

I got up first, and Kate, eyeing me, followed behind. I could feel her assessing me as I exited the room: how tall I was, how I dressed. It was unnerving.

The minute the door shut behind us and we were standing in the hall, she blurted, "That's when we really got to know each other."

"What?" I muttered. I had no idea what she was talking about and couldn't care less. My mind was focused on what I would tell Patrick once the nurse yanked open the privacy curtain.

"When I was in the hospital," she explained slowly, as if I were a five-year-old. "He felt so guilty about my broken foot that he helped carry my books to class for six weeks straight, until I was off the crutches."

"I see." A flame of anger burned in my heart. That triumphant moment of confronting David in the tea shop was quickly forgotten. I thought finding out about Kate was bad, but finding out Patrick could be attentive and sweet to another girl cut straight to my heart.

I had never seen that side of Patrick. For me, Patrick had two modes: sex and violence.

Clearly, Kate was more his type. He had never been serious about me. I was a plaything. Something to amuse him when he was bored and lonely.

Kate, oblivious to my ever-growing anger, continued, "By then, we were together all the time." She was reveling in every word, making sure each one hurt me more than the last. "He told me about you, you know. I knew you meant nothing to him. I knew why he was doing it."

My first instincts all those weeks ago had been right. He wasn't interested in me at all. He chose me as an easy target: a lonely girl with no friends. A shy person with nothing to lose. Oh, how I wished I had finished packing up my things earlier today. Then, I would be miles away from here and this hurt.

I had been feeling guilty for abandoning him on the curb. Little did I know he had never needed me. I was only a fill-in, someone to keep him warm.

Words bubbled over and spilled out without much thought. "And why was that?" My voice was like cubes of ice, hard and cold.

"You see, we have what you might call a love-hate relationship. When he met you, we were in the hate phase." She leaned up against the white wall of the hospital corridor, staring me straight in the eye, looking for any little reaction I might have to her words. "You weren't the first. In the last six months, we've probably broken up six, seven times."

I couldn't stand it anymore. I wanted to be able to listen to her and take it all in without emotion, to show her he never meant anything to me. That it was all a big joke for me, too. But the anger burned out of control.

The heavy nurse shuffled out of Patrick's room. "He's all yours, girls."

The irony of her comment was not lost on me.

I stormed into the room and whipped the curtain aside, leaving Kate still talking in the hall. I didn't need any more of her explanations. It was time to let loose all the rage inside me.

Grabbing a plastic pitcher full of ice water off the nightstand, I dumped it over the top of Patrick's head. "Fuck you asshole!" The water dripped down his surprised face and soaked into the bedsheets and his Chinese books. "You know what? You *are* a freak. Why don't you go back to your freak friends and get the hell out of my life?"

I pushed past a shocked Kate and fled from the room.

The last thing I heard chilled me to the core. "I told you she was nobody." Patrick's voice echoed in my head all the way to the elevator.

twenty-two

. . .

FOR AN HOUR I cried in my car in the hospital lot. I crossed my arms over the steering wheel and rested my head between them, sobs wracking my body. It was relief to be rid of Patrick, but I felt used and hollow. I had been only a female body to him, nothing more.

The darkness settled around my car without me even noticing. It was growing late.

To refocus my thoughts, I needed music, people, coffee, traffic. Activity of any kind. I headed to Morgan's. For a moment I dreaded running into Tim, but if I sat in the main room, maybe it would be crowded enough so he couldn't corner me so easily.

I pulled my car up to the curb and squeaked to a halt. The muted throb of music poured out into the streets. It sounded like reggae night, with a band performing on the mini-stage. It was the perfect, upbeat, loud music I needed.

I pulled on the heavy front doors to enter, and the music caved in around me. From muted to consuming in one moment, the reggae beat swirled around me, making me push that trip to the hospital to the very back of my mind.

Lining up behind several other coffee fanatics, I lost myself in my thoughts.

All through high school, I had avoided relationships. "All men were liars," according to my mother, and what other standard did I have to compare to Mickey's series of failed relationships and one-night stands? At a very young age, I decided it was smarter to stay as far away from boys as possible. They seemed to do nothing more than bring my mother grief, causing her to drink more, smoke more, yell more.

When I finally did start dating, it was out of physical need. The few boys I dated had either been experiments in sex or a warm body to make me feel less alone for a few hours.

With Patrick, I had opened that door to my heart a little bit, and it had backfired horribly. Maybe my mother was right. Maybe all men *were* liars.

Patrick was the kind of person I should have seen coming from a mile away—dark, deceptive, mysterious. I should have listened to the faint warnings in my head about him. Why would someone like him fall for someone like me? The fact was, someone like him would *not* fall for someone like me. Deep down I had known that, and it killed me to know I had pushed aside those doubts.

Look what that had gotten me: a two-timing boyfriend who had used me to try and make his on-and-off girlfriend jealous.

David had lied to me, too. He had been my first good, male friend. At least, I thought we had been friends. But after putting his wife in the hospital, attacking Tim, and then blowing up at Lucy it was obvious he was more than a liar; he was a bully *and* a liar.

"Miss? Miss?" A voice snapped me out of my thoughts. I was at the front of the ordering line and a five-foot gap of space existed between me and the counter. I looked like a complete fool. "What can I get for you?" the barista asked me.

After making my order, I turned, my gaze passing over the

tables crowded with people. Near the entrance to the small back room, I saw Tim watching the band for a moment and then he ducked into my favorite spot.

Earlier today, he had been trying to tell me something, and I had shut him down. Rudely. In fact, I had been a jerk to him for no good reason. My thoughts had been so centered on Patrick that I had completely ignored Tim. And so far, Tim had been nothing but kind to me.

Maybe my mother had been wrong.

Maybe all men weren't horrible lying bastards. If nothing else, I felt badly enough about my behavior an apology was in order.

I zigzagged my way around the maze of tables near the stage. More people had crowded inside since I had arrived, and the front room was starting to grow stuffy and claustrophobic.

It would have been a relief to walk out the door, drive back to my apartment, and hide myself under my comforter for a few days to lick my wounds. But I needed to at least try apologizing to Tim before I went home and decided what to do next.

When I reached the back room, Tim was wiping down tables and clearing a few dishes into a bussing bin. I cleared my throat to capture his attention.

He looked up at me, his hair falling his eyes. He straightened up and combed his fingers through his hair.

"Hey," I started out shakily, not sure how he would receive any greeting from me.

He stood silently, as if he was assessing me.

I gestured to an empty table, "Could we sit down for a minute and talk?"

"All right." He stashed the bin to one side.

I took the seat across from him, my heart beating a little faster.

Why was I so nervous about some little apology?

I kept my hands clasped around my coffee mug. "I wanted to apologize to you for the way I acted today."

He interrupted me curtly, "It was none of my business what you were doing, who you were talking to—"

I stopped him, "Look, I was rude to you. In fact, I acted like a fool." I took a shaky sip of coffee. I didn't want to hurt the fledgling connection Tim and I were making. I couldn't see how a man like this would ever lie to me. My mother was wrong. She just had to be.

"That call?" I said. "I wish I had never answered the phone, to tell you the truth."

"Why is that?" He leaned back in his chair, his face emotionless. I didn't blame him for giving me the cold shoulder.

I took a slow breath, the best I could do was tell him the truth and pray he believed it. "My boyfriend, Patrick? Well, it's over with him. I found out he's pretty much a big jerk."

There, I said it. No tears, no emotional craziness.

"Really?" Tim sounded skeptical, and I didn't blame him. I had practically shoved him out of my apartment when the phone rang. "This afternoon you went running off to see him, and now, suddenly, it's over? I find that hard to believe."

"Yeah, I know." I was emotionally exhausted. I didn't have the strength to argue, to prove to him what I was saying was true. Then, I looked across the table, my gaze connecting with his. I was suddenly very conscious of him, his lean body and planed face.

This man owed me nothing, but I didn't want to leave. I didn't want to turn away after my apology and go back to being the girl who ordered coffee and a scone every day.

I wanted one moment with him to feel everything, be everything I wished I could be for him. This was my chance, and I might as well take it. Screw the consequences.

I reached across the table and grabbed both his hands in mine, pulling him forward. He raised an eyebrow.

I was acting completely on impulse. And right now, I wanted more than anything to kiss him.

I don't know if Tim saw something in my eyes, but instead of pulling away from me, he leaned in. I could smell him—an earthy, soapy scent that mingled with the coffee odor lingering in the air.

It was a hard kiss. The kind of kiss you give when you've been holding back for too long, hiding too much. A kiss with a lot of unspoken meaning behind it—touch me, hold me, pull me closer.

Whoa.

And he did all those things. His hands snaked into my hair and the table was shoved out of the way, by whom, I don't remember.

The kiss was like finishing a sentence that had been left hanging since our last encounter in this very room. The hard press of his mouth against mine softened. I didn't want it to end. I slipped my arms around his neck. He was tall and lean and oh-so touchable.

He pulled away. His chest rose up and down.

I let out a gasp when his lips left mine.

Wow.

I laid my hand over his breastbone and stared up at him.

What just happened?

He reached for my hand and held it loosely, playing with my fingers. "Do you want to go somewhere with me tomorrow?"

I paused, to me those few words held so much in them—a promise of a romance, a promise of a commitment, a promise of openness. I didn't know if I could live up to all that. I knew what I *should* say, what my heart was telling me to say: *Yes.* One thousand times yes based on that hot kiss alone.

But my mother had raised a broken person who was more suited to being alone. What did I have to offer him? A few passionate kisses? A willing body? He deserved more than that, this gentle, thoughtful man.

But the word leaked out before I could stop it, "Yes." A quiet assertion, a gentle giving in to the small piece of my heart that wanted to reach out for something good, something safe something tender.

He smiled at my response, and the flash of happiness cut to my heart. I knew what would happen to him. How I would hurt him. It was inevitable. I didn't know any other way to be.

This was how my mother had raised me—to pull a man in and then to push him away when he got too close. My mother used yelling and drinking to keep men at arm's length. I worked hard at being aloof, closed up, noncommittal. If I kept up a barrier and let no one in, then how could I be hurt like my mother had been time and time again? As much as I had wanted to deny it all my life, my mother and I were one and the same. She might use different tactics, but we both ended up with the same result.

I didn't deserve someone like Tim. But the hopeful piece of my heart clung desperately to him. I should have told him "no," that he should get the hell away from me. But I had wanted one kiss for a taste of what could have been, and now I couldn't make myself walk away. I gripped his hand tightly, and all thoughts of what I might to do this man scattered.

For one moment in Morgan's my world seemed good and clean and bright once again. Just like it had the day I drove away from my mother's house.

But the dark and dirty world I knew much more intimately was ready to return the minute I turned my back. I was sure of it.

twenty-three

. . .

"YOU PROMISED you wouldn't open your eyes!" Tim made a face at me.

"That was before I knew you were going to drive like a maniac," I yelped from the passenger's seat of Tim's Chevy. Although I was belted in securely, my fingernails clung desperately to the seat underneath me. Opening one eye, I peeked out at the road, only to see a sharp drop right outside my window. I reanalyzed my decision to peek. Sometimes it was better not to know how close to death we were at any given moment.

"I've been down this way a thousand times, remember?" He laughed at my white-knuckled grip. "I grew up in Monterey. I know these roads like the back of my hand."

We had met earlier that Saturday morning at his place. He had given me directions to an apartment complex on the south side of DLI, in Pacific Grove. When I pulled up in my Festiva, he waited outside his door and waved.

It felt weird calling it our first date, but I guess that's what it was. He told me to dress for a hike, and I had done my best. I had no idea where we were going.

The car twisted along the road. He teased, "I knew I should have blindfolded you."

"No, you should have put me in a crash helmet."

At least I still had my sense of humor, even though my nerves were rattled.

"Would it make you feel any better if I told you it was only a few more miles?"

"Possibly."

"Even better...here we are!"

The car swerved gently to the right. "Am I allowed to look?"

"That didn't stop you before," he joked.

My eyes were still closed, waiting for his say-so. "Tim!" I said with aggravation.

"Go ahead."

I opened them. We had stopped next to a small kiosk where he was paying a few dollars to a stern-looking California Park Service employee.

"Where are we?" All I could see were scrubby bushes and lots of craggy rocks surrounding us.

"Point Lobos. And this is the best time of year to visit."

"It is?"

"Yep, in the fall there aren't as many tourists, and no fog."

"I can see that," I remarked with a smile. The sky was a brilliant blue marred only by a few puffy white clouds—a perfect day to be outside.

"I thought we could take a short hike around. It isn't that difficult, and the views are spectacular."

"Sounds like a plan."

Tim parked the car, and we both climbed out with water bottles tucked in our backpacks. I didn't have any hiking boots, so I had slipped on my tennis shoes that morning. I was glad to hear it wasn't a strenuous hike, or I probably would have been woefully underprepared.

He unfolded the map he'd picked up at the kiosk and

studied it for the best route to take. While he intently focused on the map, I surreptitiously unzipped my backpack, pulled out a disposable camera, and snapped a picture of him.

It was something I had picked up at the last minute, not really thinking I would take it out and use it. But the intense expression on his face as he studied the map, looking like an explorer readying to cross the Sahara, I found comical. A moment worth capturing.

After hearing the click, he looked up at me, "Hey. What do you think you're doing?" He laughed at me and covered his face with his hand, so I couldn't get another clear shot.

"Oh, come on," I whined as I snapped pictures of a shoulder, his hand, his torso. "One picture isn't going to hurt you."

"One picture?" he groaned. "More like five!" He dashed toward me to grab the cheap camera out of my hands, but I stowed it back in my pack.

He playfully tried grabbing my pack from me.

"I don't think so, buster," I squealed, as he narrowly missed catching one of the straps.

"All right, all right." He surrendered, put his hands up, and backed away slightly.

I was a little disappointed the fun didn't continue. It was easy to be with him like this, laughing and silly. On the drive here, before I thought we would surely drive over a cliff, the conversation flowed smoothly, effortlessly. Somehow, with my eyes covered, I was less tense. It made me question if my life would have been easier if I walked around with a blindfold on all the time.

"I give up," Tim smiled. "You better watch out, though, I brought a camera, too."

Not wanting to end up on the other side of his camera, I briskly changed the subject, "So, do you come here a lot?" To my ears, it spilled out like a really bad pick-up line, but he didn't seem to notice. I slipped the straps of my pack up onto my shoulders.

"I've been here a few times—"

"Well, let's get hiking! I'd love to see what's so great about this place."

"All right." With one last glance at the map, he guided us to a trailhead about a hundred yards away.

As we clambered down the dusty trail, conversation lapsed. I wished for the small, intimate space of his car again. Sitting right next to him, hearing his words close to my ear—it had made me feel as if we were the only two people in the world.

But out here—

"Look, Sabrina," he said, breaking the silence. "I have to ask you something."

Uh-oh.

That didn't sound good to me.

He was walking in front of me, leading me down the path, which made it impossible for me to read his expression.

"Ok," I said warily, wondering if I shouldn't head back to the car right now. He sounded so dead serious, I knew the topic was not going to be puppies and rainbows.

"Was it true? What you told me the other day at Morgan's?"

The first thing that popped into my mind was the kiss. That fast, hard kiss over the table in the back room. What had we talked about before that? It was pretty much a blur. "Was what true?"

"That you and Mr. Sunglasses broke up?"

Oh. That little bit of news.

"You mean Patrick?" I held my breath; I hoped Tim wouldn't turn around. My emotions from that day in the hospital were still so raw. Remembering the moment when I realized what a fool I had been was painful, but to share the details with Tim, someone I liked and respected, would be mortifying.

"Uh-huh," he said, continuing down the trail. Sweat curled the hair on the back of his neck.

Turning a bend, the rocks and trees gave way to a beautiful view of a small cove with perfect white sand and neon blue water. I stopped in my tracks, almost too stunned by the sight to move.

When I didn't respond to his question, he turned back to look at me. Squinting in the bright sunlight, he smiled, pleased at my delight of the view he chose to share with me on such a gorgeous fall day.

"Let's sit here for a minute." He guided me to a crude wooden bench crafted from two slabs of unfinished pine.

I sat and hoped he had forgotten I hadn't answered his question.

"So," he began slowly, "you were telling me about this Patrick guy?" He slipped off his backpack and set it on the ground. As he waited for my answer, he unzipped his pack and removed a digital camera.

Uh-oh. Time for some revenge?

"I told you, it's over." Maybe, if I kept talking, he would forget about the camera in his hands. "Can't we leave it at that?"

Tim removed the lens cap, and my stomach tightened.

Humiliating photo, here we come.

But he pointed his camera at the cove below instead. "I suppose," he said. Hidden behind the camera, I couldn't tell if he was annoyed with me or disappointed I didn't want to share the details with him.

I sighed, relieved he was taking a picture of the view and not me, and also relieved he wasn't pressing me any further about Patrick. "Why don't we talk about something else?"

"All right," he acquiesced. "Tell me something about your family. Any brothers or sisters?"

This topic wasn't much better. The last thing I needed to tell this nice, exceedingly normal young man was how screwed up my family was. I imagined blurting out how my mother was an alcoholic and how I had been born out of wedlock. Oh, and that I never met my father. That was classic. The perfect trailer trash family.

But I knew I had to say something, or he would start to press me for details I wasn't willing to divulge. I spat out, "Nope, no brothers or sisters. My mom and I don't get along. My dad, well, let's just say he's out of the picture."

That should be enough to keep him quiet.

To make sure, I quickly asked, "What about you? Tell me something about your family."

"I have an older brother, Jonathan. He got married last year." He aimed his camera at the horizon, squinting through the lens finder.

"Oh, does he live around here, too?"

"Nah, he went to school back East and decided to stay." The camera clicked several times as he captured a shot of the sunny day and the beach below.

"Are you two close?" I kept the topic on his family hoping he wouldn't ask me anything else.

Putting down his camera, he looked back out at the horizon. "When we were in junior high, my parents got a divorce. It was pretty rough." He capped the camera and tucked it back inside his backpack. "It was just him and me for a while there. We sort of took care of each other."

"Where were your parents?"

"My dad had an affair with some secretary, so he was gone all the time with her. My mom, well, she was an emotional wreck. When you're fourteen, you just want dinner on the table at six, like it always was, like nothing had happened. Jon and I didn't quite get why my mom couldn't get over it, you know?"

I nodded my head as I listened, but was secretly surprised such a sweet, normal-acting person like Tim could have such pain in his past. Guess I didn't corner the market on sad childhood stories after all.

I pulled one knee up to my chest. I wanted to hear more. It made me feel a little less alone to know what he had gone though. Could it be he might understand? That he might not turn his back on me if I told him where I came from? What I had experienced?

"My brother and I, we always kind of knew my dad was a jerk to my mom. It killed us to see her treated like crap." He opened up his water bottle and took a long drink. "I don't know how much more I should say—I mean, you work with my mom every day. And it was a really bad time for her. I don't think it would be fair to—"

What?

"I work with your mom?" It seemed unfathomable to me.

The only woman I really talked to at work was—

"I was wondering if she'd told you," he groaned. "Now I feel like a complete idiot. That day, at your apartment, you looked at me as if I was crazy. I had met my mom for lunch that day, and she sounded so worried about you—finals, that freak David. Anyway, I offered to stop by and check on you, since she had to get back to work. She never told me—"

"And you didn't say anything?" I was flabbergasted. All this time he had known who I was, and I had no idea. At work, Alicia and I had grown close, close enough to discuss some very personal issues. How much of that did she reveal to Tim?

Oh, God.

The whole deal with Patrick. Even that night in the meadow —I hadn't given specific details, but I alluded to what happened. Now I was mortified.

"This whole time you knew your mother and I worked together every day, Monday through Friday, and you didn't think it was worth mentioning?" I stood and slung my backpack over my shoulder.

Tim rushed over to me, "Hey, whoa, whoa, whoa!" He grabbed one of my wrists. "Where do you think you're going?"

"I feel like an idiot," I began, on the verge of tears. The pale yellow sun and brilliant sky above only made me feel worse. They were mocking me; what I thought would be a carefree date with Tim turned completely upside-down. My most tender parts had been exposed for him to see.

"What? Why?" He seemed confused by my reaction, and I didn't blame him. I was a mess. An emotional train wreck.

I wrenched the words out, wanting him to understand how betrayed I felt, "There were things I told your mother, private things. Things that stay between friends. And this whole time you knew—" My voice broke, and I couldn't stand next to him any longer. I dashed down another trail, one that turned away from the water and headed up a steep incline.

I heard him call after me, "Sabrina!"

———

The rest of Tim's words were a muffled jumble that mixed in with the buffeting winds. I didn't even care if I had to walk back to Seaside. It felt good to hike up the steep path, my legs burning, my lungs working hard. I focused on the rocky path in front of me. When I arrived at a bend that had been hidden by a clump of cypress trees, I took the turn at full speed and smacked right into an overweight woman wearing head-phones. We both went sprawling to the ground, water bottles flying, limbs tangled. Gravel on the trail skittered in all directions.

The portly hiker, dressed in a bright purple nylon track suit, wheezed irately, "Watch where you're going, young lady. You nearly killed me."

Stunned by the hard collision, I pulled my knees up to my chest and took a deep breath. I had cut one bare knee pretty badly on a rock, and both hands were stinging from the skid on the gravel.

The woman, without even helping me to my feet or asking after my injuries, wiped the dust off her ample behind and continued down the trail in a huff. The crash hadn't hurt her one bit.

"Dammit." The blood from my injured knee oozed down my leg, and I opened my pack to look for something to clean it up with.

At that very moment, Tim caught up to me. "Are you okay?"

He sounded very concerned, damn him. I couldn't even run off with dignity. Instead, I ended up sprawled on the ground, disheveled and bleeding.

Best way to save face would be to ignore his offers for help.

I didn't need him. I could take care of myself. Just watch.

I rummaged through my backpack. Wanting him to leave before I lost it, I croaked out, "Please, just go."

It seemed as if there wasn't a moment today when I could remain free of tears. The familiar sting in my eyes annoyed me. I tightly clenched my jaw to keep myself under control.

"At least let me help you," he said.

Who asked him to help?

He pulled a clean t-shirt from his backpack, which was a damn sight better than the used Kleenex I had found in my own pack, and pressed it gently to my bleeding knee.

"Does it hurt?" His concern was almost too much for me. He was too good, way too good for me.

"Why can't you leave me alone?"

"Is that what you want?" he said quietly.

There were these short moments with Tim where I could see us together as a couple. The conversation came easily with laughter and smiling. But then, the minute any serious topic came up, I'd freeze up inside. He'd soon tire of someone like me.

Before I could answer, he said testily, "You know what? Why

don't I take you back to the car? This was obviously a mistake." His brown eyes snapped.

Even though his words were not that unexpected, my stomach dropped. If I hadn't freaked out and bolted, we probably could have had a great first date. But it was better he end things early, before there was too much of an attachment, before I could really hurt him. I was being a jerk to him, and he had every right to be annoyed with me.

"Yes, why don't you do that?" I hopped up and handed him the now bloodied t-shirt.

Somewhere deep down I felt more comfortable with cruelty. Straightforward happiness? How could I have been so naive to think that was possible in my life?

For a few minutes today, riding in his car, I had felt like a different person—lighter than air, the wind blowing across my face. No troubles, no bad memories. Just me and Tim, the car and the road. How nice it would be to live like that.

Tim had stuffed the t-shirt into his backpack and handed me mine, which still sat on the trail. I took it from him, words turning to bitterness in my mouth. This was all my doing. Anything I tried to tell him would only make things worse.

"Let's go," he said, politely distant.

I limped back to his car, my knee throbbing, my hands stinging. I sat silently in the passenger seat and imagined my mother laughing at me. As if she had known all along I could never make it on my own. I was always doomed to fail.

At that moment I understood why the beer tasted so good to Mickey and the whiskey even better. I didn't want to feel like this anymore—sad, lonely, a failure in relationships. A good, stiff drink or two would at least blur the pain for a while.

Now it was my turn to lose myself in a bottle, and maybe I would never be found.

twenty-four

. . .

THE SOUR TASTE in my mouth was repulsive, the sour feeling in my stomach even worse, but I didn't care anymore. A line of shot glasses sat in front of me, and I was looking to add one more.

The bartender in the dingy, poorly-lit Doc Rickett's Bar gave me a good, long look and told me unequivocally "That's it for you, sister." He swept away all the empty glasses and turned his attentions on a pair of barely-legal blondes who sat across from me.

Secretly, I was glad the bartender had cut me off.

Drinking was not something I was used to, and one more glass might have sent me off to the bathroom to be ill. However, I was beginning to see why my mother took to it. My first shot of tequila was harsh, biting. The lime and salt helped to cut the taste. Once I got the second shot down, the world started to hum. The pain in my heart numbed, and I began to forget why I'd been so upset.

This is how Mickey survived. Pretty pathetic, but it works.

Earlier, Tim had driven us back into town. To rid us of the awkward silence, he turned the radio to a country station and cranked up the volume. He kept his eyes on the road; I kept my eyes in my lap.

I had disappointed him and acted the fool. He thought I was some normal college girl, working her way through school. I thought back to our first real conversation when he had discovered me at the bus stop. We had chatted so freely about Spanish class and which professor graded easier than another. Simple, everyday things.

But on the trail, when I found out Alicia was his mother, something in me snapped. I hadn't revealed much to her at all, but I imagined them discussing me, picking me apart over Sunday dinner. I had been a closed book, and now it was as if someone had opened me up wide, flattened my spine, and flipped casually through my pages.

So, I sat in his car, trying to distract myself from the too-quiet man next to me by pulling things out of my backpack and rearranging them: my water bottle, my sunglasses, the disposable camera.

The camera. Those goofy pictures I had taken of Tim in the parking lot. Making sure he didn't notice, I dropped the camera to the floor and kicked it under the seat. I didn't need any reminders of how well the day had begun. I never wanted to see those pictures. Ever.

He was going to drive me back to his apartment, where I had parked my car. But I told him to drop me near Cannery Row, the touristy strip right along the ocean in Monterey. The crowds and the noise would be a good distraction, and it was within a few blocks of his place.

I could pick up my car later. Besides, I knew quite a few bars were within a couple of blocks of each other.

I don't think he wanted to drop me there. Maybe he was worried? He pulled the car over right in front of the Monterey Bay Aquarium. Children milled about the entrance with their parents, middle-aged couples strolled slowly down the sidewalk, bicyclists and skateboarders clogged the pedestrian trail that ran along the old railroad tracks. It was a typical Saturday afternoon for most.

Tim might have been angry with me, but he was still a gentleman, "Are you sure I can't take you back to your car?" He turned the radio down. The twang of the music was starting to irritate us both.

I had already opened the car door. "Nope," I answered, clipped and cold. I probably sounded angry with him, but I was really angry with myself. If I expected to have a serious boyfriend or ever get married someday, wouldn't it be likely he would want to know about my family? My background? Was it so outrageous someone should ask?

I grabbed my backpack and exited out onto the sidewalk without another word. I shut the door firmly and tapped the roof with my free hand, then waved a half-hearted wave as a signal for him to take off.

Instead, his car sat there on the side of the road, engine rumbling. As if he was waiting for me to come to my senses, get back in the car, and let him take me back to my Festiva. But I continued up the street away from him. The disastrous date was over, and he didn't need to play Mr. Nice Guy anymore. I wished he would leave and forget he ever met me.

I headed toward the pedestrian trail. Less people, and it was prettier than walking past all of the cheap t-shirt shops and sellers of tacky knick-knacks on Cannery Row.

The only way I knew for sure Tim had driven off was by the distinct gunning of the Nova's engine—choppy and sputtering. The sound faded behind me, and I knew he was gone.

At that moment, a shadow passed over me. The fog was rolling in after all. The bright sunlight that had seemed so permanent, so strong earlier that day was easily overpowered by the gray morass of fog.

———

Now it was seven o'clock, and I was already intoxicated. Pretty early in the evening to be stumbling drunk around town. Since the bartender was no longer willing to serve me, I moved from my barstool to a chair and table by the small dance floor. No one was dancing this early in the evening, but the gel lights flashed anyway to the rhythm of the music. As if they alone could entice strangers to come forward and dance.

My head spun, my stomach churned, but the painful memories from Point Lobos echoed faintly in my brain. Tired, I leaned back against the wall and closed my eyes.

"Hey, gorgeous, can I sit here?"

I opened one eye to peek at who was interrupting my thoughts. An attractive guy with a goatee was standing over me. Inhibitions gone, I slurred, "Why not? Nobody else is gonna take it." I closed my eye.

"So, what are you doing here all by yourself?"

"Getting drunk." Ah, how easily honesty surfaces after a few shots of tequila.

The man laughed and sat down next to me, setting a bottle of beer on the table. Now he had my attention. My eyes were wide open.

"Say, do you think I could get one of those?" I tapped my finger on the side of the beer bottle.

He slid the bottle over to my side of the table, "Why don't you take mine? I haven't even taken a sip, I swear."

I giggled, "Thanks," and took a long sip of the bitter drink. Beer tasted better when drunk, I noticed. Come to think of it, I could barely taste at all. "I owe you one."

"Nah," my new drinking buddy replied. "I think I can afford to buy the prettiest girl in the bar a drink." He winked at me.

He was an attractive-looking fellow: dark, possibly Hispanic with a well-trimmed goatee and a small gold hoop in his left ear.

He had the whitest teeth I had ever seen, and I found myself staring intently at those teeth as he talked. I couldn't look away.

"Don't make me blush," I said. Boy, the liquor sure made me a more adventurous woman. By now the 'real' Sabrina would have headed for a quick exit. But here I was, flirting almost effortlessly with a complete stranger. I took a long sip of my beer and tucked my hair behind one ear.

"Hey, I'll be right back," he said. "I'm going to get another beer. You won't go anywhere, right?"

"Right," I affirmed, this time winking at him. I picked up the beer bottle and tipped it in his direction, like a salute, and took another drink. The sick feeling in my stomach was subsiding, and suddenly, I felt the urge to get up and move. No one else was dancing, but I didn't care. With my beer bottle in hand, I moved to the dance floor, shimmying to the music. Swaying to the rock tune playing, I felt oddly graceful. The moves came naturally to me, without artifice or pretense. When I took another sip of beer I saw my new friend watching me intently from the bar.

So, this was how Mickey did it all those years. This was how she found all those random boyfriends.

I was empowered. I felt free from myself, free from inhibitions. The beat of the music grew stronger; it boomed in my chest like a heartbeat. I was whirling, smiling, laughing.

"What's your name?"

A strong hand curved around my waist. My beer drinking companion had returned.

"Sabrina. What's yours?"

He spun me around to face him, the white teeth mesmerizing, "Ricardo."

"Nice to meet you, Ricardo."

He pulled me closer to him, and we danced together, hip to hip. My arms circled around his neck, all the while I held onto that bottle of beer. Things were spinning more quickly now.

Voice were more indistinct. I could hardly remember where we were sitting earlier. How long had I been here?

"You know," Ricardo said as we danced, the music changing to a slow number, "you have the most beautiful mouth."

"Do I?" It was all a big joke to me. Who was this guy? I was just some drunken idiot in a bar. I almost burst out laughing at the lunacy.

"You do," he said breathlessly.

He leaned in slowly and kissed me. And I felt nothing—just the buzzing in my head and the music throbbing around me.

I laughed and pushed him away.

He didn't seem that upset by my coyness; it seemed to spur him on.

He was watching me drink my beer like a hawk watches a sparrow, intently and intensely. But I didn't feel my usual self-consciousness. I liked having someone look at me with that passionate hunger, an open desire, even if I wasn't all that interested.

"One more dance, and then I'm off," I declared. Better shut things down quickly before they get out of control.

Ricardo tugged me toward the dance floor, which was now crowded with people. Spinning me around, he tried his best to convince me to stay longer. He took every opportunity to caress me, touch me. I was flattered, but that was about it. He was cute, he was candid and complimentary, but I wasn't looking. Heaven knows I wasn't looking. Not after what happened in the last few weeks.

My bottle was empty, and Ricardo was quick to notice. "Come on how about another?" He had to raise his voice quite a bit to be heard over the pounding music.

"Sure." I needed a moment to sit down and stop the spinning in my head, one more beer wouldn't hurt.

Ricardo pushed through the throngs of people who filled the

small bar. The hour was late, and the crowd was growing rowdier.

In a moment he returned with two beers, one in each hand. He offered one by holding it out to me. "Come on, please dance some more with me."

I accepted the bottle, and, although I had no real interest in dancing anymore, took his outstretched hand and headed for the dance floor.

This night was all about forgetting who I was; putting my problems on the back burner and letting loose. Maybe I wasn't completely comfortable with this Sabrina, but I sure as sugar was going to try to make it work for one night.

After an hour or two of dancing, I knew it was time to go. My stomach started to lurch—all that beer, plus the tequila—and I wasn't a drinker by any means. Now I knew why.

In the middle of a hard rock song, I walked off the dance floor, weaving around clots of people. Ricardo followed closely behind, calling out my name.

But I dashed for the restrooms before he could catch up with me. Tequila and beer were a very bad combination. What a way to find out exactly how bad.

Leaning over the toilet, retching, I longed for my lumpy futon and a big glass of ice water. I knelt helpless on the squalid restroom floor. My thoughts flashed, not to Ricardo whom I had left so abruptly, but to Tim and what he would think of me if he saw me right now. How could I have been so mean to him on our first date? Why did I have to freak like that? He was only asking questions about normal stuff—family, friends.

What the hell was wrong with me? Why did all of this secrecy matter so much to me?

After a few minutes my insides settled, and I contemplated what to do. With my spinning head, and my senses dulled by an overindulgence of alcohol, the best idea I could come up with...

BANG! BANG! BANG!

Someone knocked loudly on the restroom door.

"Hey," I heard Ricardo's muffled call. "Are you okay? Do you need some help?"

Why were men so gallant with drunken, idiotic women? I didn't really feel I was worth the effort. Why didn't this guy find the young blondes I had seen earlier at the bar?

Feeling better, but not completely sober, I rinsed out my mouth in the sink, dried my face with a rough paper towel, and opened the door a crack. Ricardo stood there, a rakish grin on his face.

"I thought you took off."

"I need to get out of here." My mind was fuzzy. I was suddenly very, very tired.

"Right now? Can't you stay for one more beer?" Ricardo frowned and looked at me with puppy dog eyes.

"I can't really. I have to get going." I shoved the door open and returned to our table. I found my backpack miraculously still on the floor and pulled out a sweatshirt. The nights were cold in Monterey, especially on nights when the fog decided to roll in.

Ricardo followed after me as I headed toward the door, "Where are you going?"

"Home. It's late." I peered at my watch in the very dark bar "See, it's almost midnight."

"That's not late! We were just getting started!"

He appeared to me as if he hadn't drunk a thing. His speech was clear, his movements fluid and smooth. He plunked his final beer on a table covered with bottles and shot glasses, and caught up to me. I opened the door, smelling the heavy, salty air outside. Fog curled around lampposts, and it was difficult to see more than a few yards down the street.

But how to get home? Even if could walk all the blocks to my car, I wasn't sober enough to drive. I didn't see a taxi.

The world tilted for a second, and then I noticed how dizzy I was. The steps in front of the door looked like a good place to clear my head. I stumbled toward the closest one, and sat down with a thunk. I had judged the distance poorly and ended up slipping onto the next lowest step.

Manny came up behind me, grabbing my elbow before I could really hurt myself. "Let me help you." He pulled me up and guided me in the direction of the parking meters behind the bar.

Even dizzier now, I mumbled, "Where are we going?"

"I'll take you home. Where do you live?"

Normal, sober Sabrina would never have told a stranger where I lived, much less let him drive me home. But this Sabrina didn't seem to have a care in the world.

"Yeah," I murmured, "take me home, please."

twenty-five

. . .

A LOUD BUZZING.

Was that in my head?

More buzzing.

I bolted upright from my spot on the floor. Nope, not in my head. It was my alarm clock waking me at seven. I must have set it by accident last night before I—

Wait a minute. Why was I on the floor?

My head was still spinning from the overload of alcohol last night. I couldn't think straight.

Oh, yeah, buzzing. Have to shut the alarm off.

I clumsily stood, wrapped myself in a blanket, and stumbled across the room to my alarm clock. My joints, stiffened from their night on the hard floor, screamed for the softness of my futon.

I tapped off my alarm.

A few more steps to the couch, and I could be comfortably back asleep.

Oops.

I had forgotten the most important part of my little jaunt last night: Ricardo.

He might have had hopeful intentions yesterday, but by the time he drove me back to my apartment I was about two seconds away from being dead asleep. So, he practically carried me up the stairs. I proposed he sleep on my futon in exchange for the ride.

It was all slowly coming back to me now.

He lived in Salinas, a good half-hour's drive, and it was late. He seemed grateful for the offer. The last I remembered, I plucked a blanket off the back of the futon, curled up on the floor with a sweatshirt for a pillow.

I rubbed at my aching neck and shuffled to the kitchen. I wouldn't be getting any more sleep on the floor, and there certainly wasn't enough room on the futon for two almost-strangers to be comfortable.

Coffee was my only option. Lots of it.

That's when I remembered my car was still parked at Tim's apartment complex. I was in Seaside, and he was at least ten miles away in Pacific Grove. Manny had a car—

Guess it was time to wake up sleeping beauty.

First, I scooped out some Folger's for my coffee maker and set two mugs on the counter. Then, I called out, "Hey, Ricardo. You awake?"

A grumble emerged from the futon.

Maybe a good prod in the back would help.

Leaving the coffee pot gurgling, I picked up my umbrella leaning near the front door and poked him several times.

That got him moving.

"Hey!" He sat up and gave me a sleepy glare. "What's with you?"

I was worried he, too, would not clearly remember last night's events and wake up confused. But he had only drunk a few beers. I was the lush last night.

My little experiment had gone awry.

I couldn't hold liquor like my mother could, and I had no

clue how to behave with a perfectly willing and good-looking stranger from a bar. It made me wonder how long it had taken my mother to perfect her self- destructive behaviors. When did she take that first drink and why? When did she push away her first potential long-term relationship and pursue meaningless nights of sex with random men?

At the bottom of it all, I knew the answer. The only man she ever spoke of with a hint of regret was my father. The man whom I knew almost nothing about. And it was regret, not anger, as I had once thought. Just like I was angry with myself now for the way I acted with Tim. There was regret there, too, and lots of anger. But not anger at Tim for anything he had done; it was anger at myself for not being able to open up about my life, my past, my family.

Mickey had been angrier with herself over losing my father than anything else. And I must have been the reminder of that failure.

It was time for me to grow up and be smarter than Mickey. I couldn't let bad things in my past ruin the present. Especially things that were out of my control. Tim wouldn't care.

I knew that now.

"Is that coffee?" Ricardo asked, running his hands through his sleep-mussed hair.

The smell of freshly brewed java filled my nose. "Yeah, you want a cup?" I returned to the kitchen to pour myself a mug.

"Sure."

"Milk? Sugar?"

"Black is good."

He was sitting up now, his clothes from last night horridly wrinkled.

Funny how Ricardo had gone from being an over-the-top flirt last night to distant but friendly this morning. Alcohol did strange things to people, I guess. The bright light of morning brought a different perspective to situations sometimes.

I sat next to him on the futon and handed him a full mug of coffee.

"Thanks," he began. "And thanks for letting me crash on your couch last night."

"No problem."

"I'll just finish this," he gestured at his mug, "and then I'll take off."

I was relieved he didn't ask for my number or anything. Last night was last night. Nothing more. He seemed to realize that, too.

But I had to ask him one more thing.

"Could I ask you for a favor?" As if this guy owed me anything. He saved my ass last night by driving me home.

"Like what?"

"My car. I left it at this apartment in Pacific Grove. Do you think—?"

"You need a ride?"

"If you wouldn't mind." God, I felt like such a needy loser. He must wonder why I didn't have any real friends to ask for help. "I'll buy you breakfast," I added.

That seemed to clinch the deal. "All right."

———

Breakfast had been awkward, but filling. Ricardo and I barely talked; we both concentrated on our eggs and pancakes.

Now, standing in the parking lot in front of Tim's building, I waved a friendly goodbye to someone I would likely never see again.

I dug my keys out of my purse. Before I unlocked my car, though, there was something I needed to do first. I didn't want to wimp out again and follow my usual patterns. Tim deserved an explanation for my behavior. And maybe he would be willing to try again.

Heading toward the main entrance of the apartment complex, I searched for mailboxes or anything that might tell me which apartment was Tim's.

On the second locked mailbox from the left I read:

T. GRANT - 202

I took a deep breath and entered the building.

———

I hesitated in front of Tim's apartment for a long while before I knocked on the door. I wished I could quell my nerves. To talk to Tim and explain myself and my life would probably be the hardest thing I ever had to do. I had never opened up before—not to anyone. Not even a diary. Somehow even putting the truth down on paper would have been too painful.

But I knew this was the only way I could move forward. If Tim, kind and gentle-hearted with his parents' bitter divorce in his past, couldn't accept me and see past my baggage, than no one could. It was a test I didn't want him to fail.

My knuckles rapped on the door, and it echoed down the empty hallway.

There was a moment before he opened the door when I wanted to flee—dash down the hallway and hide in the stairwell. My mind thought it, but I didn't let my body obey. I needed to do this.

Tim appeared in the doorway, a questioning look on his face.

"Can I come in?" I did my best to look him in the eye, to let him know I needed to talk to him while I still had the guts to do it.

He scanned my face, his brows pulled in, and he let me in without even a 'hello.'

His apartment was almost exactly what I expected, small but clean, TV in one corner, and a mountain bike hanging from the wall. He had a tall bookcase crammed full of what looked to me like academic texts. The one thing that seemed out of place was the very expensive espresso machine sitting on the tiny kitchen counter.

"So," he began, sounding unsure and maybe a little confused.

"So," I echoed, "does that thing make good lattes?" I couldn't launch right into my personal demons after yesterday's fiasco. I needed to be able to sit with him, feel him out, see if he would even give me a second chance.

But he just stood there, near the door, with his hands in his pockets. Pajama pockets.

Oh, geez.

How did I not notice the fact he was bare-chested, wearing pajama pants, and looked as if he'd woken up five minutes ago? Was I so nervous I completely blocked it out?

My face heated. "Oh, hey, I didn't mean to wake you. Um, why don't I just—" I headed for the door, my bravado fading quickly.

He put his arm across the door, "Sabrina, what are you doing here at nine on a Sunday morning?"

That bare chest was very appealing but also extremely distracting. "I came by to get my car, and then thought, hey, why not stop in and—"

"Your car? You mean, your car was here all night?" He went to the window and parted the blinds with his fingers to look out at the parking lot below.

"Yes," I answered meekly. Next would come my explanation of how I got here this morning. That was going to sound lovely.

A stranger that I met last night at a bar drove me here. His name was Ricardo, and he slept on my futon.

He waited to hear some explanation, but I didn't want it to be that. I wanted to tell him all about me. What made me tick and why. Why I could be so sensitive about certain topics. Then, if he still wanted to know how I got here this morning and why my car was parked out in his lot all night, I would tell him. Just not now.

"Can you sit down and let me talk for a minute?" I asked. My hands started to shake.

He let the blinds snap back into place and furrowed his brow. Now he knew something serious was up. "OK." He found a t-shirt lying across the back of a chair and pulled it on.

At least that distraction was taken care of.

"I want to explain myself. The way I freaked out on you yesterday. That wasn't very fair of me."

"If that's how you tell a guy you're not interested, I would say you need to work on your delivery." He moved into the kitchen tinkering with his espresso machine.

I sighed, this was going to be tougher than I thought. "This is hard for me, I wish you could understand that."

"Understand what? I don't understand you, Sabrina. It was a hike. That's it." He pressed a button, and the machine began to make a loud grinding noise. As the sound grew sharper, he grabbed two small espresso cups out of the cupboard.

I sat on his couch, knowing I wouldn't be able to talk over the noise of the espresso machine. It was loud in Morgan's when the baristas were making coffee drinks, but the noise of the espresso machine was even louder here, in this smaller space.

The grinding stopped, and he worked his magic on the machine. In a matter of moments, he was setting down two cups of espresso on the coffee table in front of me.

"Looks like you could use some caffeine," he said, pushing one of the small cups in my direction.

I took the cup and held it in my trembling hands. "It was more than a hike to me," I said softly, not daring to look up at him. I tried a sip of espresso.

"Really," he said flatly.

"I want to tell you about me," I found myself saying. "Why I am the way I am, why it made me so upset to find out Alicia was your mom—"

Tim sat back in the faded armchair next to me. Waiting.

"I'm not the girl you think I am."

"Oh, I see," Tim said. "And what kind of girl do I think you are?"

The sarcasm made me cringe. I deserved that.

"Normal."

"You're not normal?" he replied, looking at me intently, as if I should have a horn growing out of my forehead in order to qualify as abnormal.

"When you say it like that it sounds so stupid." I held the small espresso cup between my hands, trying to figure out how to explain myself without sounding like an idiot.

"Then, what, Sabrina? Spit it out. If you don't like me or whatever, just come out and say it."

"But that's just it, I *do* like you."

He hesitated when I said that. I had surprised him. My admission had thrown him for loop. "So why did you take off like that yesterday?"

"I was scared." I rose from the couch and wandered around the room. If I was busy looking at something, anything, besides his brown eyes, maybe I could think straight.

"Scared of what? Talking?"

"Yes." I picked up a book and absently flipped through the pages.

"That doesn't make any sense."

"It does to me." I faced him. I clutched the book to my chest like a shield and leaned against the wall.

"Okay, so explain it to me so I can understand."

I inhaled deeply. "I didn't grow up like Beaver Cleaver. You know, mom, dad, white pickets fences, all that stuff. In fact, I had a pretty lousy life up until now."

He sat there, looking at me, taking a sip of his espresso. He expected more of an explanation than that.

I set the book down and fiddled with a ragged edge of my sweatshirt. "I've always kinda kept to myself. You know, hiding the skeletons in the closet."

"What skeletons?" he asked.

"My mom—" *Boy this was going to be hard.* "My mom is a raging alcoholic. Not the most accessible of mothers."

He was quiet for a moment. "And your dad?"

"I don't know," I answered with a whisper.

"What do you mean, you don't know?" I think he was starting to catch on how hard this was for me. His questions became softer and his tone gentler.

"I never met him."

"Never?"

"Nope." My mouth grew dry.

"Why?"

"My mom never really told me what happened between them. She would tell me to shut up when I asked about him. I used to think I must have done something to drive him away. In fact, sometimes I think I still believe that."

"That's crazy. You never even met the guy."

"I know it's crazy, but don't you sometimes wonder if your mom and dad split up because—"

"Because of me? Or my brother? Maybe I thought that a long time ago, when it first happened. But now I know better."

I was glad to find some common ground to help him understand "Well, that's how it is for me. I really want to believe differently, but every now and then I wonder."

"So, why don't you try to find him?"

"I can't." Suddenly feeling tired, I returned to the couch.

"Why not?"

"He's dead."

"I'm sorry, Sabrina. Really sorry." Those brown eyes pulled

me in again, his sympathy reflected in them. After a pause, he said, "And this is what makes you 'not normal'?"

"Yeah. I guess." It sounded so dumb now that some of my dirty laundry was out in the open. In my head, it had all been much worse. I expected him to judge me, to look at me differently than that day we kissed in Morgan's. But he didn't.

"Do you want some more espresso?" he asked, as if we had been talking about the weather and not the most secret parts of my life.

"No, no thanks."

Do it, Sabrina.

Don't back out of it now.

"Uh, but I did want to ask you something."

Not so smooth, but at least I got the words out.

"All right." He stood in front of the espresso machine, and loud grinding filled the small apartment once again.

To be heard over the sound of the machine, I half-yelled, "Would you be willing to give our date another chance? I promise won't flip out on you."

As the espresso poured out, he looked up at me, "Next Saturday?"

"Sure," I agreed, feeling ten pounds lighter than when I walked in. "Next Saturday."

twenty-six

. . .

ONE WEEK LATER, and I was sitting in my apartment waiting for Tim. My backpack packed, my shoes tied tightly numerous times, my hair pulled away from my face in a pony-tail. I had nothing left to keep me occupied while I waited.

I looked at my watch

Another forty-five minutes?

No more laundry left to be folded, no more dishes that needed washing, not even a stray hair to wipe away in the bath-room sink.

Mail!

I hadn't checked my mail in days. Grabbing my keychain, I sped down the stairs to the mail boxes in front of my building.

I never received much mail—well, no personal mail—only bills and things addressed to 'Current Resident.' But when I opened up my box, I discovered something surprising: a thick manila envelope with my name and address typewritten on the outside. No return address.

Stacking all of my regular mail on top of the mysterious manila envelope, I carried everything to the stairwell. Tim suddenly far from my mind, I itched to rip open that big packet.

But I held back. Better to open an unexpected package in the privacy of my apartment.

I took the stairs two at a time, unlocked my apartment door, and plopped down on the futon. Tossing the bills onto my cardboard coffee table, I took the manila envelope and flipped it over in my hands. I tore at the glued flap. Inside was another, smaller manila envelope and a folded sheet of white paper.

I dumped the contents into my lap. On the front of the envelope was a familiar Fremont address and "Return to Sender" stamped in red ink across the front.

I glanced at the return address: Jack Petrosky.

My father? But he had been dead almost fifteen years. Where had this come from? How had it found its way to me?

I plucked the folded white paper from my lap and opened it, hoping it held some sort of clue as to how this manila envelope ended up in my mailbox.

You should have had these long ago.

Just one line written in an uneven, scratchy hand. Nothing more. I recognized the style of writing immediately. No mistaking Mickey's pointy lettering. By why would she do this? Why would she send me something of my father's? How long had she had this package?

Setting the note aside, I ripped open the second manila envelope, curiosity burning inside me. I knew nothing about my father, only that he and my mother had a brief fling resulting in baby girl Sabrina.

My mother had nothing but terrible things to say about Jack Petrosky—a cheat, a womanizer, a loser. Mickey had used all of these words to describe him and worse. I often wondered what the true story of Jack was, or if all her stories were lies.

The only other thing I knew about him was the small amount of insurance money I received all those years ago. Nothing but a check and a cold letter from some insurance agent.

About six or seven letter-sized envelopes were stuffed inside.

Carefully, I inspected each one. My name was handwritten on the front with the same Fremont address.

When I was about five years old, my mother and I lived in a one-bedroom apartment in Fremont, but we moved soon after my fifth birthday. Once again Mickey fell for a man who promised more than he could deliver. This particular paramour promised a home with a yard in a nice part of town. We ended up in the poorest section of Santa Clara with the recent immigrants from Mexico and Vietnam.

The house was a dump, but when the guy finally ditched my mother, we stayed. It was a better home than we'd left, and it was right around the corner from a liquor store.

Somehow these letters had never been forwarded. Could be my mother purposefully made sure they never arrived into my hands. But why? I couldn't remember one kind thing my mother ever did for me. It made no sense.

I checked the postmarks. Each letter was written within a week of my birthday. From the time I was four years old until I was ten.

Lining up each letter in front of me on the floor, I put them in date order. It was nice to just look at them without even opening them. In fact, I hesitated to open even one letter. If I didn't open them, I could imagine whatever I wanted to about my father. Like I used to do when I was much, much younger.

I used to fantasize about him being a very wealthy international businessman, a super-secret spy with the CIA, and even one of the neighbors up the street who had always been kind to me.

Now, though, I was no longer a child. Whoever my father turned out to be, I was old enough and mature enough to find out.

With shaking hands I opened the earliest letter, the one he sent for my fourth birthday, and began to read.

All the letters began with the same greeting, "My Dearest

Sabrina." That caught me from the beginning: "*dearest.*" Jack wasn't the best writer, I counted a handful of misspellings in the first few sentences, but he took the time to write these letters to me, a child he'd never met.

He didn't explain why he decided to write, but he did describe his day-to-day life as a truck driver, the loneliness of being on the road, his hopes and aspirations for me, his only child.

Each letter bore a postmark from a different state: Texas one year, Idaho the next. All postmarks were west of the Mississippi, and none were from California. Maybe he didn't have the heart to return to this particular state, maybe he didn't feel wanted.

He never mentioned Mickey.

The last two letters Jack filled with the small details that made up his day: a stop for lunch at an isolated diner outside Fallon, Nevada; seeing two coyotes cross the freeway at twilight; snippets of conversation with fellow truckers over his CB radio. Each piece gave me a greater understanding of who the man, Jack, my father, really was. Not a wealthy man, not an educated man, but a hard-working man who took pride in his job and pride in me. He called me "the one good thing" he had ever accomplished in his life.

I curled up on the futon with the last letter clutched in my hand. Tears welled up. How different would my life have been had I read these letters each birthday? Would Mickey's indifference toward me have been easier to bear? Just knowing that this stranger, my father, cared about me, dreamed about what I must look like, would have made such a difference.

Inspired, I picked up a pen and some lined notebook paper and wrote. For a good solid hour I wrote a letter to a dead man, a stranger, a father. I opened up my heart and told him about my life, my first boyfriend, learning to drive a car, my favorite ice cream flavor. Even after my hand began to cramp, I kept on, filling ten pages with my writing. I signed it "Love, Your Daughter, Sabrina," and placed it in an envelope. With the last bit of energy and emotion I had, I addressed it to Jack Petrosky and then set the envelope on the counter.

When I finished, I thought again of my mother and the note that she'd enclosed with my father's letters. For all these years I thought my mother hated me and saw me as a nuisance. If she truly hated me, she would have burned these letters or thrown them away. But saving them and then taking the time to send them to me?

Maybe my mother had a heart after all, a soft spot for her daughter. I thought back to the day I left for Monterey and the sweater my mother had taken out of my bags. I had, at the time, believed she only kept that sweater out of spite. But as I replayed the scene in my head, perhaps Mickey's anger at my leaving wasn't anger. Maybe she was hurt. Maybe I was the one thing she'd managed to hold on to all these years while everything else—her boyfriends, any money she ever made—seemed to slip through her fingers.

Maybe, when I left, she was divested of the one positive thing in her life. And that sweater was a reminder of me, hoping someday I would come back for it. Thinking I wouldn't leave it behind forever.

Instead of the aching, empty space in my chest I had when I thought about my mother, I had a warm sensation. A clean, clarifying sensation of knowing who I was and where I was going. Even if my mother never had the courage to admit her love for me, I now knew it was there. The love of a mother who didn't know how to give love.

I didn't leave home to start my life over. No, I left home to continue my life. From this spot, I could see the road was clear in front of me. There was no reason to look back at places I'd been.

Jack described in one of his letters to me that looking ahead to his next stop was the best moment of his morning. The road was never the same, even roads he traveled many times before.

He always saw something new, something surprising. In fact, that was one of the reasons he liked being a truck driver.

And now I could understand why.

A knock on the door brought me back to the present, and I got up to answer it. I wiped away the undried tears on my face. When the door opened Tim stood there with his backpack in one hand.

I smiled, happy to see him. Truly happy.

"Hey," he greeted me, "are you all ready to go?"

An instant flame sparked in my heart. A tenderness grew there, that wanted to flourish. He always made me feel that way.

"Yeah," I answered him. "Let me just grab my pack."

"You got lucky, you know. They were forecasting fog for the whole weekend." He smiled his slow, sweet smile at me. "You never did get to see my favorite spot at Point Lobos."

He had laid out his heart for me; he had been all along.

I grabbed the manila folder stuffed with my father's letters and carried them with me out the door.

"What are those?" He tilted his head to the side.

As we started down the stairs, I took a letter out of the package. "Here." I handed him a yellowed envelope. "Would you like to meet my father?"

He took the letter, even though I knew he didn't quite understand what I meant. But he would soon.

On our way down to his car, I grabbed his hand and squeezed. Tim stopped halfway down the stairs and looked at me with his soft brown eyes. Eyes that could melt me completely. How easily he could stop me with that look. It had been that way almost from the very beginning.

He kissed me gently, and my heart opened like a morning glory opens to the first rays of sunlight.

THE END

author bio

Britt Zane is reliving the 90s through her debut novel, *Blond Boy*. She likes 'Buffy the Vampire Slayer,' gelato, and a good bargain. She'll never be caught dead listening to anything but The Cure and Nine Inch Nails.